SABRE'S EDGE

***Also by Ralph Cotton
in Large Print:***

Powder River
Gunman's Song
Jackpot Ridge
Ralph Compton: Death Along the Cimarron
Vengeance Is a Bullet
Webb's Posse

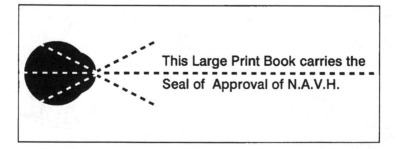

SABRE'S EDGE

Ralph Cotton

Thorndike Press • Waterville, Maine

Copyright © Ralph Cotton, 2003

Published in 2004 by arrangement with NAL Signet, a
division of Penguin Group (USA) Inc.

Thorndike Press® Large Print Western.

The tree indicium is a trademark of Thorndike Press.

The text of this Large Print edition is unabridged.
Other aspects of the book may vary from the original edition.

Set in 16 pt. Plantin by Ramona Watson.

Printed in the United States on permanent paper.

Library of Congress Cataloging-in-Publication Data

Cotton, Ralph W.
    Sabre's edge / Ralph Cotton.
      p. cm.
    ISBN 0-7862-7105-1 (lg. print : hc : alk. paper)
    1. Arizona Rangers — Fiction. 2. Bank robberies —
Fiction. 3. Sheriffs — Fiction. 4. Arizona — Fiction.
5. Large type books. I. Title.
PS3553.O766S23 2004
  813'.54—dc22   2004058814

For Mary Lynn . . . *of course.*

And to John and Paula Herd and
Kimberly Weatherly,
with much appreciation.

As the Founder/CEO of NAVH, the only national health agency solely devoted to those who, although not totally blind, have an eye disease which could lead to serious visual impairment, I am pleased to recognize Thorndike Press* as one of the leading publishers in the large print field.

Founded in 1954 in San Francisco to prepare large print textbooks for partially seeing children, NAVH became the pioneer and standard setting agency in the preparation of large type.

Today, those publishers who meet our standards carry the prestigious "Seal of Approval" indicating high quality large print. We are delighted that Thorndike Press is one of the publishers whose titles meet these standards. We are also pleased to recognize the significant contribution Thorndike Press is making in this important and growing field.

Lorraine H. Marchi, L.H.D.
Founder/CEO
NAVH

* Thorndike Press encompasses the following imprints: Thorndike, Wheeler, Walker and Large Print Press.

Chapter 1

Ranger Sam Burrack and his prisoner pressed closer to Sabre Ridge, coming from the south across the sand flats. Through the wavering heat and the stabbing glare of sunlight, they looked like raging ghosts from some netherworld. In the far distance beyond them, a dark storm cloud stood high in the air, filled with brown dust it had sucked up from the desert floor. In a thin line of shade along the edge of the boardwalk, old Pip Richards had sat watching the storm twist its way east for the better part of two hours. Then his attention had turned to the two riders in the distance as they rode up out of the endless ground this side of the hill line. Pip only glanced out toward the riders now and then, protecting his eyes while he whittled a worthless twig of hickory into a worthless pile of curled shavings.

Pip had no idea who the two riders might be, but he knew that nobody in their right mind rode the sand flats this time of day: not at this time of year. *Trouble? Could be*. Pip glanced across the street toward the saloon, where laughter spilled through the batwing doors above the sound of a tinny piano. He spit and shook his head. Well, if it *was* trouble, it wasn't *his* trouble. Whoever that was riding in, he wasn't going to go blind watching them. In this land of great distances, it would take these two at least another hour to get to Sabre Ridge — that's if both their horses held up . . . and not counting heatstroke or snakebite, Pip thought.

Speaking of heatstroke — he kicked a boot at a skinny hound that had dared to slink across the dusty street and creep into his strip of shade. Then he went back to whittling. He gave the two riders no more thought until the soft fall of hooves came near him and stopped, the sound of them quieted by the tinny piano filling the street. Only then did Pip glance back up as the white barb horse with a black ring around its eye scraped a hoof on the ground before him, and only then did old Pip notice that the rider on the second horse — a frothed and blowing dun — sat slump-shouldered, with his wrists crosstied to his saddle horn. *A prisoner?* It danged sure is! And my goodness, he thought, *look who this prisoner is!*

Pip squinted into the sharp glare of sunlight, looked the ranger on the white barb up and down, then cut his eyes to the man on the dun. On most occasions, Pip would have chastised a person soundly for riding two big, hot, smelly horses into his shade and interrupting his thoughts. But since it wasn't real clear what he'd been thinking, and since he detected no sign of tolerance in the bearing of this lawman in his black linen suit and tan riding duster, Pip decided it best to keep quiet. He squinted back at the prisoner long and hard just to make sure he could believe his eyes. *What's going on here . . . ?*

A well-worn badge shone on the ranger's chest, partly hidden by his faded riding duster. He wore a pearl gray sombrero that kept his features hidden, as if his face had backed into a black hole beneath the wide brim. A long-barreled .45 pistol lay in a hand-tooled holster along the ranger's leg, tied in place almost at knee level by a strip of rawhide. Something about that big pistol rang a bell, but Pip couldn't place it right off.

"I'm looking for Sheriff Hugh Boggs," the ranger said. Then his voice stopped flat, no introduction, no *good day* or *hot, ain't it* or nothing else. Ordinarily, Pip might have just told a person to go straight to Hades. But something about all this was starting to pique his interest. *A ranger's badge . . . that big pistol!* Yep, now Pip made the connection. He knew who this man was, too. *This prisoner . . . The Ranger! Whoooie!*

Pip leaned his head sideways, trying to make out the face behind the voice, but the glare of harsh sun behind the Ranger kept him hidden — nothing more than a dark hole in the dazzling sky. Across the dirt street, two women watched a young man load staples onto a buckboard, and Pip glanced past them toward the Hung Dog Saloon, then back at the dark hole as he pointed the shaved hickory twig.

"He'd more than likely be over there, Ranger," Pip said, squinting then looking back down and squeezing his eyes shut for a second to chase away the swirl of sun glare. "You'll find that our sheriff does most of his work leaning on one elbow." He spit and made a contemptuous grunt. "You can tell him I said it — makes no difference to me." Pip spit again.

"That's about to change," said the Ranger. Then, without another word, he tipped a finger to his sombrero, turned his horse and, leading the prisoner on the dun, reined across the street to a hitch rail. Pip stood up slowly when he saw the Ranger step down from his saddle. The Ranger only spun his white barb's reins, but he tied three half hitches and a safety in the reins of the dun while the prisoner sat tied to his saddle horn.

"I'll be cracked," old Pip whispered to himself, watching the Ranger walk into the saloon with his duster and black linen coat pulled back behind his holster, the pistol butt riding near his hand. Pip scratched the twig against his scraggly beard stubble. This day was getting better and better as it went along.

Inside the Hung Dog Saloon, the Ranger stopped in the middle of the floor and said in a quiet voice that still caused faces to turn toward him even amid the melodious ring of the piano, "Sheriff Hugh Boggs, I need the use of your jail. I have a prisoner bound for Territorial Court."

A quietness settled along the bar. The piano slowed to a halt. Drinkers turned to face the Ranger, some holding beer mugs or shot glasses in their hands. In the center of the bar, a long rawboned face looked at him from beneath a drooping hat brim. "I'm Sheriff Boggs. Do as you please. The jail is thataway. See my deputy about it." He pointed an uninterested finger off to-

11

ward the dirt street, then turned back to the bar. Amused drinkers stifled their laughter but made little effort to conceal their smiles.

The Ranger stood silent for a moment longer — long enough to make the bar crowd uneasy. "Uh, Sheriff," said a beer-happy voice. "He's still here."

Boggs half turned, still paying little attention to the seriousness of the man facing him. "Is there something else I can do for you?" Boggs said, sounding a bit testy.

"Yep, you can go along with me to your jail. We can talk things over while I lock up the prisoner."

"You and me? Talk things over?" Boggs seemed mildly amused at the suggestion. Now, for the first time, he looked the Ranger up and down. But with the effects of rye whiskey slowing him, about all he really noted was that the Ranger was a few years younger than himself. "Son," he said, "if you think I'm going out in this heat just to accommodate you, you must be out of your mind."

"Is that your whole say on the matter?" the Ranger asked quietly.

"Yep, that pretty much sums it up," said Boggs. "Only thing would get me out in the heat today is something life threatening."

"I see . . ." The Ranger looked all around the bar as he spoke, taking in faces, placing them alongside wanted posters that had come across the captain's desk back at the badlands outpost. At the far end of the bar, he saw a sweaty black face tucked between a low-mantled hat brim and a dusty, damp bandanna. The face tried to avoid him, yet Sam felt the eyes staying fixed on him. He'd have to get back to that one, he thought. But first things first. He raised the big pistol from his holster as he stepped forward.

Outside of the Hung Dog Saloon, Pip stood up from his whittling spot at the first sound of commotion. Fearing gunshots might erupt at any second, he took a cautious step back, ready to bolt for the shelter of an alley beside the harness shop. But then he stopped cold at the sight of the saloon doors bursting open as Sheriff Hugh Boggs sailed through them without touching the boardwalk and landed in the dirt street, raising a cloud of dust.

The Ranger stepped out slowly behind Boggs, the big pistol still in his hand, the swinging doors batting wildly on their spring hinges. "I wouldn't have come here

13

if it wasn't *life threatening*," he said to Boggs.

Some of the drinking crowd started out the doors as the Ranger stepped down toward Sheriff Boggs, but they stopped and pressed back as the Ranger turned and faced them. Sam searched for that same sweaty black face among the onlookers, but he didn't see it. The man was either still inside or else he'd taken off out the back door as soon as Sam and the sheriff had left.

"What's going on over there?" Dave Pollard, the town harnessmaker, asked Pip. He'd walked out of his shop at the sound of the scuffle from the saloon. Now he stood behind Pip. Pollard craned his neck, looking out above his spectacles and wiping his hands on his work apron.

"Cracked if I know," Pip said without turning. The two of them stared as the Ranger walked calmly over to Sheriff Boggs, who lay struggling in the dirt, trying to raise himself on his hands while his feet scraped back and forth, raising more dust. "He just rode in, went into the saloon, and —" Pip stopped himself. He wasn't going to be blamed for directing the Ranger to Boggs, no sir. "There you have it."

Above the harness shop, Clare-Annette stood at the window in her petticoat, wiping her neck with a wet rag and watching the street below. She giggled. "You ain't gonna believe this," she said over her shoulder. "Somebody's dragging Boggs to the water trough and . . . oh *my God!*" She giggled again and dropped the rag at her feet. "He's dunking him . . . *dunking* him. Baptizing his worthless ass like a —"

"What are you talking about?" Swan Hendricks stepped up from the bed, pushing her dark hair back with both hands as she swept across the bare wood floor to the window. She was naked beneath the thin cotton gown. Perspiration held the fabric against her flat stomach.

"Look," Clare-Annette said. "I swear, it's the funniest thing you ever saw!" She let out a short squeal.

But Swan's eyes turned hollow with recognition when she saw the man in the tan duster slouching the sheriff's head up and down in the trough. Her hand went to her throat. "Oh no," she whispered. "It's him!"

"*Yeeee-hiii!* Give it to him *good!*" Clare-Annette shouted through the open window, but not one of the gathering townsmen looked up.

"Don't do that, you fool," Swan hissed, pulling Clare-Annette away from the window.

"You're kidding." Clare-Annette pulled loose and leaned back toward the window. "After all that hateful ole whiskey-sucker has done to us? You oughta be waving a flag!"

"That's him, Clare." Swan's voice trembled. "The one I told you about. The one who killed Montana Red Hollis, Bent Jackson, and all the others!"

Clare-Annette jerked back from the window and faced her. "You mean — ?"

"Yes, it's Burrack . . . Sam Burrack . . . *The Ranger*. That's him right there, as I live and breathe."

"I think you're mistaken, Pip," Dave Pollard said, staring across the street with his mouth hanging open, wiping anxious hands on his leather apron.

"Cracked if I'm mistaken," Pip snorted. "I seen him back in Raylean Crossing a couple of years ago. He cleaned that town up good and proper, back when there weren't a man before him could stand against all the cutthroats and hell-raisers. I couldn't make him out in the sun right off, but I can now. That white horse with the

16

black circled eye once belonged to an outlaw named Bent Jackson. The Ranger kilt him dead, then took his horse. It's him all right . . . cracked if it ain't."

In the street, the Ranger pulled Sheriff Boggs up from the trough, dragged him, leaving a wet smear of mud, and dropped him half on the boardwalk and half in the dirt. The townsmen stayed back a cautious distance and watched Sheriff Boggs cough, gag, and flap his wet arms.

A young desk clerk wearing red sleeve garters stood out front of the Miller Hotel, his mouth agape. Fuller Wright, the sheriff's deputy, had run over from the jail office and was watching from a safe distance, gathering his nerve as the Ranger walked over to where Sheriff Boggs' hat lay in the middle of the street. Now Fuller bit his lip and slipped a hand to his pistol butt. The Ranger saw it, stopped and turned toward him. For a second, Fuller's hand trembled. Then he raised it away from the holster. The Ranger nodded, reached down with his pistol barrel, picked up the sheriff's hat on the end of it and walked back to Boggs. He let the hat slide off his pistol and fall at the sheriff's feet. Boggs' voice was a strangling rasp. "You *rotten* . . . *dirty*. . . . You've no right at all . . . coming in here . . . pistol-whip —"

"Save the talk, Boggs," said Sam from beneath the brim of his broad sombrero. His voice sounded determined. "You'll need all your strength for the Abbadele Gang. They'll soon be coming."

"Gang?" Sheriff Boggs wiped a hand down his wet face. "The Abbadeles are not a *gang!* They're working boys . . . drovers, for crying out loud! And I reckon they will be *coming here* — they come here nearly every *weekend!*" He shook his dripping head. "*Gang,* my aching ass! You're crazy, Ranger."

"Call them what you will, Boggs," the Ranger said. "I've got one of them prisoner." He wagged his pistol barrel toward the man on the dun horse. "Him and some of the others robbed a bank over in Riley. I'll be needing your jail for a few days."

"Huh, what?" Boggs squinted and for the first time noticed the slump-shouldered man on the dun horse. He stopped short and stared for a second, stunned. Then he said, "Oh Lord, Ranger. What have you just done to this town? That's Dick Abbadele himself!"

The prisoner straightened a bit and smiled a tight smile, his brow narrowing, his eyes dark and full of warning. "Howdy, Sheriff

Boggs," he said in a low, rasping tone.

"Howdy, Dick — I mean, *Mr. Abbadele*," Sheriff Boggs replied, correcting himself, his voice shaky as he struggled the rest of the way to his feet, snatching his hat off the ground. "I — I hope you don't think anybody in Sabre Ridge had anything to do with this."

"Let the blame fall where it falls, Sheriff," Dick Abbadele said, a little warning in there beneath his leveled gaze. "I don't expect to be here long, eh?" His eyes glinted. "I've tried to tell this fool who I am, but he won't listen. Maybe for all our sakes, you can talk some sense —"

"That's enough out of you," the Ranger said, cutting him off. "Pull your nose back where it belongs, or I'll flatten it into your face." He stepped toward Dick Abbadele with the pistol barrel raised.

"Sure thing, Ranger," Dick said; then his eyes passed across Sheriff Boggs and lowered.

Boggs pointed a shaking wet finger at Dick Abbadele and said to the Ranger, "You're not laying a hand on that poor man in this town, Ranger. Badge or no badge, I won't tolerate you mistreating a man who hasn't even been before a judge and jury, let alone —"

"Shut up, Boggs," the Ranger said. He reached his free hand down and brought up the long knife from out of his boot well. "If you want to do something for this *poor man*" — he pitched the knife into the dirt at Sheriff Boggs' feet — "cut him loose from the saddle horn and escort him to your jail."

"I'm not putting him in my jail, Ranger." Boggs stood firm. Deputy Fuller Wright stepped over beside him, gazing at the Ranger with an uncertain look on his face.

"Fair enough," the Ranger said, stepping back with his eyes on Boggs and his deputy. He reached down, uncinched the saddle on the dun horse and shoved Dick Abbadele, saddle and all, off into the dirt street. Dust billowed. The onlookers gazed, startled. "Get out in the middle of the street, Abbadele," the Ranger said.

"Do what?" Dick Abbadele spit dust from his lips, the saddle out from between his knees and hanging from his tied hands as he brought himself up onto wobbly legs. A dark bloodstain shone on the lower left side of his shirt.

"You heard me," the Ranger said. "Get out there and lie down now. I'll just pound a stake into the ground and tie you to it. Seems the good sheriff here doesn't care

20

whether or not you bake in the sun."

"Boggs, damn it!" Dick Abbadele shot a hard glance at the sheriff. "You can't let him treat me this way!"

"He's wounded?" Sheriff Boggs stepped forward, his deputy coming with him a step behind, the two looking closer at the blood on Abbadele's shirt. "You didn't mention it."

"Yeah, he's nicked a little," the Ranger said. "Nothing that a few hours out here in the hot street won't cure, I reckon. You can explain it all to his amigos once they get here." He sliced a glance at Dick Abbadele, then back to the sheriff. "Well, what's it going to be — bake him in the street or cool him out in your jail, Sheriff?"

"Dick — I mean, Mr. Abbadele, we need to get you attended to," Boggs said, stepping closer. "We probably should get you over to the jail, all right?"

The Ranger just listened and shook his head.

"Yeah," Dick Abbadele said, his tone arrogant, threatening. "You do that, Boggs. You best see that nothing bad happens to me, if you know what's good for you."

Chapter 2

The afternoon wind blew in from the south-
west, a scouring breath of hell: dry, hot and
merciless in its intent. Dust billowed up on
the flat, endless horizon, the low sun shim-
mering red behind a wavering veil of fire.
The Ranger looked out through the open
door, watching evening move in slow across
the desert, stretching the town's shadow
long across smoldering sand and clumps of
parched wild grass. Where was she? *Come on,
Maria, get on in here. Where did you go?* His
eyes traced his trail back out of town and out
across the sand flats until the earth ended in
a silver swirl. No sign of her.

He and his partner, Maria, had split up
out there. Maria had gone off chasing two
of the Abbadele Gang before he'd had time
to stop her. He'd been ahead of her when
he saw where Dick Abbadele lay up among
the rocks, ready to fire down on them. It
was either slip in and up after Dick
Abbadele or take a chance on putting a
bullet in Maria as she rode closer. So the

Ranger had made his move and taken Dick Abbadele down. But somewhere in the stir of it, Maria had vanished. *Where to . . . ?*

"I demand to know how long you expect me to hold him here," Boggs said, interrupting the Ranger's thoughts. Boggs scrubbed a towel through his wet hair. He glanced at Dick Abbadele, who stood inside the cell, holding onto the bars with both hands, staring down and scraping one boot against the floor.

"Until I say otherwise," the Ranger replied. He returned to his silence and remained in the doorway of the sheriff's office, forcing himself to take his mind off Maria and his eyes off the fiery basin out there in the distance. He'd go looking for her as soon as he got things settled here. For now, she was on her own out there. He looked back along the dusty street, watching the last of the horses at the hitch rail stand with its head sideways to the hot wind.

The other horses had gone off one and two at a time, their owners slipping from the saloon, glancing in all directions as they batted boot heels and slung reins and rode off into the wavering furnace of sand. The big pistol hung in Sam's hand as he studied the last horse against the backdrop of swirling dust. He'd unfastened his holster belt from around his waist earlier and now had it looped over his shoulder. Behind him, Sheriff Boggs slapped the wet, muddy towel down on his battered oak desk and ran a shaking hand back across his wet, tangled hair.

"You have no right . . . no jurisdiction here!" Boggs' voice sounded liquor thick and quivering on the edge of explosion. "You could've had the decency to call me away from the saloon!"

"I tried," said the Ranger, still scanning the town without turning to face him. "You didn't listen."

"For God sakes!" Boggs whined. "You shamed me in front of the whole town."

"I abide scant tolerance for drunkards," said the Ranger without so much as a glance over his shoulder. "You shamed yourself. You represent the law here, Boggs. If you want to be a drunk, drop the badge and take to drumming whiskey." He snapped a sharp glance over his shoulder, then back to the horizon. "Apparently, it better suits your nature."

Boggs gritted his teeth and clenched his thick red fists. His shirt lay open and wet against his chest. Red curly hair lay plastered to his chest like frayed rope. His .44

hung against his thigh, but even in his rage he dared not reach for it. The Ranger would kill him. Somehow, even with his back to him and his eyes and mind trained far away into the torrent of hot dust, this man would sense or smell or somehow know that he'd reached for his gun, and Boggs' life would spill onto the dirty floor. Boggs knew it.

"I have a right to know, for crying out loud!" Boggs lowered his voice in a deep breath. "This is my damn jail here. This is my town!"

"Because he's a thieving, murdering dog," the Ranger said without facing him. "The whole Abbadele bunch are thieves and murdering dogs. Right, Dick?" He tossed the question over his shoulder toward the cell, then turned back and gazed out toward the lone horse at the hitch rail.

"You got nothing on me," Dick Abbadele hissed from his cell.

"We'll see, won't we?" The Ranger shrugged, then changed the subject, nodding over toward the lone horse standing at the hitch rail. "That big cut-eared gray horse there," he said. "Who rides him?"

"Huh?" Boggs stepped over, still scrubbing grit from his wet hair. "Heck, I don't know. Why?" He ran his hand across his face and around to his neck. He needed a drink — needed it bad. Perhaps for a split second, he had pictured his gun in his hand, had pictured himself squeezing the trigger on the Ranger; but if he had, the thought of it had struck an empty sickness low in his guts. Now the emptiness needed filling. "I don't keep tabs on who rides what horse around here."

"You should; it's part of your job to know," said the Ranger. Without giving Boggs time to reply, he asked, "Is it a big colored fellow, stands about two heads taller than anybody else? Wears thick eye-glasses and talks real educated-like?"

"I said, I don't know —"

"Because if it is, I've got his name on my short list."

"Oh? Is there some reward money on him?" Boggs craned his neck and looked over at the big brush-scarred gray horse. Its right ear stood an inch shorter than its left, clipped short by a rifle bullet years past. The Ranger turned and stared at him. "I mean . . . if there is, it *might* be him," Boggs added. "But I ain't saying nothing more unless we're partners on it."

"You'd cash in on him, but you let these other outlaws run free here?" the Ranger asked, already knowing the answer.

26

"Well, he is an outsider." Boggs shrugged.

"You're a piece of work, Boggs. I bet I have to dunk you a few more times before I leave here." He grinned, turned and walked over to the cell while he dropped the holster from his shoulder and swung it around his waist.

Boggs stepped along behind him and threw the wet towel in the corner behind the dust-covered woodstove. "Straighten *me* out? How dare you come in here, *out of your jurisdiction,* and start muscling me around in my own jail!"

The Ranger spoke to him over his shoulder as he stared into Dick Abbadele's eyes. "What about the Abbadeles? You gonna side with them when they get here?"

"No! But I ain't siding with you, either. The Abbadeles have done right by this town. They come through all the time. I've had no problems with 'em. Sure, they get a little wild, but that's just how it is. They spend money here when they've got it. This town depends on them."

"And when they don't have money to spend, they go and steal some. Right, Dick?"

"I ain't saying nothing else to you," Dick Abbadele hissed.

Pushing up the wide brim on his big gray

sombrero, revealing a jagged scar running the length of his cheek, the Ranger turned and faced Boggs. "And you let them come here to spend it . . . free as birds."

"Now, hold on," Boggs said. He pointed a finger. "If the law has a problem with Frank, Toot, Big Bob or Tillis Abbadele, I've heard nothing about it. Until I hear otherwise" — Boggs glanced toward the cell and raised his voice enough for Dick Abbadele to hear it — "they're as welcome here as anybody else, long as they mind their own business. That's more than I can say for you." He saw Dick Abbadele's eyes slice across him from within the darkness, then disappear.

"I've got their names on my list," the Ranger said. "They'll come here to get him, and I'm going to arrest them. If they go along with me, fine. If they put up a fight, I'll kill them in *your* street. You might just as well get used to the notion of it and save yourself a lot of consternation." He reached inside his coat.

"I don't want to see your so-called *list*. I've heard all about it." Boggs had raised a hand, but he dropped it when, instead of pulling out his list, the Ranger pulled out a long, thin cigar and bit the tip off it. He spit out the tip and stuck the cigar in his mouth. Boggs wiped his palms on his pants and bit the inside of his lip.

"Oh, I've got my list right here," the Ranger said, tapping a finger against his lapel, "and I'll pull it out when the time comes. Meanwhile, if you've got any sense at all, you'll go tell your townsfolk what's about to happen here in the next couple days and get 'em ready for it. You're gonna face the Abbadeles with me."

Boggs jutted his chin. "If I don't?"

The Ranger adjusted his holster, buttoned one button on his duster, turned and walked toward the door, the key to Dick Abbadele's cell shoved down in the hip pocket of his black linen suit. "There ain't no *if-I-don't,* Boggs. You're going to do it. Might as well sober up and dry off your shooting gear."

"Damn it!" Boggs slammed a fist against the wall beside Dick Abbadele's cell.

"Another thing," said the Ranger. "I'm leaving this prisoner under your protection while I ride back out there this evening. If he ain't here when I get back, I'll just figure it's your way of calling me out into the street."

"Lord, Ranger, that's a straight-out threat," said Boggs, his face turning even paler.

"I'm glad we both understand that," said the Ranger. He patted the key in his vest pocket. "Is this the only key to that cell?"

"Yes," said Boggs flatly.

"Then if he's not here, it means you had plenty of time to think about things while you had that door removed." Sam touched his fingers to the brim of his sombrero and headed for the door. "I'll give you this key as soon as I get back."

Boggs said, "You've come here for no other purpose than to start trouble, Ranger. I hope you're damn proud of yourself."

"It's trouble that needed starting," the Ranger said over his shoulder, pulling the door shut behind him.

With the Ranger gone and Sheriff Boggs standing alone in the office, Dick Abbadele shook the cell bars with both hands. "Come on, Sheriff, let me out of here. I know there's more than one key to this cell. Nobody would be that stupid."

Sheriff Boggs gave him an embarrassed look. "There was never any thought of needing *two* keys," he said.

"I'll be damned," said Dick Abbadele in disgust. "Then you best get somebody over here to jerk this door down or pick this lock. I want out of here!" He shook the bars harder.

"Damn it, Dick!" said Boggs, his voice quivering with the need for a drink. "You heard him. He all but said he'd *kill* me if I turn you loose."

Dick Abbadele stared at Boggs for a moment in disbelief. Then he slumped, shook his head and walked to the dirty cot in the shadowed corner of the cell. "Looks like it's time you made a decision, Sheriff."

The Hung Dog Saloon stood silent when Sam once again stepped through the batwing doors and looked all around. Empty bottles and half-full beer mugs stood along the bar and on tables covered with wet circles of mud where the glasses had sweated and run down into fine brown dust. Tobacco juice lay in dark, wet strings across the dirty plank floor. At the far end of the bar, the big black man stood as if he hadn't moved an inch since Sam's first visit. Sweating over a mug of beer and a bottle of rye whiskey, he stared at the Ranger through a pair of thick eyeglasses, threw back a shot and lifted the beer mug. White foam capped his lip, and he sucked it away.

"Jefferson Eldridge Shadowen," the Ranger said, stepping over to the other end of the bar. He raised his hands slightly and spread them along the edge of the deserted bar. "Also known as Big Shod," Sam added.

"That's correct," the black man said, his voice sounding refined and articulate. "I know who you are, and I'm not greatly impressed. So whatever you came here to do, either do it straightaway or leave me in peace." He threw back another drink and chased it with beer. "I know I'm on your so-called short list."

"Um-hm, that's right." The Ranger nodded, reached a cautious hand inside his duster, pulled out a match and cocked his thumbnail on the tip of it. The unlit cigar moved to the corner of his mouth. "But let's talk a minute, unless you're in a hurry." The match flared, and he raised it to the tip of his cigar.

"It's too hot to be in a hurry," the black man said, "and I have nowhere to go. If you want a drink, you'll have to oblige yourself. The bartender thought of something he forgot to do at home when he saw you coming." He almost smiled, but stopped himself. "You seem to have a way of clearing out a drinking crowd."

"Everybody's guilty of something, I expect. My coming around just reminds them of it." He drew on the cigar and let a stream of smoke roll out of his mouth. "Now you, on the other hand" — he pointed the cigar toward him — "you had more reason to run than the rest . . . but you didn't."

"I told you: It's too hot to hurry. I'm tired of running." He hefted the mug, sipped, set it down and spread a tight, tired smile. "How do the Lakota say it? *Today is a good day to die.*'"

"Something like that." The Ranger spread open his duster, hooked it behind the butt of the big pistol, then brought his hand back up on the bar. "Best I can recall, you used to work for the law, didn't you? You were even a lawyer for a spell, weren't you?"

"Yes, for a spell, as you put it," said Shod.

"Before that, you were a lawman. Federal law, wasn't it?" the Ranger asked.

"You know it was," said Shod, giving up very little about himself.

The Ranger studied the tip of the cigar as if considering something. Then he said, "Took to drinking and lost your badge."

"You've got that backward. I lost my badge, *then* took to drinking. I practiced law while I was down in —"

"Yeah, now I remember," the Ranger

said, cutting him off. "Took to using that Eastern education of yours down in *Tejas*. Guess them ole southern boys figured their law didn't need any practice, huh?" He smiled, then added: "And you shot a man down once for calling you a bad name." The Ranger shook his head slowly. "That must've been some really bad name. What came over you, anyway?"

"You had to be there to appreciate it," Shod said. "It wasn't so much calling me the bad name as it was calling me the bad name from behind a cocked pistol. I get real touchy about things like that."

"I bet you do. Now you're on the run, same as every other gunman and rounder on my list."

"After today, I don't plan on being on your list, one way or the other." He slid the beer mug to the side.

The Ranger raised a cautious hand. "Still just talking here. I haven't called you a bad name, have I?"

"If we're gonna do it . . ."

"Well, I ain't real sure we have to. I knew the man you shot. Only problem I had with it was that somebody didn't do it sooner."

"Yeah?" Shod cocked his head. "Then why have I been on your list the past year?"

"I just wanted to give you some room, see what you did next. See if you was gonna go straight or crooked. All I've heard is that you're hunting bounty now."

"A man has to make a living. If you call bounty hunting *living*." He shrugged one shoulder. "Are you telling me we're not going to draw loaded pistols and see how many holes we can shoot into one another?"

The Ranger smiled. "That's an eloquent way of putting it. But that's exactly what I'm trying to tell you . . . unless you feel like we really should." He shook his head. "I'd just as soon we didn't. You've pulled your time in the badlands. Don't worry about me looking for you. I never did: not very hard, anyway. Besides, I've got too much to do here to have to worry about you throwing down on me."

Big Shod nodded. "Yes, you do. I saw who you brought in. You must be wanting to die."

"No, just doing my job here. Figured I'd bring him alive and draw the rest of the gang in." He gave a slight smile.

"Do you realize how many Abbadele men there are out there?" Shod wagged a thumb toward the distant badlands.

"Quite a few, as I recall," the Ranger

said. "But I only want the ones who robbed the bank over in Riley."

Big Shod shook his head slowly. "It won't matter to them. They're all beans in the same bucket, so to speak. You'll have to face all of them."

"Yes, I expect I will." The Ranger nodded.

"The Abbadeles seem to be well-respected here in Sabre Ridge," said Shod. "The Abbadele brothers themselves, anyway. I don't know about the men who ride with them."

"I know," said the Ranger. "The sheriff was kind enough to let me know that I've come here to start trouble with some highly regarded citizens."

"Citizens," Shod said flatly, almost offering a trace of a smile. He studied the Ranger's eyes for a second, then shrugged again. "Well, whatever works for you, Ranger. Good luck."

"Then you and I are caught up?" the Ranger asked, and he stepped back from the bar, turning slowly, and started to leave.

"Yep. But just one thing, Ranger," Big Shod said in a low tone.

"What's that?" the Ranger stopped and asked without turning around.

"The bartender who left here? I forgot to tell you. He's Earl Dobson. He went home to get a shotgun full of nail heads. Said you've been looking for him for two years."

"I was wondering if you was going to tell me or not." The Ranger let out a breath. "Earl Dobson. Yep, he's on my list, all right. He killed a man and his wife. Has he got many friends here?"

"A couple of fellows left here with him. You know how that goes. Anything to stay in good with a bartender."

"Yeah, anything for a free round, I reckon." The Ranger drew his pistol, let his coat fall closed and eased the barrel down through the false pocket flap of his riding duster. Then he dropped his cigar, stepped on it, flipped up his collar with his free hand and walked out the door. He had no more time to spend: He had to get out there and find Maria.

Big Shod moved to the middle of the bar with his beer mug, reached over and filled it from the tap. He stood still for a moment until he heard a voice call out from the street. "All right, Ranger! You want me — here I am!"

"Us, too! We're gonna —" another voice yelled, but it stopped short beneath three rapid blasts of pistol fire.

There was no sound of a shotgun. Big Shod stood in the ringing silence of the empty bar, shook his head and raised his beer mug with a thin smile. "So long, Earl," he said, throwing back a drink.

Chapter 3

Bob Abbadele sidled up to the large steer as it pulled and fought against the rope around its neck. On the other end of that tightly drawn rope, Lenbow Decker and Tommy Walsh dug their heels into the dirt, trying to handle the steer's weight. "Damn it, boys," Big Bob said, talking as he worked. He grabbed the steer by both horns and twisted its head quickly upward. At the same time, he swept his right boot sidelong, knocking the powerful animal's forelegs out from under it. "I always say, when rustling and cross-branding gets to be harder work than lawful cattle ranching, it's time to roll up our blankets." The steer hit the ground on its side in a spray of dust. Decker and Walsh felt the earth shudder beneath their feet.

"Jesus," said Len Decker, wide-eyed, always impressed by Big Bob's strength.

"Hell, that ain't nothing," said Tommy Walsh, keeping his talk between himself and Decker while they both watched Big Bob stoop down and tie the steer's hooves together. "It's just an old Mexican trick . . . all in using your weight and balance just right. I saw my pa do it a thousand times. I could do it myself if I wanted to."

"Then let's see you do it," Decker said.

"I don't want to," Walsh said. He spit and handed Decker his handful of rope. "I was born for better things than throwing beeves." He walked to where Frank Abbadele, the eldest of the Abbadele brothers, stood near the small fire. Frank put his right boot down on the long handle of a branding iron. He rolled the iron back and forth with his boot, watching the end of the iron glow red hot. Sweat streamed down Frank's face into his thick red-gray beard. He raised his hat and mopped his palm across his brow and back along his wet, salted-red hair. His hair fell long and limp to his shoulders. He shoved his long hair back, then lowered his hat to hold it in place. He gazed out across the flat, endless stretch of desert to where a tall brown windstorm swirled thick and high into heaven.

"I expect this work would go some easier if everybody showed up when they're supposed to," Frank said, answering his brother Bob. He took a step back as Tommy Walsh reached a gloved hand down for the branding iron, picked it up and hurried toward the downed steer with it.

Big Bob leaned to one side and watched Walsh stick the iron to the steer's rump. Burnt hair sizzled and smoked. The steer bawled and struggled to toss its head up. But Big Bob held it pinned to the ground almost effortlessly. "Jesus," said Lenbow Decker again, watching as he coiled the long, unused end of the rope.

"I don't know if you've noticed, Brother Frank," said Big Bob, "but Toot's got something eating his guts out lately. He ain't got his mind where it ought be — that's the problem." He turned his face from the smell of singed skin and hair until Walsh raised the smoking branding iron and hurried back to the fire with it.

Frank nodded at the distant dust storm. "I reckon if Toot, Dick and Tillis got caught in that twist of dirt, they'll not be back before dark."

"I reckon," said Big Bob, "but I doubt if that's anything they're worried about. You ever want to slow them to a walk, just tell them there's work where they're headed." He untied the steer's hooves, grabbed it by its side and seemed to pitch it up onto all fours. The steer bolted away across the corral.

"Jesus!" said Lenbow Decker for the third time.

Walsh shook his head in reproach. "Damn it to hell, Lenbow, quit using the Lord's name in vain," he said.

"In *vain?*" Decker looked puzzled. As the two spoke, they gathered closer to Frank Abbadele but stayed back away from the heat of the fire.

"Yeah, *in vain,* damn it!" said Tommy Walsh, yanking off his hot leather gloves. "I might be a no-account cattle rustler, but by God, I come from good Christian people. I don't like that kind of talk. It's bad luck. It causes bad stuff to happen." He dropped his branding gloves in the dirt, then reached behind his back, untied his batwing chaps and let them fall.

"You mean you're scared you'll go to hell?" asked Decker. "Because if you are, I've got some bad news for you . . ." He let his voice trail.

"It's just a peculiarity I have, is all. So cut it out," said Walsh. "I ain't afraid of going to hell. I don't even believe in hell. I don't believe in none of that religious malarkey. I just don't like that kind of talk."

Lenbow Decker grinned as he fished a bag of tobacco and papers from his shirt pocket. "If you don't believe in none of it,

42

why does it bother you what people say?"

"It just does." Tommy Walsh took out his own bag of tobacco and began rolling himself a smoke. "See, a man don't have to believe in hell not to want to go there, does he?"

Decker shrugged, busy rolling his own smoke. "I don't know. Take me, I believe in hell and the devil, but I still don't do nothing to keep me from going to hell."

"Then you're what's called a damned fool," said Walsh matter-of-factly, running the twisted cigarette in and out of his mouth, wetting and firming it. "If I believed in hell and the devil, I'd damned sure take some steps for myself."

"What kind of steps?" Decker asked.

"Just steps," said Walsh, suddenly feeling pressed by the conversation. "Don't ask so many questions. I think religion is a personal thing, ought not be discussed freely."

"But you don't believe in it," Decker persisted with a wry grin.

"Stop crowding me, Decker," said Walsh. "Hell and the devil ain't something to play around with."

"But if you don't even believe in —"

"Both of you shut up," said Frank Abbadele, cutting Lenbow Decker off. "You're getting on my nerves."

"Speaking of hell and the devil," said Big Bob Abbadele, "look who's coming here." Over a short rise came a big, sweat-streaked chestnut barb in a full run. "Now we'll hear what's taking everybody so long getting home."

"Slow down, Brooks," said Frank Abbadele, as if the rider could hear him from a hundred yards away. Craning upward on his toes, Frank's expression turned curious. The rider looked small in the saddle, his duster tails flapping straight back behind him. "Is he drunk or hurt? He's riding awful funny."

"He always rides that way," said Big Bob. "You just ain't noticed."

"That's embarrassing, a grown man flopping up and down that way," said Frank. "Are you sure that's Brooks?"

"It's Brooks," said Big Bob.

They drew to a halt as the horse slowed to a trot the last few yards and swung sideways in front of them. "It's good to see you all," said the rider, his face pale, his eyes red-rimmed beneath his hat brim. "I was afraid I'd run into more of them damned *comadrejas*."

"You ran into *comadrejas?*" asked Bob.

"Yep, but I ducked away from them before we rode into that twister," said Brooks.

44

He took a deep breath, then said with a look of dread, "Boy oh boy, have we got some trouble coming! Has any of the others showed up yet? We all got scattered apart in that twister. Has the law been through here?"

Frank and Big Bob looked at one another. Then Frank said, "Slow down, Brooks. What the hell are you talking about? Where's our brothers?"

Lester Brooks took off his hat and slapped fine dust from it against his trouser leg as he spoke to them. "I know you ain't going to like this, Frank, but Dick and Tillis got a wild hair about robbing that little bank in Riley. My boy, Kirby, was going with them, so I went along, too. I knew it was a bad idea!"

"Damn it!" said Bob. "They all knew we've been trying to lay low for a while. Didn't I make that clear?"

"Yes, you did," said Brooks, raising a canteen by its strap from his saddle horn and uncapping it as he talked, "but what was I supposed to do? Tillis had Kirby all stoked up to go, telling him there was a big parcel of cash came in from back East just waiting for the pickings. I figured I better go, keep an eye on things."

"Shit," said Frank. He looked out across

45

the land at the big, thrashing brown cloud in the distance. "Where's Toot? With Dick and Tillis, I expect?"

Brooks had turned back a mouthful of warm water from his canteen. He swished it around in his mouth, then spit a stream before answering. "Toot?" Brooks shook his head as if considering it. "Naw, Toot didn't go to Riley. He split off before we got twenty miles from here. He was acting strange again, you know?"

"Then where the hell is he?" asked Frank. "He left there with Dick and Tillis. He's been gone all week!"

"I don't know where he goes when he gets in that crazy frame of mind," said Brooks. "It's bad enough I got my own boy, Kirby, to look out for. Anyway, somebody got on our trail before we hit the twister. Don't know if it was *comadrejas* or that ranger and his woman or some other lawman or what. But Dick stayed back to see — said he'd put an ambush on them from up in the rocks. Since then, I ain't seen none of them."

Frank and Bob perked up. "That ranger?" Frank asked. "What about that ranger?"

"Oh, didn't I say?" said Brooks. "It was that ranger, Sam Burrack, who got onto our trail just outside of Riley. If it wasn't him, it was his double . . . riding that big white horse with the black ring around its eye. That's the horse he took from Bent Jackson after he killed him deader than hell."

"I heard that story," said Frank, getting impatient with him. He and Bob gave one another a wary look.

"That's all we need," said Bob. "That bloodthirsty ranger down our necks."

"Take it easy, Brother Bob," said Frank, not wanting to look overly concerned in front of the men. "Let's make sure Brooks knows what he's talking about before we go off with a bend in our backbone."

Big Bob's face reddened a bit, but he settled down. "I'm just saying we don't need no trouble right now."

"I know that, Brother Bob," said Frank. "But we've heard enough to know something's up out there. Let's get some horses under us and see what the hell's going on." He turned back to Lester Brooks. "Did they make any money off that bank job, or was that a waste of time?"

"No, sir! It weren't no waste of time. It was a good haul!" said Brooks, his eyes lighting up at the subject turning to money. "I bet we took out over thirty thousand dollars from that little, pint-sized bank! I never seen so much money come from a place that small."

"No kidding?" Frank Abbadele said, getting more interested in details now that money was involved. "Who carried it?"

"Dick carried it," said Brooks, "just like he always does."

"How many of you went along?" Frank asked.

"There was eight of us, counting Dick and Tillis," said Brooks. "There was me and Kirby, the two Knox brothers, Billy Stone, and Doyle Royal."

"That's a lot of cutting," said Big Bob. "Thirty thousand ain't so much when you divvy it eight ways."

Frank gave him a look, ignoring his remark, and said, "I say let's get going, see if we can find Dick, first of all." He grinned. "I worry about any brother of mine out there packing that kind of cash around. I'd hate to see him pull his back out carrying it."

"Want me and Walsh to get some horses saddled?" asked Lenbow Decker.

"Hell, yes." Frank Abbadele gave him a stern look. "Are you still standing here?"

Seeing Decker and Walsh head for the livery barn, Brooks said, "I'll just turn this

48

horse in, get one that ain't blown and ride with you."

"Yeah, you do that, Brooks," said Frank. Then, as soon as Brooks gigged his tired horse toward the barn, Frank turned to his brother Bob.

Before Frank could say anything, Bob said, "I feel like kicking Dick's ass up around his neck, doing this after us all agreeing to lay low awhile."

"What about Tillis?" asked Frank. "You feel like kicking his ass, too? 'Cause you can bet he's in it up to his chin."

Big Bob made a sucking noise, slicing air through his teeth. Tillis Abbadele was the gunslinger of the family, the one most likely to blow somebody's head off if something they did or said struck him the wrong way. "We're going to have a very serious talk once this is all settled," said Bob. "I promise you that, whether Tillis likes it or not."

Frank only grinned flatly. "You're missing the picture here, big brother. Didn't you hear Brooks? We're talking thirty thousand dollars. All we got to do is round everybody up and get the kinks jerked out of this thing."

"But like I said," Big Bob replied, "that's thirty thousand cut eight ways."

Frank shook his head, his grin widening as he raised his big Colt and checked it, blowing a fleck of dust from the tip of the barrel. "You're *still* not getting the picture. I can see I'm going have to teach you how to add and subtract."

Maria led her limping paint horse by its reins, the sound of the wind still roaring in her ears although the worst part of the storm had passed nearly an hour ago. Looking back over her shoulder, she saw the long, twisting, brown cloud move across the land like some ancient raging demon. She hoped Sam had made it out all right. Turning her eyes back in the direction of Sabre Ridge, she hoped Sam was still alive. *Stop it!* she chastised herself. Of course he was alive. And if Sam were here right now, she knew he would be telling her not to think about him until she knew she was out of trouble herself. Looking around the wind-tossed inferno at jagged rock ridges reaching upward from an endless bed of sand, she had to agree. She was afoot in the badlands desert, a hostile place not known for its mercy toward beast or humankind.

But that was only looking on the bad side of her situation, Maria reminded herself. Fortunately for her, she knew this terrain. She had lived in this land longer than she cared to remember, until Sam had found her and rescued her from the *comadrejas*. At the thought of the *comadrejas*, she darted a wary glance right and left, raised the rifle she'd been letting hang freely in her gloved hand and cradled it in her arm. Her hand slipped in closer to the rifle's trigger, feeling better there as she scanned the winding trail before her. She was certain Sam had made it past the worst of the storm when he split off from her and went to take care of the rifleman up in the rocks above them. That being the case, she had every reason to believe he'd soon be looking for her. She knew of an old mining shack two miles ahead just off the main trail, tucked inside a towering rock hillside. Her best move would be to get there and wait and keep an eye out for Sam, at least until morning.

The two-mile walk took longer than she'd anticipated, her pace slowed more and more by the limping horse. By the time she stepped up on a flat rock and looked down at the sun-bleached shack, cactus shadows had started to stretch long across the hot, wavering sand.

Behind her, the paint horse blew out a

breath and shifted back and forth uncomfortably, keeping its weight off its bruised hoof. "Don't worry," Maria said. "Soon we will have you resting, and I will find you some water." She took a step back and rubbed the paint's muzzle. Then, looking down at the shack, she froze at the slightest glimpse of someone walking past the side window. "Easy," she whispered to the horse, stepping farther back out of sight. She inched carefully forward and watched the window but saw nothing more. Looking all around the rocky yard, seeing no signs of tracks, whether of men or beasts, she whispered to the horse as if it could understand her words. "We are not going to spend the night up here. We are going down there. You must be very quiet, *sí?*"

Taking her time, Maria led the paint horse down a steep, rocky path that approached the shack from a blind side, where there was no window facing her. At a distance of twenty yards, she stood partly hidden by rock and said to the half-open door of the shack, "*Hola?* My horse is lame, and we are both in need of water. May we come forward?" She kept her hand around the poised rifle stock, her finger across the trigger.

After a moment of silence with no response from inside the shack, instead of calling out again she wrapped the horse's reins around an edge of protruding rock and stepped forward, keeping an eye on the half-open door. Stepping lightly across the creaking boards of the porch, she laid a hand against the door and slowly opened it a few more inches, peering into the shaded darkness.

"Hola," Maria said quietly. "I know you are in there: I saw you." Listening closely, she heard labored, panting breathing coming from a far, dark corner. A woman's breath, Maria told herself. "Are you all right?" she asked.

A weak voice whispered through the darkness. "You are a woman . . ."

"Sí," said Maria, although it was not a question. "I am a woman. Are you hurt? Do you need help?"

Maria heard the faintest sound of sobbing come from the darkness and could not tell if it was tears of pain or relief. "Oh please . . . yes," the voice said. "I — I need help. I'm . . . having a baby."

"Oh my," said Maria, hearing the young woman's words and sensing the sincerity of them. She swung the door open and stepped inside. Still using caution, but hurrying across the shack toward the figure lying in the corner, Maria looked down in the afternoon gloom at the sweaty black face staring up at her.

"There's a lamp . . . over there," the young woman said with much effort, pointing at a battered table against the back wall. "I — I tried to light it, but I . . . hurt too bad."

"*Sí*," said Maria. "You lie still. I will get the lamp." She hurried to the table, checked the lamp, then lit it. In a moment, she was kneeling beside the woman, the soft lamplight falling in a wide circle around them. "What are you doing out here?"

"I came to my baby's father here. But there was a terrible windstorm," the woman said, her hands clasped to her large, glistening belly. "It came so fast, without warning. I lost my burro . . . most of my belongings. I must have been knocked unconscious." Her right hand went to the back of her head, and she winced in pain at her own touch.

"I, too, was caught in the storm," said Maria, leaning forward and looking at the knot on the back of the woman's head. "The storm has shaken many things loose from the badlands." She thought about the *comadrejas*, then said, "We must not have a fire or a light here after dark." In the lamp-light, Maria could see that the woman had taken a blanket and made a pallet for herself on the hard floor. She lay naked, her dust-streaked dress lying in a heap beside her.

"I know," said the woman. "My child's father has warned me about the *comadrejas*."

"Oh?" said Maria. "Then the child's father is from around here?"

The woman made no reply but was instead stricken by a sudden sharp pain that drew her full attention. Maria felt her hand being clasped and squeezed tightly. As the woman's pain subsided, Maria reached in with her bandanna and wiped her sweaty forehead. "We will talk later. Now we must get prepared."

The woman nodded in agreement. "When my birthing pains became closer together, I didn't know what to do to get prepared," the young woman managed to say, seeming to have drawn strength from having someone beside her.

"You have done well, considering," Maria said, reaching for the dress. "But let's get this back on you. That was not a good idea. The night will be cold." She looked at the dress, seeing that it was a large, shapeless gingham. Then she helped the woman slip the dress over her head and gather it above her large, tight belly. Looking all around the dusty abandoned shack, Maria's eyes fell upon a goatskin of water lying alongside a pair of saddlebags. "But what on earth are you doing out in these badlands?" As she spoke, Maria set the lamp a few feet away from the blanket, stood up and stepped over to the goatskin, picking it up, seeing that it was full.

"It's a long story," the young woman said, her voice slicing short against renewed pain in her belly.

"I understand," said Maria, realizing that this was no time to press her with questions. "I will be right back. I have to —"

"Wait! Where are you going?" the young woman asked in panic, cutting Maria off.

"I have a blanket, a cooking pan and some other things on my horse," Maria said. She smiled, hoping it would reassure the young woman. "Don't worry, I will not leave you here alone. We will have this child together."

Outside, along a higher terrace of ridgeline, three dust-covered figures moved afoot until they were able to look down on the shack and the paint horse standing nearby. "Ramoul, Santaglio," said the white man to the two men following him in a low crouch, "how many of de bullets do we's have between us?" The white man had lived so long with the *comadrejas* that he had taken on their broken accent, a garbled combination of French, Spanish, Apache and border English.

Behind him, the two dusty, sweat-smeared faces looked at one another. Then Ramoul said, "I have dis many bullets." He held up three bony fingers. "But my *pistole*, it is full ob de dirt."

"Then get it cleaned, damn it," said Fuller. "We have got to have dis horse so's we can join de others!"

"Look!" said Santaglio, drawing their attention to Maria as she appeared from the shack and walked toward the horse.

"Quickly!" said the white man. "It is only a woman! Rush her before she gets into de saddle!"

"Bud she has de rifle!" said Ramoul.

"Huh-uh, not me," Santaglio said.

"You cowardly *bastidos!*" the white man growled, standing, holding his big cap-and-ball pistol up, cocking it. "If we scare her, she will run away! Must I do id all myself?"

Turning with a long, wild yell, the white man leaped from ridge to ridge, firing a shot as he charged downward toward where Maria stood beside the big paint horse.

"He is right!" yelled Ramoul. "Come on! We scare her away!"

"I don't think so," said Santaglio, shaking his head warily. But Ramoul hurried down behind the white man, waving his dirt-jammed pistol over his head.

Santaglio batted his eyes as he saw Maria's first shot nail the white man in his chest and send him backward mid-yell, a spray of blood blowing out of his back. Behind him, Ramoul saw what had happened and realized how foolish he'd been, trying to scare her, especially with a jammed gun. He veered, making a leap for the white man's pistol, hoping to give himself a fighting chance.

Maria levered a fresh round into her rifle chamber, watching the second *comadreja* go down and snatch up the fallen pistol. She waited for a second, knowing he had to rise up slightly at least to take a shot at her. She aimed coolly and steadily, her eyes locking onto her target even as she attended peripherally to the upward ridges behind him. When he raised onto his knees and held the big cap-and-ball pistol out with both hands, she squeezed the trigger and saw him flip backward, his blood and brain matter showering a red mist across the rocks.

As calmly as Maria had taken the shot, she levered a fresh round into the chamber with the rifle still pressed into the pocket of her shoulder. She scanned the terraced ridges in anticipation, unable to see Santaglio running away in a crouch, still shaking his head at what a bad idea this had been. He wasn't about to tell the other *comadrejas* the truth about what had happened out here, that he had run away, leaving the white man and Ramoul lying dead and unavenged in the dirt. He'd have to think of something more heroic. Maybe he could even work this to his advantage.

Well, that settles it, Maria thought to herself. The storm had scattered the *comadrejas* everywhere. They would be crawling out from under rocks like snakes. Now it made no difference whether or not she had a fire and a light throughout the night. The rifle shots had announced her and the black woman's presence. Her choice was simple now. She couldn't move the woman until the baby was born. All she could do now was take the horse inside the shack and make a stand against anything that came creeping out of the night. She looked out past the harsh, barren ridges and took a deep, resolved breath, hearing a long moan of anguish coming from the shack behind her. "Come on, Sam," she whispered aloud. "Where are you?"

Chapter 4

The Ranger had no time to waste getting back on the trail looking for Maria. While a drift of burnt powder still hung in the air, he took his horse, Black-eye, to the livery and paid the stable boy a full dollar to wipe the horse down and feed and water it. Then he'd taken the only rental horse available, a tall, scrappy red stallion, and he'd saddled the big brute as the animal blew out a breath and stepped sideways, trying to duck out from under the saddle. "I've got no time for this right now," Sam said. He stayed close against the stallion's side, getting the saddle on before the animal could outmaneuver him. The stable boy stood in front of the stallion, holding the reins with a worried look on his face.

"What's this stud's name, young man?" Sam asked, taking the reins and grabbing the stallion's bridle close to the chin while the animal jerked and whinnied and shook his head.

"He's a wild herd stud from the Northern

Territory. The stable owner calls him Red Devil," said the boy, staring wide-eyed at the big thrashing ball of red fury in the Ranger's hand.

"That seems to fit," said the Ranger. "Is he always this friendly?"

"I've never seen anybody get a saddle on him that quick," said the stable boy. "To tell the truth, nobody has rented him since I've been here. He's a bucker and a biter. If he doesn't settle down, the owner is going to geld him as soon as he gets back to town."

"Ouch!" the Ranger said, turning to face the big wild animal. "Did you hear that, Red Devil? This could be your last chance to redeem yourself."

The stallion had settled a little, but the Ranger could tell there was more to come. "A bucker, huh?" He ran a gloved hand down the red muzzle and looked deep into the raging eyes. "Well, it makes no difference. We're just going to have to get along, you and me," he said. Then he said to the stable boy, "Son, open that door for me."

The boy looked dubious. "Hadn't you better get on him first? He gets loose out into the corral, he could be hard to catch."

"We'll be all right," said the Ranger.

The boy stepped back and swung the

doors open, making sure he got out of the way as he saw the stallion perk its ears and collect itself for a quick lunge. "Watch it, Ranger!" the boy shouted.

Sam had seen the move coming: in fact, had been counting on it. As the stallion began to bolt out of the barn, the Ranger grabbed the saddle horn, ran the first few steps with the stallion and swung up into the saddle, taking away the stallion's opportunity to buck him right away. Now the stallion had lost the edge. He spun and kicked, but with the Ranger keeping his head high, the big brute began to realize the man on his back was there to stay. Still, he ran high-headed in a wide circle around the corral, snorting, whinnying and trying to toss his head around for a bite at the Ranger's leg. "Now throw that gate open!" the Ranger called out to the stable boy.

Across the street from the livery corral, Big Shod stood watching. He smiled slightly to himself as the boy opened the corral gate and the Ranger raced out on the red stallion and disappeared in a rise of dust along the trail toward the badlands. Sitting on the boardwalk a few feet from Shod, Pip Richards whittled at a new stick. "Now, there goes a man in sore need of transportation," Pip commented, fanning the dust the stallion had raised. "That is one powerfully *mean* red stallion."

"That is one powerfully *determined* ranger," said Shod.

"Yep, I reckon." Pip nodded and spit, then turned his gaze up at Shod. He squinted, even though the sun glare was no obstacle to him from where he now sat. "You're that colored bounty hunter, ain't ya?"

Big Shod stared at him for a silent moment, then said, "I *am* colored; I *am* a bounty hunter. Does that help you any?"

"I meant no offense," said Pip.

"None was taken," said Shod.

Pip nodded, took a couple of long slices down the wood with his pocketknife and watched the curled shavings fall to the dirt between his feet. "Will you be here when the Abbadeles come calling?"

"That's a possibility," said Shod, offering no more than was asked of him. "Why?"

"Just curious," said Pip, taking another long slice down the stick. "I figure, you being a bounty hunter . . . the Abbadeles ought to be a good catch."

"Oh?" Shod cocked his head in curiosity, eyeing Pip. "I've heard of no bounty on any of the Abbadeles."

"No," said Pip, "but most of the men

riding with them are worth a whole lot more dead than they ever will be alive." He spit. "Just thought I'd mention it."

"Really?" Shod remarked. "And what's your interest in all this?"

"Nothing," said Pip. But then he seemed to consider something and added, "I could use some pocket money for tobacco, come to think of it."

"I see," said Shod, looking out again in the direction the Ranger had taken.

"Of course, none of this means anything if our drunken sheriff turns Dick Abbadele loose, I reckon."

"I think you're probably right, old timer," said Shod, turning his glance toward the jail as he spoke. "Excuse me." He turned and started toward the jail.

"Where you going?" Pip asked, almost standing up in his curiosity and following him.

Shod held a hand out, halting him. "I'm going to see the sheriff. Let him know that I'm volunteering my services to keep an eye on the jail. Make sure nothing happens to Dick Abbadele."

"He's ain't going to like that," said Pip, a faint, knowing smile coming to his lips.

"Then he'll have to learn to live with it," said Shod.

★ ★ ★

The baby arrived in the middle of the night. So did the *comadrejas*. Maria had heard running footsteps beyond the bolted door as she finished wiping the baby girl down with her wet bandanna. Calmly, she spoke to the slumbering black woman. "April," she said quietly, having learned the young woman's name during the rigors of childbirth, "here is your brand-new daughter."

April stirred, her eyelids fluttering for a second before she took a firm grasp on consciousness. "Is she . . . ? Is she . . . ?" April's voice faltered.

"She is fine," said Maria, holding the blanket-wrapped baby out to its mother's weak but willing arms. "Now you must hold her. We have visitors." Keeping her voice calm and steady helped some, but not enough to keep April from shaking with fear.

"Oh God, please!" said April, partly to Maria and partly in prayer. "Please don't let them harm this child!"

"Shhh, we will be all right," Maria said, trying to sound more confident than she was right then. There was no telling how many *comadrejas* the storm had blown up from the depths of the badlands. Standing up, picking up her rifle, Maria paused before turning toward the window where she had closed and latched the wooden shutter and said, "But if something should happen to me, you must find the strength to take the baby and make a run for your lives on the horse."

"I can't! I'm not a good rider," said April, her voice sounding frightened. "I could never manage on a horse with this baby."

"Then I must give you this pistol with only *two* bullets in it," said Maria, touching the pistol on her hip. Her voice took on a dark, serious tone. "Do you understand what that means you must do?"

"My God, I could never do such a thing!" April said, appalled by the very thought of it.

"Then do not tell me you can't ride and carry the baby," said Maria. "If worse comes to worst, you must both die escaping, or you must die by your own hand. It is harsh, but it is how things are."

"I know," said April, summoning up a stronger voice. "I'm sorry." She held the baby close to her bosom. "What are you going to do?"

Maria shrugged. "My choice is certain. I am going to fight them."

"Then I'll lay the baby somewhere safe and help you fight them," said April.

"For now," said Maria, "take care of the baby. If things get bad, there will be plenty of fighting for both of us."

"I will do my part," April said bravely.

"*Sí*, of course you will. I do not doubt you," said Maria respectfully.

She walked to the shuttered window and looked out through the gun slot that had been installed for this very type of situation. Outside, a full moon stood high above the badlands, bathing the clearing out front of the shack in purple-shadowed light. "This place was built to hold off the Apache. The *comadrejas* are not nearly so fierce. So perhaps we will be all right." Maria spoke boldly, yet looking out through the gun slot at the many shadowy figures moving forward to the closest cover of rock, she felt a dark chill go up her spine. There were too many *comadrejas* to count. On the next terraced ridgeline, a campfire raged, a sure sign of the outlaws' confidence in their large numbers.

Suddenly a voice called out from less than thirty yards away. "Hey jou — the woman in the shack! Lesten to me. You are not going nowhere tonight, you bet! You come out wid jour hand high up! Maybe we keel you quicklike, *sí?*"

Maria raised the rifle to the slot but did not stick the barrel out lest there be someone waiting to grab it and render her powerless. Instead, she rested the very tip of the barrel at the inner edge of the slot and cocked the rifle. She made no reply to the voice outside; there was nothing to say. Let them do all the talking, she reminded herself, having heard that safe bit of advice from Sam during their time together. *While they talk, you plan,* Sam always said. She could picture his wry smile. *While they plan, you shoot . . .*

"I know jou hear me in there — jou with the rifle!" the voice called out. "Jou must die. Jou killed our friends . . . My brothers, *mis hermanos!* Now jour blood will run in great streams! Jour head will be upon a pole for the crowd to pick out jour eyeballs!"

"Don't let him spook you, April," Maria said over her shoulder, still keeping her attention on the rifle slot. "The *comadrejas* always talk better than they fight. They are dangerous, but they are also cowardly swine who are good at boastful threats but do their best fighting against women, children and unarmed —"

"Yiii!" a voice screamed in rage right outside the rifle slot, cutting her words off.

69

One of the *comadrejas* had been standing with his back against the wall, waiting for her to shove the rifle barrel through the slot. He had listened to her insults until he could take no more. He shrieked and pounded on the thick wooden shutters. Maria fired quickly through the slot and heard his body hit the ground with a thud. Footsteps pounded away from the shack. Maria acted fast. Now that the porch was clear, she shoved the rifle barrel through the slot and fired three shots as rapidly as she could lever rounds into the chamber. One shadowy figure fell and tumbled to a halt, dead. Another figure fell but crawled away screaming.

Two bullets thumped against the front of the shack. Maria pulled her rifle in and dropped below the window ledge, waiting. In a moment, when no more shots came, she rose up and looked out through the rifle slot. She saw figures moving back farther away. On the ridgeline, figures moved between her and the firelight as the *comadrejas* gathered to plan their next move. *While they plan, I shoot . . .* She shoved her rifle barrel forward through the gun slot, took a close aim at the figures around the fire and, although she knew her ammunition was worth more than gold to

70

her, fired three more quick shots.

At the end of her firing, Maria heard a man cry out in pain. *Good,* she thought. *Now that they know they are dealing with a shooter, they will not take us so lightly.* She looked over at April and the blanket-wrapped baby and offered a smile, hoping it didn't look too contrived.

"That will make them think twice before rushing us," she said. Then, as April tried to offer a brave smile in return, Maria said to herself, turning back to the window, *Sam, please hurry. If these weasels hit us all at once, we're done for. . . .*

A half hour later, the voice of the same *comadreja* called out to the shack, this time from farther back among the cover of rock. "This will be jour last chance to come out wid jour hand up! After dis there is no more of the warning! We will set fire to the shack and jou will die choking on smoke and jour own blood!"

From her position at the window, Maria heard April let out a short gasp. "Do not be frightened," Maria said. "If they thought we were so easy to handle, they would not be asking us to surrender."

"But if they set fire, what will we do?" April asked, her confidence waning.

"Don't worry," said Maria. "They're not

71

going to set fire to this shack unless all else fails." She nodded toward the paint horse standing against the far wall. "Everything they want is in this shack. If they burn it, they kill the horse and lose whatever goods we might have. They're stupid, but they're also greedy . . . too greedy to risk killing the horse. That's one reason they haven't shot this place to pieces."

"Then what will they do?" April asked.

Maria considered it. "They'll try to browbeat us, scare us, maybe get lucky and manage to get a shot through this gun slot." As she spoke, she leaned slightly and gazed out through the gun slot. "If they think they have time, they'll wait us out. Eventually we will run out of water and food . . . and ammunition. But we are a long way from that happening."

"How do you know so much about them?" April asked.

"I was once their prisoner," Maria said flatly, in a tone of voice that suggested she didn't want to discuss it any further.

"Oh, I see," said April, taking the hint and falling silent, holding the baby securely against her bosom.

"Are jou coming out now?" the *comadreja* shouted.

Maria didn't bother answering. She

turned to face April and the baby and smiled. "You are feeling much stronger already, *sí?*"

April only nodded in reply.

"All right den," said the *comadreja,* "do not say I didn't warn jou!"

Three shots hit the outside of the thick plank window shutter. Maria ducked away in reflex and crouched down until she realized the shots had stopped. Then she took a quick glance through the gun slot and said to April, "They are low on ammunition — good! It is one more thing in our favor."

Outside, the *comadreja* leader said, "it is so terrible, this *violencia!* I always say, why is it we cannot get along together? Huh? Can jou tell me that?"

Maria gave April a knowing glance. "Yes, they are low on ammunition, and they need our horse and supplies. Otherwise, he would not be talking this way."

"I think there is a *solucion* for jou," the voice called out. "Do jou want to hear it?"

Again, Maria refused to answer.

"All right den, I will tell jou," said the voice. "Send us out the horse . . . for killing my friends. Den jou can go on jour ways."

"Be prepared," Maria said to April.

73

"They might hit harder this time." A concerned look came to her face. "If they are desperate for ammunition and supplies, they might even go ahead and burn us out."

"But you said we —" April's words were cut short by two rifle shots hitting the front of the shack at once.

"I know what I said," Maria replied, wincing a bit as a bullet thumped against the front of the shack, "but it is all pure speculation until we live through it. Be prepared for anything." The last of her words were drowned beneath a heavy volley of rifle and pistol fire. As soon as it stopped, Maria ventured a peep through the gun slot. She saw torches pass from hand to hand near the fire. She hesitated before telling April, but when she turned to face her in the thin lamplight, April saw the look on her face. A shot thumped against the thick shutter.

"They are lighting torches," said Maria.

"Oh no," said April. "Then they are getting ready to burn us?" Two shots thumped against the shack.

"I do not know," said Maria, stepping over to her. "But if they are, you must be ready to ride out through them the way we discussed it." She stooped down, laid her rifle on the floor and took the blanketed baby into the crook of her arm. Then, with her free hand, she helped April struggle to her feet. Carrying the baby, Maria helped April walk over to where the paint horse stood against the wall. The horse stretched its neck toward them and touched its muzzle to the blanket in curiosity, sniffing the scent of the newly born infant. Now pistol and rifle shots came steadily.

"Stand here and be ready," said Maria, giving April the baby and placing the paint horse's reins in her hand. "I must see what they are doing."

Hurrying to the window, snatching up her rifle on the way, Maria glanced out as bullets began to pelt the front of the shack heavily. She saw the torches hurrying down from the fireside toward the shack. "Be ready; here they come," she said with urgency to April. Then she stuck the rifle out through the gun slot, took careful aim on the first in a line of running figures and sent him rolling to a halt, the torch flying from his dead hand. The others scattered for a moment, but then they regrouped and made another run toward the shack.

The *comadrejas* ran in a wide circle in front of the shack, hurling their torches in turn as they passed, then hurried back to the cover of rocks. Maria fired as rapidly as she could, dropping one, then two, then a third. But in spite of her deadly rifle fire, two torches came dangerously close to landing on the front porch. One of the two actually licked at the porch edge on the drift of a breeze. Maria held her breath, watching the flames try to get a hold on the dried wood. Three more torch-holding *comadrejas* came running forward from behind the rocks. Maria managed to press them back with rapid shots.

Atop the shack, Maria heard running footsteps and saw dust jar loose from the ceiling. She jerked her pistol from her holster and fired twice. Still the runner moved back and forth on the roof. She could picture what he was doing, jamming the torch down at any spot he felt the flames might take a quick hold and begin to burn. She fired again, yet the shot had no effect. She followed the footsteps back and forth with her pistol barrel, trying to get a fix on a target. She almost pulled the trigger. Then she stopped herself as the loud report of a big .50-caliber rifle roared above the other gunfire. Maria's heart leaped in her chest. "Sam!" she cried out.

Above her, a large billowing cloud of dust gathered as the weight of the man on the roof flew backward and began to roll wildly downward. Maria's eyes followed the sound until the man's body left the roof and hit the dirt with a loud thud. *"Santa Madora!"* Maria quickly made the sign of the cross and closed her eyes for a second in thanks.

"What?" April called out from across the room.

"It's Sam!" Maria said, wiping a hand across her watery eyes. "I knew he would find us!" She hurriedly shoved her rifle back through the gun slot and began firing at the fleeing *comadrejas,* hearing the big .50-caliber Swedish roar steadily from the rocks higher up. "Now we will see whose blood runs in a great stream," Maria hissed under her breath.

Chapter 5

As soon as Sam's shot sent the *comadreja* on the roof plunging to the ground, he scanned the purple moonlit night as he fired and made plans for his next move. He had wanted to get around on the other side of the campfire to a ledge directly above. From there he could have shot down into the camp and sent the men scattering downward. *Comadrejas* were fierce fighters when they had every advantage on their side, but take their warm fire away and reduce their ability to band together and embolden one another, and Sam knew their defenses would crumble. But with the shack starting to burn along the edge of the front porch, Sam realized he had to end this thing quickly. He stood up, dusting his knees, watching rifle fire blossom steadily from the gun slot of the shack. There was little doubt in his mind that Maria was the person on the other side of the thick wooden shutters.

Seeing short flames rise up in several places where the *comadrejas* had stuck the torch to the roof boards and brittle wooden shingles, Sam said to the red stallion, "Come on, Devil. We better get down there." With his big Swedish rifle in hand, he led the stallion quietly and quickly down a winding footpath toward the shack, having to first give an extra tug on the reins to let the stubborn animal know he meant business. Well-hidden in the dark rock shadows, Sam listened to the sound of the *comadrejas'* gunshots thump and ricochet off the rocky ledge where he'd been only a moment ago. At the bottom of the path, he hurriedly wrapped the stallion's reins around a deadfall of sun-bleached piñon, then took up a prone firing position ten yards away.

Inside the shack, Maria listened intently and only breathed easier when she heard the sound of the big rifle resume firing, this time much closer than before. She had slowed her firing, realizing that the *comadrejas* had began to back away now that the odds had tilted slightly. Maria looked over at April, still standing beside the paint horse, and said, "They are leaving. We will be all right now."

"Who is Sam?" April asked, holding the baby firmly to her bosom.

"He is my partner, the Ranger." Maria

smiled, letting go of some of the tension. "We were on the trail of a band of outlaws when the storm separated us."

April looked apprehensive. "You didn't mention him."

"No," said Maria, "I have had no opportunity to mention him. But I knew he would come looking for me. I just wasn't sure when he would get here."

"I see," said April. Maria watched as the young woman seemed to grow weak. She eased herself down to the floor and sat slumped, still holding the reins to the paint horse in her hand.

"Are you all right?" Maria asked. She was hesitant to leave her firing position at the window and go to April, knowing Sam might need her help out there. Yet outside the big rifle fired steadily, the sound of it seeming to overpower the return fire of the *comadrejas*. Sam just about had them on the run, Maria thought.

"I — I'm all right," said April, sitting on the floor, her legs tucked under her. "These outlaws you were chasing — who are they?"

"They are the Abbadeles," Maria said, seeing something at work here. "Have you heard of them?"

"Yes," said April, "I have heard of them. What have they done?"

"They robbed the bank in Riley. Two men are dead because of them." She watched the young woman's eyes as she spoke to her.

"I have to tell you something," April said, lowering her dark eyes. On the ceiling, smoke seeped in and spread out along the rafters. Maria saw it but wasn't alarmed now that she knew the *comadrejas* had lost this battle.

"Yes? What is it?" Maria asked.

"My baby," said April, clutching the infant to her as if what she was about to say might cause Maria to try to take it from her. "Her father is an Abbadele. He is Toot Abbadele. We're going to be married and leave this country . . . now that the baby is born."

"Oh my," Maria said, almost in a whisper. Immediately she questioned whether this was something Toot Abbadele had told an impressionable young woman or if this was something April had fashioned in her mind.

Before Maria could say any more, April said, "But Toot wasn't with his brothers in Riley when they robbed the bank. He was with me. We spent three days together, making our plans. We're going to live in Mexico, a place Toot knows about where people won't mind that I'm colored or that our baby is only half-white."

Maria gave her a dubious look.

"It's the truth, I swear it," said April.

Before Maria could respond, the Ranger called out from the rocky front yard. "Hello, in there! Maria, is that you?"

"*Sí*, I am here, Sam," Maria called out through the gun slot. "Are they gone?"

"They're trying to be," Sam said. Above the shack on the ridge where the campfire glowed, the sound of cursing and horses' hooves resounded. "Watch for me," Sam said to Maria. "When I get to the porch, throw the door open."

"All right," said Maria. "Ready when you are." She stepped to the door, un-latched it and stood with her hand poised on the knob. When she heard Sam's running footsteps hit the porch, she opened the door, then quickly slammed and latched it behind him. They embraced, but only for a second as Sam's eyes swept the room and saw the face of the woman holding the baby. "Sam, you can't believe what kind of night it has been," Maria said between the two of them. Beside April, the paint horse grew restless at the smell of smoke and the sound of brittle wooden shingles crackling in the flames atop them.

82

Sam drew a quick mental picture of what had gone on, his eyes meeting Maria's for a second, seeing the look she gave him. "I know it's going to be interesting," he said, "but let's get you both out of here first."

Outside, the firing had stopped as the large band of *comadrejas* scurried away into the night. Maria carried the baby and led the paint horse to the spot where Sam had left the red stallion. Sam supported the woman, looping her arm over his shoulders while making sure he kept his gun hand free in case any *comadrejas* had stayed behind and lay in wait for them among the rock. They continued on until they reached a small clearing hidden on three sides inside a wide crevice. Maria took the blanket she'd thrown across the paint horse and spread it on the sand. Sam helped April seat herself on it, then stood back in the moonlight and watched her take the baby from Maria's arms.

"We can't risk staying here too long," Sam said, looking back toward the shack and seeing that the fire had engulfed it. "The weasels are on the run now, but they could turn around and come back. The storm must've wiped out their supplies. I've never seen so many of them on the prowl all at once."

"As soon as she rests for a moment, we will be on our way," said Maria. She nodded down at April and said to the Ranger, "Sam, I want you to meet April." As April raised her dark eyes to him, Maria added, "April, this is my partner, the ranger I told you about."

"Ma'am." Sam touched his fingers to the brim of his sombrero, then looked at the bundle in April's arms. "And who is this one?"

"This one is too new to have a name yet," said Maria. "This is April's daughter, born when the *comadrejas* first attacked us."

He stooped down and gently laid a hand on the back of the blanket-wrapped baby and said as if the child could understand, "This big ole world certainly didn't give you a hospitable welcoming. But let's hope that's all behind you now."

"Sam," said Maria quietly as she stooped down beside him, "there is something you need to know about the baby's father."

"Oh?" Sam just looked at her, already picking up something from her tone of voice.

"This is Toot Abbadele's daughter," Maria said.

When Sam only gazed into April's eyes,

Maria continued, saying, "She said they are going to be married and live in Mexico. She said that Toot could not have been with his brothers when they robbed the bank in Riley, because he was with her."

Sam stood up and rubbed his chin, considering the situation. "Ma'am, I have Dick Abbadele in jail in Sabre Ridge. Once his brothers find out, it's a sure bet they'll be coming for him. Whether Toot was in on the bank robbery or not, if he makes a fight against me alongside his brothers . . . Well, I'm afraid there's no good going to come of it."

April's voice trembled slightly as she drew the baby closer to her and, looking back and forth between Sam and Maria, said almost in a whisper, "You'll kill him, Ranger. Or at least you'll try to. Just come out and say it clearly."

"All right, ma'am." Sam gave Maria a glance, then said to April, "If he stands with his brothers, I'll kill him. That's as clear as it can be said." He considered his next words before asking her, "Ma'am, you said you were with Toot for three days. Where did the two of you stay?"

"We were at the Saldemar spread, near the border. We didn't leave until the day before the storm hit. Juan Saldemar made us welcome there. Toot befriended the Saldemars back when they needed help. Since then, Juan and Toot have become very close."

"I see," said Sam. "Very close." He nodded. "Do you realize the Saldemars are as big a gang of outlaws as the Abbadeles?"

"I don't know that the Abbadeles *are* outlaws," she said in defiance. "I think a person is supposed to be innocent until they're proved guilty."

Enough said, Sam told himself upon hearing her reply. He saw before him a young, impressionable woman who could not force herself to see the truth. It made no difference what he said: to this woman, Toot Abbadele could do no wrong. He gazed at the infant in her arms. This was not the time to push her on the matter. She had enough problems facing her, he thought. "Ma'am, you're right. Innocence or guilt is up to a judge and jury to decide. It's not something we'll settle tonight." He offered her a patient smile. "You rest yourself for a spell. Then we'll get you and the baby to Sabre Ridge."

April nodded in reply and let the infant rest down onto her lap. "I will hold the baby for you," Maria offered, stepping in and reaching down. But April shook her bowed head and hovered over the child as if protecting it from harm.

Maria withdrew her arms and looked at Sam. Together they stepped back from April and the baby and moved to a spot a few feet away where they could watch the narrow trail for any sign of lurking *comadrejas*. In a moment, Maria looked back over her shoulder at April sitting with her head bowed in slumber over the sleeping baby on her lap. "Do you suppose she is telling the truth about Toot Abbadele being with her instead of robbing the bank?"

"I don't know," said Sam. "But she's got a lot riding on keeping the man alive and out of prison. I'd have a hard time believing her if it came down to her word against anybody else's. Either way, it's like I told her. If Toot stands with his brothers against me, I'll have to kill him."

"This poor girl has chosen a hard road for herself, Sam," said Maria, looking back at April and speaking softly. "I wish we could help her."

"So do I, Maria. I'd like to help her, but only if it comes in the course of me doing my job. I can't bend things to suit her, and she evidently isn't seeing the same Toot Abbadele I know about."

"But maybe he is innocent this time," said Maria.

"Maybe he is," said Sam, stone-faced. "You heard what I told her. Can I be any more fair and still wear this badge?"

"No," said Maria. "I am only wishing the best could happen."

"Me, too," Sam said. "But some of that responsibility has to rest on her shoulders. This woman made her own choice, having Toot Abbadele's baby. If he deceived her, or if she refused to see what he was, either way it's her string. She'll have to play it out."

"*Sí,*" Maria said quietly. "It is her string. But it is also the baby's."

"I'm sorry," said Sam. "I reckon I just get a little bitter sometimes, watching folks mess up their lives for foolish reasons."

"Is love a foolish reason?" Maria asked, a trace of a smile coming to her lips.

"Yep, the most foolish reason in the world." As he spoke, Sam reached up with his right hand and gently brushed a wisp of hair from her forehead. He returned her smile. "Also the strongest reason I've ever seen." He looked past Maria's shoulder to where April sat sleeping on the ground, the baby lying quietly in her lap. "Do what you can for them. With Toot

Abbadele in their lives, they'll need all the help they can get."

"Look who's coming here," said Frank Abbadele, sitting atop his horse at the front of the four riders above a creek bed. Summer had reduced the creek to a thin trickle that meandered down from the hill line miles to their west. "Tell me if that ain't those two high-living Texas outlaws, the Knox brothers, coming this way."

Beside him, Big Bob wiped dust from the end of a field lens and raised it to his eyes, gazing long and closely before saying anything.

"Well?" said Frank. "Is it or not?"

Bob replied without lowering the field lens. "Yep, it's Terrence and Hirsh, all right."

Frank gave a sliver of a smile to Decker, Walsh and Lester Brooks sitting on their horses behind Big Bob. Lester shook his head. "You've got eyes like a bird of prey, Frank. There's no discounting it." Walsh and Decker nodded quietly in agreement.

"Well, guess what *bird of prey*," Big Bob said with a critical twist to his words, still looking out at the riders. "Brother Toot is riding double with Terrence . . . in case you didn't see that."

89

Frank Abbadele craned upward in his saddle without answering. Big Bob lowered the lens and rubbed his eye. Then, seeing Frank try to look closer at the riders, he held the lens out to him. "Here, stick this in your eye. It ain't no disgrace."

Frank only turned a look of disdain at the lens. "You stick it some place yourself, Brother Bob. I see well enough."

"Suit yourself." Big Bob raised the lens again and gazed out across the hot, wavering landscape. "Uh-oh," he said after a second study. "It looks like Toot's got himself a goose egg on the side of his head."

"I've got a dollar says his horse threw him. But let's just see if he'll admit it." Frank spit in a show of disgust and wiped his hand across his mouth. "You can't keep this bunch in horses anymore. We lose more horses than we steal in cattle."

Nobody responded. "Well, hell, come on then — let's go hear his version of it." Frank batted his boot heels to his horse's sides and rode it forward. The others followed close behind him.

With both parties of riders moving steadily toward one another, it still took a quarter of an hour before they met atop a low rise of sand beneath the thin shade of an up-reaching saguaro cactus. As soon as the Knox brothers reined their horses to a halt, Toot Abbadele slid down from behind Terrence Knox, stretched and touched his fingers to the large knot on the side of his head.

"I'm damn glad we've met up with yas," said Terrence Knox as he and his brother stepped down from their saddles. "Riding double has just about pulled my horse down to a crawl."

Frank Abbadele looked the men up and down, then said to Toot, "Where's your horse?"

Toot Abbadele reached for a canteen being offered to him by Lenbow Decker. He gave Frank Abbadele a harsh look and took his time answering, untwisting the canteen cap and wiping his palm across the rim before raising it toward his lips. "Good to see you too, Brother Frank," he said wryly. He took a mouthful of warm water, swished it and spit it out. "Damned if I know where my horse is. It got sucked right out from under me when that big blow came through. I hit a rock and can't remember much else." He poured a few drops of water into the palm of his hand and bowed his head into it, rubbing dried, dark blood until it came loose from the small gash in his swollen head.

"You don't remember nothing else, but you remember hitting your head on a rock?" Frank asked sarcastically.

Toot seethed and stared off into the distance for a moment to keep his temper. Then he said evenly, "No, Frank, I don't really remember hitting a rock. But since rock was the only thing lying around, I just figured I'd take a chance on saying that's what I hit. Now, if you suppose I might have hit something else, I'd be pleased to hear your take on it."

"Cut it out, both of you," said Big Bob.

"We've had a rough time, sure enough," said Terrence Knox, trying to change the subject to keep Bob and Toot's argument from turning violent. "We lost Dick somewhere in the ridges. Lost track of Kirby and Billy Stone in the wind. Billy went flying straight up, spinning like a pinwheel, his horse spinning right next to him! I never seen nothing like it in my natural life!" His eyes went to Lester Brooks. "You're the first ones we've seen alive, except for Toot. How'd you manage to get out of it?"

Brooks shrugged. "Faith in the Lord, I reckon." His eyes went across the land, then back to Terrence Knox. "What about my boy, Kirby? You didn't happen see him spinning like a pinwheel, did you?"

"No, Brooks," said Terrence, his voice turning serious as he answered, seeing that the older outlaw hadn't appreciated his flavor of excitement over the storm. "I wasn't making fun of poor Billy. I know that must be a hell of a way to die." He paused as if out of respect for the deceased, then said, "To answer your question, though: No, I did not see what happened to Kirby. But I've got to be honest. I don't hold out much hope for him. This storm came straight from hell and ain't likely to stop till it gets back there."

As Terrence and Brooks talked, Frank Abbadele noticed Toot staring out across the flat stretch of hot desert floor. "What's got your nose drawn to the hills, Toot?" he asked. Above the line of jagged badland hills, a thin streak of smoke stood on the still air.

"Nothing," Toot replied, turning his eyes back to the gathering of men. "It's just that I heard gunfire over in there last night — heard it for a long time."

"Yeah, so?" said Frank.

"I don't know," said Toot. "It just struck me as odd. No sooner did that storm rip through than I started hearing shooting. I thought maybe I'd go investigate . . . if I had a horse, that is." He looked all around the group.

"But you don't," said Frank. He nodded at the smoke. "Probably some wagon travelers come upon by *comadrejas*."

"Or it could be Dick, or even Tillis," said Toot. "I thought we might ought to at least check it out."

"And so we will," said Frank. "As soon as we scour the rest of this hellhole and scrape up the rest of you big, bad bank robbers." His eyes went from one to the other of the men, each of them getting the point. "Maybe next time, you'll think twice before going off doing what we all agreed not to do."

"Tillis and Dick both said it was all right with you," said Terrence Knox, "else me and Hirsh here wouldn't have done it. Ain't that right, Hirsh?"

Hirsh Knox only nodded. Having a terrible stammer caused him to remain quiet most of the time.

"We're not going to talk about it now," said Frank. "But there's going to be some changes made around here. I tell you men something, I ain't just talking to air out my chewing tobacco." He looked all around. "Any sign of that crazy ranger out there, Terrence?"

"No, but that's who Dick stayed back to ambush," said the young Texas outlaw. "Maybe that's what the shooting was last night, some *comadrejas* having that ranger for supper. That would be a huckleberry for you, wouldn't it?"

"Yeah," said Frank absently as he gazed back and forth across the land. "Say what you will about the *comadrejas,* they stay true to their calling. They know they're some no-good sonsabitches, and they don't try to hide it. If the Ranger is out there, they'll pick his bones clean."

"I don't think the Ranger is out there," said Terrence. "What about you, Hirsh? What do you think?" Again his eyes went to his brother, who stood quietly beside his horse.

Hirsh Knox swallowed a knot in his throat and struggled with his words. "Ahhh, he-he-he — tha-tha — ju-ju —"

"Never mind, Hirsh," said Frank. "We understand." He looked down at Terrence Knox. "You had to get him started, didn't you?"

"He does the best he can, Frank," said Terrence in a solemn tone of voice. "He can't help if it he don't talk as good as the rest of us."

"I never said he could help it, Terrence,

but you can," said Frank. Turning from Terrence, he said to the others, "Somebody give Toot a ride. We're going to ride over to where that storm hit and see if we can find where Dick was going to ambush that ranger. Anybody finds any of Dick's gear, I want it brought to me, *pronto!*"

As the Knoxes mounted their horses and Toot stepped up behind Lester Brooks, Lenbow Decker said to Tommy Walsh, "Dick's *gear?* What's he talking about, wanting his gear brought to him? Does he mean Dick's saddle and such?"

Tommy Walsh grinned and said in a lowered tone, "Offhand, I'd say he's talking about that stolen bank money." They heeled their horses forward after the others.

Chapter 6

The Abbadele party rode on another ten miles before coming upon more of the men who'd been scattered by the storm. This time it was Lester Brooks who spotted his son, Kirby, and another man sitting on the ground next to their horses at a dry water hole. Lester had split off from the others long enough to take a look on the other side of a low, sloping hill dotted with cholla and mesquite bushes and caught the two young outlaws by surprise. The young gunman with Kirby was not one of the men who had ridden with the Abbadeles to the bank robbery in Riley. Seeing him aroused Lester's clannish nature. As soon as he had greeted his son, Lester turned his horse to the other outlaw. "You're Charlie Whittaker," Lester said as if the name were an accusation of some sort. "I've heard of you."

Both young men stood up, dusting themselves off. Whittaker said, "Well, it's good to be heard of, I reckon."

"What are you doing here?" Lester asked bluntly.

"Easy, Pa," said Kirby. "We ran into one another an hour ago. Whit here has been telling me about getting run out of Sabre Ridge yesterday. Guess who by?"

Keeping his eyes narrowed on Whittaker, Lester said, "I haven't the faintest idea."

"The Ranger," said Kirby, watching his father's face for a reaction. "We was right about him being on our trail, I reckon. Whit here said the Ranger rode in with Dick Abbadele in tow. Said word has it the Ranger is out to take down all the Abbadeles."

"Is that a fact?" Lester asked sarcastically.

"It sure is," said Charlie Whittaker. "The Ranger went straight to the Hung Dog, dragged ole Sheriff Boggs out by the nape of his neck and dunked him in the water trough!"

"I'd have given anything to see that," Kirby Brooks said. The two young outlaws laughed aloud.

Lester Brooks stared at them with contempt. "You think that's funny, do you?" he growled at his son.

"Well, Pa, you have to admit," said Kirby, still chuckling under his breath, "the sight of Sheriff Boggs being dunked in a horse trough ain't something that —"

"Sheriff Boggs has been damn good to

this bunch," Lester snapped, cutting him off. "I see no humor in him being humiliated in front of his whole town, do you?"

"No, sir," said Kirby, seeing the seriousness of his father's eyes. "Not if you put it that way, I don't."

Lester Brooks turned to Charlie Whittaker. "And you. You say you rode all this way just to warn the Abbadeles about Dick being in jail?"

"I was headed this way anyway," said the young outlaw. "But yeah. I figured it was something the Abbadeles would want to know."

"So you figured you'd stick your nose in and maybe get on somebody's good side?" Lester asked in a growl.

"Easy, Pa," said Kirby. "Whit's my friend . . . has been for a long while."

Lester looked at his son as he calmly drew his pistol from his holster. "You tell me one more time to take it easy, I'm going to bend this barrel over your thick head."

"Sorry, Pa," said Kirby.

Lester let the pistol hang in his hand. He turned back to Charlie Whittaker, still expecting an answer. "Well?"

Whittaker shrugged. "Sure, I'd like to get on the Abbadeles' good side. I admit it.

I'd like to make myself useful . . . get myself a place riding with them. Why not? I'm as good as the next when it comes to handling cattle . . . or a gun, too, for that matter."

Lester grinned, seeming to settle down a little. "Right enough. I reckon it's every young man's dream to better himself. I shouldn't blame you for that. Can you make a good pot of coffee?"

"Some of the best, I've been told," said Whittaker.

"That's a plus," said Lester. "Is that horse of yours sound enough for long travel?"

"Oh yeah!" Whittaker nodded, seeing that he might be on the right track with the Abbadeles.

"He won't spook under gunfire?" Lester looked the horse up and down as he asked.

"No, sir. He'd stand under cannon fire, I reckon." Whittaker grinned.

"Good. We can use him," said Lester. He raised his pistol and shot the young outlaw dead. As Whittaker's body hit the ground, Lester snatched the reins to his horse, noting how the animal had barely flinched at the sound of his pistol shot. "He wasn't lying about the horse," Lester said.

"Good God, Pa!" Kirby shrieked, stunned by the suddenness as well as the callousness of his father's act. "You killed him! He never done a thing to you! He was a friend of mine, and you just killed him!"

"Hush, Kirby," said Lester. "Couldn't you see what he was trying to do?"

"No! He was just wanting to ride with us! We could have had some good times together, me and him."

"He was all ready to root you out of your spot in the bunch, Kirby, you damn fool. You heard him say how good he makes coffee, how good he can handle cattle, a gun?" Lester nodded as he spoke. "I just done you a hell of a favor killing that turd."

"Pa, I've got no friends my own age," Kirby protested.

"You don't need no friends, boy, least-wise not outside our own circle. Friends will get you killed every time." With smoke curling from his pistol barrel, Lester flipped out his spent cartridge and replaced it as Frank and Bob Abbadele led the rest of the riders over the slope toward them. "Here they come," Lester said to his son. "Don't let them hear us disagreeing. Someday, when you're leading your own bunch, you'll thank me for looking out for your interests."

"Damn, I hope so, Pa," Kirby said, staring down at Charlie Whittaker's body bleeding into the dirt. "For both our sakes."

Lester just stared at him.

"What's going on here?" Frank Abbadele asked, sliding his horse to a halt as Big Bob did the same beside him. Behind them, the others halted, raising dust. "Who's that?" Frank nodded at the body on the ground.

"It's that punk, Charlie Whittaker," said Lester, lowering his pistol into his holster. Looking up at Toot Abbadele, who'd switched over to riding double behind Tommy Walsh, Lester said with a half grin, "He brought you a horse."

Toot stepped down from behind Walsh and took the reins to the sweaty dun gelding without questioning Lester. Frank gave Whittaker's body a quick glance, then dismissed it, saying to Toot as Toot stepped into the saddle, "Try to hang on to this one."

"I'll do my damndest." Toot gave his brother a cold stare in response and pulled the dun over beside the rest of the riders.

Frank crossed his wrists on his saddle horn and said to Kirby, "I suppose you also got sidetracked by the storm?"

"He sure did," said Lester, not giving

Kirby a chance to speak for himself. "But listen to what he found out for us from Whittaker." Lester turned to Kirby. "Go on and tell him, son, about Dick and all."

"What about Dick?" Frank demanded.

Kirby pushed up his dusty hat brim and said, "Whit told me he saw that crazy ranger bring Dick into Sabre Ridge, tied to his horse and beat all to hell. Said the Ranger took over Sheriff Boggs' jail and threw Dick in it."

"Damn it," said Frank. "In broad daylight, in front of everybody, a damned lawdog rides in and takes over a man's jail. Sounds like he's inviting trouble."

"I'd say he is," said Kirby. "Whit said the word around Sabre Ridge is that the Ranger is determined to take down all of us."

"That's awfully ambitious for one man wearing a tin badge," said Frank. He paused in contemplation, then let go of a tense breath and said with resolve, "Well, I guess that settles the mystery of where's Dick." He asked Kirby, "What about Tillis or Doyle Royal? Did you hear anything about them?"

"Not a word about them," said Kirby. He shrugged. "It's like Tillis and Royal have dropped off the earth."

"What about any saddlebags?" Frank asked. "Did Whittaker say if it looked like the Ranger was carrying the bank money?"

"Whit never said." Shooting his father a dark glance as he spoke, Kirby added, "We didn't get to talk that long."

"Get mounted then," Frank said to Kirby and Lester. "I still want to see the spot where Dick lay in wait for the Ranger."

"Frank," said Toot, "you just heard him say Dick's in jail. What's the point in riding out there? I got somewhere I need to be!"

All day Frank had noticed Toot constantly glancing over toward the hill line where the smoke had drifted in the air. "What's got your tail in a knot, Toot?" Frank asked. "If you tell us, maybe we can help straighten it out."

"There's not a damn thing got my tail in a knot, Frank," Toot snapped at him. He jerked the horse's reins around toward the hill line. "I don't need to tell you every move I make!"

"If it concerns this family, you do," said Frank. "We've got Tillis missing and Dick in jail. You better stay close, see if you can help out some."

"Help out how?" said Toot. "All we got to do is ride in any time we're ready and take Dick away from that ranger. You don't even need me for that; if you do, you can wait until I get back. It isn't like Sabre Ridge is going to lynch one of us Abbadeles." He batted his boots to the dun's sides and rode away, raising dust.

"I'll go talk some sense to him," said Big Bob, getting ready to heel his horse forward.

But Frank stopped him. "Let him go, Brother Bob. Whatever's bothering him, let him get it out of his system."

"Whatever you say," said Bob, staring after Toot. "Anyway, he's right about the Ranger. All we got to do is ride in and take Dick out of that jail . . . pull it down with ropes if we have to. The Ranger can't stop us — not by himself."

Frank grinned. "He's not by himself. I heard he travels with a Spanish woman these days."

"Either way," said Bob, "it's no problem getting Dick away from him."

"No, I doubt if it would be," said Frank. "But I can't help wondering if us riding in and breaking Dick out of jail ain't playing into the Ranger's hands some way."

"I can't see how," said Big Bob Abbadele.

"Neither can I," said Frank. "That's what keeps me puzzled." A moment of silence passed. Then he looked over his shoulder at the rest of the men and back at his brother. "The Ranger wants us to ride in and make a jailbreak — so let's not do it. Instead, let's have some fun with him."

"Have fun? With the Ranger?" Bob shook his head warily. "I don't like the sound of that, Frank. What the hell are you talking about, having fun with him?"

"Sometimes you worry too much," Frank said. "I'm saying, if the Ranger wants to bring us down . . . hell, let's be obliging. He can't make that bank robbery stick on us, especially not in Sabre Ridge."

Seeing Frank was getting ready to spur his horse away without saying any more on the matter, Bob said, "Frank, what have you got in mind? Tell us something here."

But Frank only grinned. "I'll tell you what I've got in mind just as soon as we go see if Dick hid that bank money out there."

At midmorning, the Ranger and Maria rode into Sabre Ridge side by side, Maria on the paint horse carrying the baby, April cradled in Sam's arms, sound asleep against his chest. Pip Richards stood up from the edge of the boardwalk and shook wood shavings from his boot tops. He walked along sideways, craning his neck for a better look until the Ranger and Maria turned their horses to a hitch rail out front of the Miller Hotel. By then, several other townsfolk had turned their attention to the Ranger, having either seen or heard of what had happened between him and their sheriff. Through their window above the harness shop, Clare-Annette and Swan Hendricks saw the Ranger arrive and hurriedly stepped out onto the flat roof and stood looking down, giggling between themselves like two schoolgirls. Swan started to wave, but Clare-Annette grabbed her wrist and stopped her, seeing Maria cast a sidelong glance in their direction.

"I see you have developed a following here already," Maria said quietly, stifling a slight smile.

"A following?" The Ranger's face reddened. "I hardly think so." As he spoke, he looked at Pip Richards moving along the edge of the street with them, and up at the two women. "He's the town whittler," Sam explained. Out of courtesy, he looked at Pip, touched his fingers to the brim of his sombrero, then offered the same gesture to the women. "I saw those two watching from the window when I stuck the sheriff into the water trough. They seemed to get a kick out of it." At Sam's courteous acknowledgment, the two women ventured a modest wave in reply.

"You did not tell me about the sheriff and the water trough," said Maria.

"It must have slipped my mind," the Ranger replied, stopping his horse at the rail. "He'd been drinking and seemed to have a hard time understanding what I intended to do here. The dunking cleared his head quite a bit." Sam smiled and eased down from the saddle, taking April with him, keeping her cradled against his chest.

"I bet it did," Maria commented. She tossed a glance at the water trough. "And now he is on our side in this Abbadele situation?" She smiled at how gently the Ranger handled the young woman, without even awakening her.

Speaking softly for the sleeping woman's sake, Sam said, "Let's just say the sheriff and I have an understanding." He stepped onto the boardwalk.

April stirred for a moment without fully awakening. "Where is my baby?" she asked in a weak, sleepy voice.

"She's right here," said Sam. "Don't worry, Maria is taking good care of her. You rest. That's the best thing for you."

Stepping down with the baby in her arms,

Maria moved ahead of the Ranger and opened the door to the hotel for him. "Do you suppose there will be any difficulty getting a room here with her and the baby?"

"I doubt it," said the Ranger. "The clerk saw me dunk the sheriff."

Maria smiled and shook her head as the Ranger stepped inside the hotel lobby.

But the Ranger was right. The desk clerk who rushed from behind the counter to direct them to a divan in the lobby was the same young man who had watched the sheriff dunked in the water trough. "My goodness, what have we here?" he asked, looking April up and down as the Ranger laid her down gently.

"She became a mother last night," Sam said, discounting any other possible meaning in the young man's question. "Is that a problem? You do let rooms to new mothers with infants, don't you?"

"Oh . . ." The young man looked baffled for a second, but then responded. "Of course. New mothers are always welcome here. I'm Philbert Newman. Although I'm not the owner, I speak for the Miller Hotel when I say that mothers with small children have always been welcome here."

"Good," said the Ranger. There was a silent pause.

The clerk's eyes went to the baby, then to Maria, then back to the Ranger, who seemed to be waiting for something. "Well?" said the Ranger. "Can you rustle us up two adjoining rooms, one of them overlooking the street?"

"Oh! Yes! Of course," said Philbert, gesturing the Ranger to the polished wooden counter. "Please follow me. We'll just get you to sign our guest registry and get you settled in upstairs."

The Ranger offered Maria a wry grin and said in a lowered voice, "There, see how easy that was?"

Moments later, inside the shaded coolness of the rooms, the Ranger parted the thin curtains with his fingers and looked down upon the street. The townsfolk who had ventured forward for a look had now dispersed, except for the old whittler and the two young women on the front roof of the harness shop. Sam saw the two smile his way as he looked in both directions to see what sort of view the hotel afforded him. There was a blind spot to the left, coming into Sabre Ridge from the north, he noted. But aside from that, he had a good view to the south, east and west. It would have to do, he told himself. Giving the young women a slight wave of his gloved fingertips, he let the curtain close.

"If there is a town doctor here, we must have him look at these two," Maria said quietly. "They seem to be fine, but I will feel better if we get a doctor's opinion."

"I'll look for a doctor's office on my way to see about the sheriff and my prisoner," the Ranger said, turning to Maria as she placed the infant between two pillows on the bed beside April. He stood quietly for a moment watching Maria attend to the sleeping baby. He smiled and said, "I couldn't help but notice earlier how handy you are with a baby. You seem to be a natural at it."

"Oh?" Maria blushed slightly. But then she caught herself and said, "More handy than I am at shooting *comadrejas?*"

"I best think that over awhile before I answer," the Ranger said, leveling his sombrero as he turned and left the room.

Chapter 7

Sam stopped by the office of Sabre Ridge's only physician and asked the elderly doctor to go check on April and her baby. From there the Ranger went to Sheriff Boggs' office. On his way, he noted how the eyes of every townsperson on the street turned toward him in curiosity. Pip Richards crept along the opposite side of the street until finally the Ranger took a patient breath and waved him over. Without stopping, the Ranger asked, "What's your name, sir?"

"Pip Richards, at your service," Pip replied gamely. "I already know your name, Ranger. I was in Raylean Crossing when you cleaned that mess of gunfighting trash out'n there."

The Ranger slowed a step and looked Pip up and down. "That was quite a place, Raylean Crossing."

"Yep, it was," said Pip. "I can name you every man you shot, the one who shot you, what date it was and where you fell in the street. That was the first time I ever saw a man show up for a shoot-out carrying a big sharpshooter's rifle. A big engraved Swedish gun, as I recollect. Do you still carry it?"

The Ranger looked impressed. "And now you live in Sabre Ridge."

"I've been here two years come June. Anything you want to know about anything in Sabre Ridge, I'm your huckleberry for it."

"I can see you are," said the Ranger. "Did you ever consider a job with a newspaper?"

"A newspaper?" Pip scratched his head with the tip of his whittling stick. "What for?"

"Never mind," said the Ranger. "I was only making a joke."

"A joke? About working for a newspaper?" Pip looked puzzled. "Where's there any joke in that?"

"I said never mind." The Ranger shook his head as he walked.

"We had a newspaper here for nearly a year. Then it got struck by lightning," said Pip, seeming unable to let go of it. "But I never worked for it. A couple of times I helped deliver some to the barbershop —"

"Stop it," said the Ranger. "How about giving me an update?"

"An update?"

"Yes, an update." The Ranger continued walking. Pip was only a short step back, but still beside him. "Has everything been quiet here since I left last evening?"

"Well, now, let me see," Pip said studiously yet beaming at the very notion of being asked for a town update. "Okay, first off, that bounty hunter over there." He pointed to where Big Shod stood leaning against a boardwalk post straight across from the sheriff's office. "Him and Sheriff Hugh Boggs had a heated discussion over Dick Abbadele."

"No kidding?" The Ranger smiled slightly. "How'd you know about it?"

"I was just standing outside the open window there, minding my own business, when they went at it. The bounty hunter warned Sheriff Boggs what would happen to him if Dick Abbadele escaped. Said, 'Sheriff, there's a lot worse things going around that can befall a man besides getting dunked in a horse trough.'" Pip laughed and wheezed under his breath. Then he collected himself and said, "That big feller sure talks fancy for a . . . you know."

"What?" said Sam. "You mean for a *bounty hunter?*"

Pip caught the Ranger's indifference to

the man's race. He grinned and said, "Yep, that's what I mean. For a bounty hunter, he talks right fancy."

"I knew that's what you meant," said Sam. They walked on. Pip fell silent for a second, and Sam could tell the old man was busting to ask about the young black woman who'd ridden in on the Ranger's lap. "Did anything else go on here? Any Abbadeles show up?" But the Ranger knew better. If any of the Abbadeles had ridden into town, it would have been the first piece of information out of the old man's mouth.

"Naw," Pip said, dismissing the question with a swipe of one hand. "Ranger, I couldn't help notice that you rode in here with a young colored woman on your lap."

"That's right," said Sam, already having decided to keep the story about Toot Abbadele being the baby's father a secret . . . for the time being, at least. "We found her under attack by the *comadrejas*. Do you suppose she has any folks living around here?"

"Didn't she tell you?" Pip asked instantly.

The Ranger caught the edge in the old man's voice and saw the sharpness in his eyes as he glanced into them. He came

115

back quickly. "She couldn't. She's been unconscious most of the trip. I just thought you might know of any families around here."

The Ranger's statement was meant to challenge Pip. "Don't worry, I know about every family within miles of here. There's only one colored family ever lived around here that I know of. They lived three days north on the high grasslands. Their name was Hedgings, but they've been gone quite a while." Pip scratched his head again with the whittling stick as they neared the boardwalk where Big Shod stood watching them come closer. "You suppose she's any kin to them?"

"I don't know, Pip," said the Ranger. "You're the one who's supposed to know everything around here." He offered Pip a slight smile and a curt nod, letting him know that their walk together had ended. Pip slowed to a halt and watched the Ranger step up onto the boardwalk beside the black bounty hunter.

"I'll be keeping you informed on anything I happen to hear, Ranger," Pip said, lingering in hopes of being welcomed into the conversation. He tipped his hat to both men, adding, "You, too, Mr. Shod."

"You do that, Pip," said the Ranger.

"We'll be much obliged." The Ranger stared at him until Pip Richards saw he was no longer welcome and backed away, then turned and walked back to his spot of shade out front of the harness shop.

"The old man doesn't miss much, does he?" said Big Shod, staring after Pip Richards in the sharp glare of midmorning sunlight. Across the street, the bony hound had slipped into Pip's shade while he was gone. Pip cursed the animal as he approached it, causing it to slink away and disappear under the boardwalk.

"No, he doesn't," said the Ranger. Then, looking Big Shod up and down, he asked, "What's keeping you here? I figured you be gone on your way by now."

"Didn't he tell you?" Shod replied, nodding toward Pip Richards.

"He said you had some words with the sheriff over my prisoner," Sam said. "He never said why." The Ranger looked toward the jail, then back at Shod. "You're not one of those kind of people who like to stick around to watch the fireworks, are you?"

"Only if it's the Fourth of July," said Shod. "The fact is, I grew concerned about your prisoner leaving town while you were gone. I thought I better inform the sheriff that my services as a professional tracker and manhunter were on your side. I may even have told him that you asked me to keep an eye on things until you returned, in case he needed any help. I hope that's all right with you."

The Ranger just looked at him. "How did that set with him?"

"Not good," said Shod, "but he seemed able to reconcile himself to it after he saw I meant business. Evidently that dunking you gave him cleared his head more than you realized."

"Much obliged for your help," said the Ranger. "But if you don't mind me asking, what's your interest in all this? Don't tell me it's just to see justice done."

Big Shod offered a thin smile. "No, it's not about justice. It's about bounty money. Pip made me realize there are quite a few men with the Abbadeles who have prices on their heads. I figured it might be wise for me to hang around here and back your play. Perhaps I can earn some money out of it at the same time."

"Suit yourself," said the Ranger. "I always like to encourage the free enterprise system . . . so long as you don't get between me and my job."

"I wouldn't dream of it," said Shod. "By

the way, I saw the young woman and the baby ride in with you and your partner. Who is she?"

The Ranger quickly considered telling him, but then decided it would keep until later. "Beats me," he said. "Maria found her last night, ready to give birth. We haven't had much chance to talk to her yet."

"Sure you haven't," said Shod, not buying the Ranger's answer for a second. "Whatever you say." He nodded toward the sheriff's office. "I suppose you're headed over to check on your prisoner. Want some company?"

"Yep, let's go," the Ranger said.

The eyes of the townsfolk along the street turned toward them as they left the boardwalk and walked to the sheriff's office. Noting how the Ranger seemed to pay no attention to being the town's object of interest, Big Shod said in passing, "I still haven't gotten used to people watching my every move. Sometimes I feel like a carnival act, wearing a gun for a living."

The Ranger smiled thinly. "Sometimes we probably *are* like a carnival act to these folks."

Big Shod nodded in agreement. "Then we should at least get paid for it."

"We do," said the Ranger. "We just don't sell tickets."

At the sheriff's office, Sam stepped through the door first, taking both Sheriff Boggs and Dick Abbadele by surprise. Sheriff Boggs stood leaning against the open door of a cell, a cup of coffee in his hand. At the sheriff's desk in the center of the room sat Dick Abbadele, sprawled back in a chair, both feet on the desk, a plate of food on his stomach, a white cloth napkin on his chest. He had just tipped back, taking a long swig from a foamy mug of beer.

Taking a quick glance around the office, seeing the empty cell, the Ranger stopped cold inside the open door. "Jailbreak!" he said. Then he snatched his pistol from his holster and fired two quick shots into the floor inches from the legs of Dick Abbadele's chair. Splinters exploded from the rough plank floor as Dick Abbadele hurled himself upward in a spray of food, beer and scattered paperwork. Two more shots pounded the floor, nipping close to Dick Abbadele's heels as he raced into the cell and up onto the bunk. He stood spread-eagle against the wall.

"Boggs!" he screamed. "Do something!"

"No! Ranger!" shouted Sheriff Boggs.

"Hold your fire! For God sakes, there's no jailbreak here!"

Standing inside the open door behind the Ranger, Big Shod had stepped to one side and instinctively reached for his gun. But upon seeing what the Ranger was doing, Shod let his hand relax on the gun handle. He kept himself from laughing at the sight of Sheriff Boggs standing with a streak of coffee down the front of him, his tin coffee cup lying on the floor at his feet where he'd dropped it.

The Ranger reluctantly lowered his pistol and looked at Sheriff Boggs standing as if in shock. The sheriff's gun belt hung from a peg on the wall ten feet away. "Oh," he said. "My mistake then. I came in, saw you standing without your weapon, a prisoner sitting at your desk. You can see how I might have figured he'd gotten the drop on you, can't you?" Before the sheriff could answer, Sam stepped back outside onto the boardwalk and gazed past the shocked onlookers toward the hotel just in time to see Maria running down the dirt street, her rifle in hand. Sam waved her to a halt, letting her know there was no cause for alarm. Maria came to an abrupt stop and gave him a critical look. Sam smiled and shrugged. As Maria turned back toward the hotel, Sam stepped back inside the sheriff's office. "You were saying, Boggs?" he asked.

It suddenly struck Boggs that the Ranger had made no mistake. The whole thing had been orchestrated to teach him some sort of lesson. "Damn it, Ranger!" Boggs kicked his coffee cup away. "That's the most disrespectful, the most irresponsible, thing I've ever seen!"

The Ranger stepped forward now and slammed the iron bar door to Dick Abbadele's cell. All humor had gone from his eyes. His pistol still hung in his hand. "I'll listen real close, Boggs," he said, his voice a sharp slice of anger, "while you tell me everything you know about disrespect and irresponsibility."

Boggs only had one step back before he met the wall, but he took it as the Ranger advanced on him. "Now, damn it, Ranger, take it easy!" Boggs said, running out of courage fast. "We're both lawmen here."

The Ranger stopped and stared into Boggs' eyes from only inches away. "If you ever call yourself a lawman again in front of me, I'll pistol-whip you into the ground, Boggs. I give you my word on that."

"I — I'm doing my job here, Ranger," said Boggs, trying to hold onto some shred of self-respect in front of Dick Abbadele. "I kept your prisoner here just like you asked me to. I am an elected public servant doing what I'm paid to do." He carefully avoided referring to himself as a lawman, Big Shod noticed, taking it all in, seeing a glint of satisfaction in Dick Abbadele's eyes as he stepped down from atop his bunk.

"You might be elected. You might wear a badge. You might even convince yourself that you're upholding the safety of this town," said the Ranger. "But you're nothing but a drunken joke to the Abbadeles or any other bunch of outlaws who happen to look at how you run this town and decide it's time they take it over. Look at yourself, Boggs. You disgrace this office. You disgrace any man who's ever tried to stand up for what's right in this land." He nodded at the food and plate lying strewn across the floor. "Allowing a prisoner to sit and eat at your desk, put his boots up on it while he swigs beer? What kind of decent sheriff would ever do something like that?"

"Ranger," said Boggs, summoning enough courage to speak up for himself, "I wouldn't allow just *any* prisoner to do that. But I happen to know Dick Abbadele. I know all the Abbadeles. They're friends of mine. I told you that." He shot Dick Abbadele a quick, nervous glance. "Ain't that right, Dick, about us being friends?"

"Like one big happy family," said Dick Abbadele, grinning, stepping forward and lounging against the bars, one arm out and dangling loosely over a cross member. He gestured toward a tin bucket of beer sitting on a shelf. "Why don't you be a sport, Ranger? Hand me that bucket and a mug so I can — *Ayiee!*"

Abbadele's word cut short into a yelp of pain as the Ranger rapped his pistol barrel across the back of his hand. "Ask me something else," said the Ranger. "See if you like my answer any better."

"Damn you!" Dick Abbadele shouted, holding his aching hand. "Wait till my brothers get through with you! We'll see who gets the final say!" He turned his rage on Sheriff Boggs. "You better start taking care of this situation, Boggs! Don't make me tell my brothers you ain't on our side."

"Dick, please!" said Boggs, his face reddening under the Ranger's harsh glare.

"See?" said the Ranger. "That tells me a lot about where you stand with the Abbadeles. It ought to tell you a lot, too . . . if you haven't had your mind soaked in whiskey so long that you refuse to see what a sorry fool you are."

"Ranger, I can feed prisoners what I damned well please," said Boggs, getting more mouthy now that he watched the Ranger lower the pistol into its holster. "And if I allow one to sit at my desk, that's nobody's business, either. Besides, this man is not convicted of anything. For all I know, I could have an innocent man sitting here in jail."

"Oh, he's guilty, sure enough," said the Ranger.

"But that's not for you to decide," said Boggs. "That's up to a judge and a jury. Until then, I'll treat this man the way I myself would want to be treated under the same circumstances."

"He's my prisoner, Boggs," said the Ranger. "Until a judge says otherwise, I better not catch him sitting outside that cell." He looked over at Dick Abbadele standing by his bunk and nursing his sore hand. "Next time I see you out of that cell, I'll just figure you really *are* making a jailbreak. I won't shoot holes in the floor, either."

The Ranger turned and nodded at the tin bucket of beer sitting on the shelf. Big Shod picked it up, took a long sip and looked into Dick Abbadele's eyes as he licked foam from his upper lip. Then he tipped the bucket and poured the rest of the beer onto the floor.

"I suppose you'll expect me to clean that up," Sheriff Boggs said to the Ranger.

"Clean what up?" said the Ranger. He and Big Shod turned and walked out the door.

As soon as the two had left, Dick Abbadele looked at Sheriff Boggs through the cell bars and said, "Now that he's through shoving his weight around, get back over to the restaurant and get me some more food. Get some more beer, too." He rubbed his hand across his dry lips and growled under his breath, "That damn Ranger. I can't wait till I get him in my gun sights."

Sheriff Boggs looked at him. "No offense, Dick, but you *had* him in your gun sights. And he's still alive."

"Next time he won't be," said Dick Abbadele.

"Next time," Boggs whispered to himself, shaking his head.

Outside, walking along the boardwalk, the Ranger said to Big Shod, "You might find it hard to believe, but I hate treating Boggs that way."

"Boggs is a fool, Ranger, and he's a

danger to everybody in this town, himself included. What if that had been some of Dick Abbadele's friends instead of you and me walking in there a while ago? Boggs wasn't even armed. He'd be lying dead in his own blood right now."

"No," said the Ranger. "If that was one of the Abbadele Gang instead of us, Boggs would be running to get them some beer. But I get your point, Shod. Boggs has never seen the bad side of these men. He's let them have free run here, and so far they've always come here on their best behavior, I reckon. Wait until they show up wanting their brother out of jail and find out I'm not going to let it happen. Boggs will see a whole different breed of cat."

"Yes, I suppose he will," said Big Shod. "You've definitely put a cramp in everyone's lifestyle by coming here." He nodded toward the Hung Dog Saloon, where the piano music drifted out, sounding slow and lonely coming from the empty bar. Out front of the saloon, the hitch rail stood bare. In the doorway, the bar owner stood leaning with his hands in his pockets beneath his white apron. "Apparently outlaws and gunmen made up most of the drinking crowd. Without it, the saloon might as well close up." He shook his head. "How does a town allow itself to get in this shape?"

"Some places it happens suddenly," the Ranger said, "as quick as a snap of lightning. Other places, like here, it sneaks up gradually. A town doesn't realize it's being overrun by a bad element until it's almost too late to do anything about it." He nodded back in the direction of the sheriff's office. "But no matter which way it happens, it always starts because the law has gone lax. Times get good, people get to living better, the law starts letting things go unattended." He gave Shod a glance. "But I needn't tell you that. You've seen it."

"Yes, a hundred times," said Shod. "People like Boggs come into office because folks start thinking it doesn't matter who's wearing the badge so long as they keep drunks off the streets and properly tax all the whores."

"But there's always something in the badlands waiting and watching like a hungry wolf," said the Ranger. "Soon as a town gets too fat and lazy and lets itself go, something rolls in and takes it apart." He looked out toward the badlands. "A sheriff that stands drinking when he should be walking his town's borders, seeing what's coming in, is nothing but the first nail in a town's coffin."

A silence set in. The two men stopped in the street. The Ranger continued to stare off into the distance as if searching for an omen. Finally, Big Shod said, "I've heard it said that you dislike working in a town, Ranger. That there is too much civil formality to suit you."

"*Civil formality*," the Ranger said, repeating Shod's words in a bemused tone. "That's an elegant way of putting it. But I reckon it's true, however you want to say it. Town is where the trouble comes to after it's begun to boil over the edge. I like to catch trouble out there before it gets off to a good start."

"Do you think you've managed to do that here?" Shod asked, gazing out toward the badlands with him.

"No," said the Ranger. "If I'd caught it out there, I wouldn't be waiting for the Abbadeles to come riding in here. I like working without the risk of a lot of innocent bystanders getting in the way."

"Is that another way of saying you don't like having any witnesses?" Shod asked.

The Ranger took a deep breath and said, "Every once in a while, that lawyer side of you just slips right out, doesn't it?"

Big Shod smiled. "I struggle with it constantly."

Chapter 8

The riders' shadows stretched long across the desert floor, moving like dark whispers across rock, cactus and scrub juniper along the trail leading to the large adobe hacienda outside of Circle Wells. From his shooting range behind the hacienda, attorney at law Parker Dennison had spotted the two riders a half hour earlier, when they were no more than black specks on the distant horizon. Now, in the shade of the adobe shooting pavilion, he poured himself another glass of wine and raised it to his lips. His cap-and-ball dueling pistol lay beside the silver-trimmed case where its twin rested in its fitted bed of dark velvet. "Shall I reload for you, sir?" asked Sturgen, Dennison's personal valet.

Looking out at the two riders, who were now closing in on the hacienda at a loose trot, Parker Dennison said, "No, Sturgen. I won't be doing any more shooting this evening."

Also watching the riders approach,

Sturgen asked, "Shall I bring out more wine from the cellar, sir? And more glasses, of course?"

"No," said Dennison. "But do bring a bottle of whiskey and some *large* glasses."

"Some of the fine Kentucky bourbon, sir?" asked Sturgen.

Dennison winced at the thought. "No, no . . . not the bourbon. Some of that cheap Cincinnati Charm. These boys won't mind at all. In fact, just some double-cut rye would do if there's any lying around gathering dust."

"Double-cut *rye?* Lying around here, sir? I should think not." Sturgen lifted his nose toward the riders with contempt. "But I'm certain I can find something to be appreciated."

"Thank you, Sturgen. Have the gate boy let them in. Then you personally accompany them back here. We wouldn't want those two to get lost inside the house, would we?"

"No, sir. I daresay we certainly would not!" Sturgen replied.

Parker Dennison sipped his wine as Sturgen moved briskly from the shooting pavilion back to the hacienda. Then, still watching the riders approach as he picked up the dueling pistol and began reloading it, Dennison said to himself, "Now, what do we have coming here, I wonder?" Even as he dropped a lead ball down the pistol barrel and tamped it down against the load of gunpowder with a short ramrod, Dennison stopped for a second and placed a hand to his stomach, making sure his single-shot Derringer lay snugly in his vest pocket. *One can never be too well-armed with these kinds of clients,* he reminded himself.

Moments later, outside the iron gates of the hacienda, Lenbow Decker and Tommy Walsh stepped down from their sweaty horses and slapped dust from themselves as a young Mexican houseboy lifted the heavy latch to allow them to enter. Sturgen, having already set up a full bottle of whiskey and tall glasses in the shooting pavilion, now stood back a few feet from the main iron gate, his hands calmly folded behind his back.

"God almighty," said Lenbow Decker as the two stepped inside the main gate and looked around. "This is where I've always wanted to go to when I die!" In the center of a large, tiled courtyard lined with exotic flowers stood a tall fountain made up of four larger-than-life-sized marble angels collectively holding a giant water urn above their heads. Water spilled down onto a wheel of smaller urns, where the weight of it kept the large wheel in motion.

"It's nice enough, I reckon, for something made out of mud." Tommy Walsh looked around also, but he tried to shrug it off as if he weren't impressed. Then he said to Sturgen, "I'm Mr. Walsh. This is Mr. Decker. We're here to see Mr. Dennison. He got a telegraph telling him we was on our way."

"Gentlemen, I'm Sturgen, Mr. Dennison's proper man's man. Of course Mr. Dennison is aware of your arrival. He awaits you."

"Well, I reckon he'll await no longer then, because we are as here as we'll ever be. We rode all night and all day." He poked a thumb over his shoulder at the two sweat-streaked horses standing outside the gate. "See to it our horses are attended proper-like," Tommy Walsh said, giving Sturgen a superior grin.

"Yes, sir, to be sure," said Sturgen. He gave a quick sign to a young man who had just appeared outside the main gate. The young man gathered the horses' reins and hurriedly led them away to a smaller gate leading to the livery barn behind the main compound. Then Sturgen stepped forward with his hands extended and an unpleasant expression on his face.

"May I take your hats, sirs?"

"Take them where?" said Lenbow Decker, looking distrustful.

"No, but much obliged, Sturgen," said Walsh, taking off his dusty, sweat-stained hat but not offering to give it up.

"Very well then," said Sturgen, looking relieved. "If you will follow me . . . I know Mr. Dennison is eager to speak to you both."

Decker and Walsh grinned at one another like two schoolboys and followed Sturgen through the cool darkness of the elaborately furnished home. Stepping out the rear door, they saw Parker Dennison stand up from a Spanish hand-carved chair beneath the shooting pavilion. "May I present Mr. Decker and Mr. Walsh, sir," said Sturgen.

"Very good, Sturgen," said Dennison. Then, gesturing to Decker and Walsh for them to join him, he said, "Gentlemen, please, make yourselves at home." He spread a hand toward the bottle of whiskey. "A refreshing drink to settle the dust while Sturgen hurries our cook along in preparing dinner." He raised the whiskey bottle and filled two tall glasses while Decker and Walsh came to a halt and stood staring, their eyes appearing to already taste the fiery amber as it trickled from the bottle. "There now. Enjoy. I know you've had a hard ride getting here."

"I'll say so," Tommy Walsh said, reaching down and picking up the glass. "We rode all night and all day," he said for the second time. He took a long drink of whiskey, Lenbow Decker joining him.

"Whooiee!" said Decker, letting out a whiskey hiss. "That tastes just like sweet Cincinnati Charm whiskey. Best whiskey east of the Mississippi!"

"Well, indeed it is, sir!" said Dennison, shooting Sturgen an I-told-you-so look. "And let me say, it's a pleasure meeting a man who knows good whiskey."

"It's always been my favorite," said Decker, taking another sip.

Walsh, still not wanting to look overly impressed, said, "My favorite, too . . . unless of course there's some double-cut rye a feller can lay his hands on."

"I'm sorry, Mr. Walsh," said Dennison, "but when it comes to double-cut rye, I can't seem to keep it on the place." Again he gave Sturgen a look.

"If that will be all, sir," said Sturgen, "I'll straightaway see about dinner."

"Thank you, Sturgen," said Parker Dennison, dismissing him with the toss of a hand. "We'll just seat ourselves here and enjoy our drinks."

The two sweaty, dusty outlaws plopped down into finely upholstered chairs as Dennison winced and pretended not to notice.

"Now then, gentlemen," said Dennison, rubbing his palms together. "What can I do for my dearest friend and favorite client, Mr. Frank Abbadele? Have the Abbadeles once again been singled out and unjustly persecuted?"

Tommy Walsh said, "Mr. Dennison, you must be a mind reader." As Walsh spoke, he pulled out a thick, wrinkled envelope from inside his shirt and pitched it onto the table beside the dueling pistols and the whiskey bottle.

For the next half hour, the attorney listened to the two outlaws tell him about the Ranger jailing Dick Abbadele. While the three talked, Sturgen hurried the cook along, helping the old Frenchman grill steaks over a bed of mesquite coals in the separate kitchen off to the side of the main hacienda. At dinner, as Dennison and the others gathered around the table, Sturgen opened a fresh bottle of wine and began to pour it. But Dennison stopped him. "Here, Sturgen," he said, "let me serve our guests while you prepare us both for a trip to Sabre Ridge."

Sturgen looked as if his boss had hit him with a hickory club. "To Sabre Ridge, sir? Both of us?" He swallowed a tense knot in his thin throat and prepared to hear Dennison repeat himself.

"You heard correctly, Sturgen," said Dennison. "I've been summoned to Sabre Ridge. We're both going. My good friend Frank Abbadele needs my help. No power on earth could keep me from going to a friend in need of my legal counsel." He beamed, looking back and forth from Decker to Walsh, the thick envelope of money Walsh had handed him bulging inside his lapel pocket. "Gentleman . . . *bon appetit!*" He raised a tall glass of wine in one hand and the bottle in the other. "Then on to Sabre Ridge, where I will make quick work of this high-handed ranger! Onward to victory, gentlemen!"

The Ranger stood on the boardwalk out front of the hotel and watched the high rise of dust boil up from the desert floor. "Finally," he whispered to himself, feeling a sense of relief at the sighting of riders. It had been three full days since he'd sent Dick Abbadele fleeing into his cell, bullets nipping at his heels. Things had been tense but respectful between Sam and Sheriff Boggs ever since. But there had been an aura of tension engulfing Sabre Ridge like the steady buildup of pressure before a violent storm. Sam would be glad to see this thing with the Abbadeles come to an end. After all, he wasn't here to cause trouble for the town, although looking around, it was easy to see why some townsfolk might think so.

The Hung Dog Saloon had sat nearly empty day and night, business so poor that the piano player had left town on the southbound stage, along with the two young sporting women who had greeted Sam's arrival the day he and Maria rode in with the woman and baby in their arms. Well, this tense lull was about to end, Sam thought, letting his hand rest on the pistol butt of his tied-down Colt. He stepped back onto the boardwalk long enough to pick up his big Swedish long-range rifle. Then he stepped down and started walking toward the jail. Ahead of him he saw Big Shod step out of the shade and stand watching the riders grow larger as they approached town.

Sam stepped off the boardwalk onto the street far enough to look up at the half-open window where Maria stood holding the baby in her arms. She had also seen the rise of dust and now the large numbers of riders as they seemed to come up out of the hot belly of the earth. Her gaze left the riders on the horizon and went down to where the Ranger stood looking up at her. He gave her a short nod.

"Here, April, take the baby," Maria said, turning from the window to the chair where April sat brushing her hair.

"What's wrong?" April asked.

"I think the Abbadeles are here," said Maria.

"Oh . . ." April took the baby but started to rise up from the chair.

"No," said Maria. "You stay here. It will be dangerous out there."

"But Toot will be there!" April protested.

"*Sí*, but for your baby's safety, and your own, you must stay here." Maria picked up her rifle from against the wall and quickly checked it as they talked. There was no use trying to convince the young woman not to venture down onto the street. Sam had already spoken with the hotel clerk and told him to keep the woman from leaving the hotel should something of this nature come about. Sam thought of everything, she reminded herself, levering a round up into her rifle chamber as she headed for the door.

On the street, when the Ranger walked up beside Shod, the bounty hunter had just finished cleaning his wire-rimmed eyeglasses and put them back on. Under his arm he cradled a sawed-off ten gauge shotgun. Keeping his eyes peeled on the desert, he said, "Better late than never, right, Ranger?"

"I can't understand what's taken them so long," said Sam, a trace of suspicion in his voice. "I can usually call these things a lot closer."

"Nobody's perfect," said Shod. Looking at his face, the Ranger saw a nerve twitch in his tight jaw.

"You're right," said the Ranger, watching the riders, judging their arrival. He stepped back and leaned his big Swedish rifle against the hitch rail. As he returned to Shod's side, the bounty hunter nodded at the big rifle and said, "I see you don't plan on any of them getting out of range, making it out of here alive."

"Not if I can help it," said the Ranger. "They've had four days to think about why they're coming here. If they don't know they came to kill me, they should've asked more questions."

140

"So far I like your line of thinking, Ranger," said Shod.

"Have you checked your wanted posters?" Sam asked.

"Yep, some new ones came in on the stage yesterday," Shod replied. "I wired Circle Wells, had the printer there send me a personal stack just like the ones the sheriff gets. The only difference is, I actually look at mine."

"Anything interesting?" Sam asked.

"Yes, if you're a bounty hunter," said Shod, his hand resting on his pistol butt as the riders drew closer. "Apparently, the Abbadele brothers themselves are the only ones without prices on their heads. Some are small, hardly worth the trouble. But I have four here that total close to two thousand dollars. I need a payday bad, Ranger."

"All right," said Sam. "Just let me do my job first. Then you do yours."

"I assume you'll first give them a chance to surrender?" said Shod.

"Yep," said the Ranger. "Sounds stupid, but I have to make the offer."

"You're right. It does sound stupid . . . in this case, at least. The Abbadeles aren't about to surrender to you or anybody else."

"I know it," said Sam, "but that's how the law works."

"Sure it is," said Shod, lifting his pistol enough to loosen it in his holster, then keeping his hand on the butt. "That's why I gave it up."

"You haven't given up law work," said the Ranger. "You're just working it from a different approach." Sam watched the riders begin to rein down at the edge of town.

"Whatever you say, Ranger," said Shod. He glanced back over his shoulder and saw Maria walking up to them, rifle in hand, a big Colt pistol holstered on her hip.

At the edge of the town, Frank Abbadele let the men gather abreast. Then he heeled his horse forward at a slow walk. Aside from the Knox brothers, Lester and Kirby Brooks, and Walsh and Decker, three others had joined them on the trail to Sabre Ridge: Bennie Pearl, Otis Harpe, and a new man, Kurt Jones. They formed a V behind Frank and coaxed their horses forward. Before dropping his horse back a step behind his brother, Big Bob said, "I sure hope to hell you know what you're doing, Frank."

"Stick with me, Brother Bob," said Frank Abbadele. "We'll come out of this stronger than we've ever been."

Frank stepped his horse closer toward the jail, the others right behind him until, at a distance of twenty yards, the Ranger stepped forward and called out, "That's close enough. I have Dick Abbadele in jail for bank robbery and murder. The rest of you are under arrest on that same charge. Throw down your guns easy-like, with two fingers." The Ranger had already drawn his big Colt and cocked it as the riders gathered at the edge of town. He stood, feet shoulder length apart, poised, ready, convinced that they weren't about to give up their guns. To his left, one step back, stood the bounty hunter. To the Ranger's right stood Maria.

Frank Abbadele raised his hands chest high, showing no cause for alarm. Seeing the look on the Ranger's face, Frank Abbadele said, "Keep your dogs chained, Ranger." He offered a strange, mirthless grin. "I'm Frank Abbadele." He thumbed over his shoulder toward his brothers. "That's Big Bob and Toot. Tillis ain't with us right now. We heard about our brother, Dick, and we heard about the bank robbery. It's all been a misunderstanding. We're here to straighten everything out."

"Watch it, Ranger," Shod whispered.

Sam nodded slightly. Then he said to Frank Abbadele, "I haven't seen any guns drop yet. Either drop them or use them."

Frank chuckled under his breath, then said, "Ranger, you seem real eager to turn this into a gunfight. But it's not going to happen." He said over his shoulder, "Men, we want to do whatever we can to be obliging. You heard the Ranger. Ease those guns up and let them fall."

On the boardwalk, Sheriff Boggs stepped out of the sheriff's office, unarmed, holding his hands raised a cautious distance from his empty holster. Behind him stood Dick Abbadele, the sheriff's pistol in his hand, his free hand holding Boggs by the shirt collar. "Nobody move!" Dick shouted. "Or I'll blow this fool's head off!"

But as soon as Dick Abbadele made his threat, the Ranger, Big Shod and Maria all three half-turned, facing him without taking their eye off the other gunmen. "Do what he says, Ranger! For God sakes, he'll kill me," Boggs pleaded.

Before the Ranger could say anything or make a move, Frank Abbadele shouted at his brother, Dick. "Damn it to hell, Dick! Get your stupid ass back inside that jail! Or I'll shoot you my own damned self!"

"What?" Dick Abbadele looked stunned.

"You heard me!" Frank shouted. "Now get the hell back inside! We're giving ourselves up here! We never robbed any bank, and we're not going to be accused of it."

Seeing that the Ranger looked ready to raise his pistol and fire, and hearing the seriousness of his brother Frank's voice, Dick dropped the sheriff's pistol as if it had turned red hot. "Sorry," Dick said, turning loose of Boggs' collar. He jumped backward inside the office and slammed the door.

Sheriff Boggs stood in bewilderment, staring wild-eyed back and forth. "What's going on out here?" He looked at Frank Abbadele. "Frank, he could have made a getaway! I swear he could have. I wouldn't have been able to stop him! This wasn't none of my doing anyway: arresting Dick, putting him in jail!"

"Shut up, Boggs," said Frank Abbadele, "and don't worry about it." He laughed a little now that his brother was safely inside, the door shut behind him. "Some jailbreaks work, others don't. I hope you can get plenty of beer and fried chicken. Me and the boys are giving ourselves up to the Ranger. You know how Brother Bob here likes his fried chicken."

A ripple of laughter rose from the men.

Frank turned to the Ranger and raised his pistol from his holster with his thumb and first finger. "Here you go, Ranger. I'm raising it with two fingers, just like you asked." He dropped the pistol to the hoof-rutted ground. "I want you to know, that's a new Colt double-action Thunderer. Just had it shipped to me from Denver. It didn't have a scratch on it."

Maria started to take a step forward to pick up the pistol, but the Ranger stopped her with a raised hand. "Tell your boys to do the same," he said to Frank Abbadele. "This thing can still take a bad turn."

Frank turned slightly in his saddle. "Boys, are you all deaf? I said raise them and drop them. Now, let's get it done."

"I'm having bad thoughts about this, Frank," said Toot, sitting three places back on Frank's right. "How do we know that we'll get —"

"Shut up, Toot!" Frank shouted, cutting his brother off. "We want to abide by the law, don't we, like any good, respectable cattleman?" Frank turned to Sheriff Boggs and said, "Boggs, get a bag or something to put these guns in. Take good care of them for us."

"Sure thing, Frank," said the sheriff, hurrying back inside the office. In a moment, he returned with a large flour sack and stood with the top of it held open.

"All right, men," said Frank Abbadele. "Let's get it done."

Slowly the men raised their pistols with two fingers and let them fall. The Ranger and Shod shot one another a glance. Maria stepped up closer beside the Ranger. "What is he up to, Sam?" she asked. Sheriff Boggs rushed down from the boardwalk and held the flour sack open. Pistols fell into the sack; rifles began to stack up across the sheriff's arms.

Under his breath, the Ranger answered, "Maria, I don't have the slightest idea." They stood and watched as Boggs rushed back to the boardwalk with the heavy load of firearms. The Abbadele Gang stepped down slowly from their horses and stood with their hands raised.

Chapter 9

Sheriff Boggs had stepped down and helped Maria and Big Shod collect the weapons and pile them on the boardwalk temporarily, a safe distance from the Abbadeles. As the gang waited, lined up with their hands raised, the Ranger called out, "Toot Abbadele, you're not under arrest. Step out of the line."

Frank Abbadele gave his younger brother Toot a curious look, then turned to the Ranger. "What are you trying to pull now, Ranger? Of course he's under arrest. He's no different than the rest of us."

But Toot had already stepped out of line. "Can I have my gun back?" he asked.

Ignoring Frank's question, the Ranger said, "You can have it back, but you better make sure it doesn't point toward any one of us." He nodded toward Maria and Big Shod.

"Ranger," said Frank Abbadele, "I'm in charge of this bunch. I've got a right to know why Toot ain't being arrested along with the rest of us!"

"You're not in charge now, Frank," said the Ranger. "You're just a prisoner like everybody else." He wasn't about to answer to Frank Abbadele.

"I'd like to know that myself, Ranger," said Toot. He'd started to step over and pick up his pistol, but he stopped first, long enough to hear what the Ranger had to say.

From the other end of town, a dusty two-horse buggy came riding in from the desert. Maria, the Ranger and Big Shod looked at it drawing closer. Then the Ranger said to Toot, "You're going free because you've got a witness who says you weren't in Riley the day the bank was robbed." As he spoke, the Ranger stared into the young outlaw's eyes to see what truth might reveal itself.

"What the hell? A witness?" Frank cut in.

"A witness!" said Toot, echoing his brother's words. The Ranger saw him begin to get excited at the prospect. "Where is she!" Toot looked back and forth wildly, already putting two and two together, knowing it was April the Ranger was talking about. "Is she all right, Ranger?" He looked back and forth again before the Ranger could even answer. "April!" he shouted. The two-horse buggy came closer along the street, causing onlookers to move out of its way.

"April?" said Frank. He looked at his brother Bob. "Who is he talking about?" Then it dawned on Frank. "Hold it, Toot!" He grabbed his younger brother by the arm. "You don't mean that little nigra gal, do you?"

"Yeah, that's who," said Toot defiantly. "Her name is April." He shook Frank's hand off of his arm.

"I don't give a damn what her name is," Frank sneered. "I told you not to go around with her anymore!"

"I know what you told me, Frank," said Toot. "But there's things in this world you've got no say-so about and this is one of them."

"We'll see about that!" said Frank in a threatening tone. "I better not catch you around her anymore!"

As if Frank Abbadele was no longer even there, Toot asked, "Ranger, where is she? Is she all right? I've been going out of my mind!"

"She's all right, Toot," said the Ranger, seeing sincerity in this young outlaw's concern for the girl. He nodded back toward the hotel. "She's back there. She's weak,

150

but she's getting stronger every day."

"And . . . ? And . . . the baby? Did it? I mean . . ." Toot's words trailed. He had already leaned a step in the direction of the hotel and was ready to bolt into a run.

The Ranger forgot himself for a moment and offered a trace of a smile. "Congratulations, young man, you have a beautiful baby daughter."

Toot Abbadele looked stunned and delighted. "Can I . . . ? That is —" He pointed toward the hotel, suddenly not sure what he could or couldn't do.

"Get on out of here," said the Ranger. "Go see your little girl."

Toot Abbadele raced across the dirt street, through the parting collection of onlookers.

"A baby?" said Frank, outraged. "There better not be no baby! Get back here, Toot! Damn it to hell!" Frank shouted. The Ranger put his hand flat on the outlaw's chest, stopping him from going after his younger brother. "You damn fool!" Frank shouted at Toot. "You didn't even remember your gun!" Feeling the Ranger's hand holding him back, he swung himself free and said, "Take your stinking hand off me, Ranger! Nobody touches me!" His right hand went instinctively to his empty holster.

"It's in the pile, Frank," the Ranger said, leaning close to his face, keeping the words between themselves. "I'll have him go fetch it for you, though . . . since he's good at doing whatever you tell him to."

"You won't rile me into a gunfight, Ranger," said Frank. "I'm on to how you operate. I'm not falling for it."

The two stood almost nose-to-nose, Frank Abbadele's fists clenched tightly. Behind him, Big Bob cautioned him. "Easy, Frank. You said the key to this was for everybody to keep a cool head, remember?"

The Ranger listened and watched, wanting any clue he could get as to what was going on in these outlaws' scheming minds. Frank Abbadele forced himself to take a deep breath and calm down. Behind him, the Ranger heard a booming voice say, "Here, here! That'll be enough of that!" but Sam wasn't about to take his eyes off of Frank Abbadele to see who it was. Maria and Big Shod both stood behind him; he knew his back was well covered. "That man is a client of mine, sir!" the voice said. "Stand away from him!" But the Ranger ignored the voice.

"Who are you?" Maria demanded, stepping in front of Parker Dennison and blocking his path with the tip of her rifle barrel. Big Shod kept a wary eye on the outlaws, who stood with smug expressions on their faces.

"Your firearm doesn't frighten me, young lady," said Dennison. Yet he raised his hands slightly and stopped all the same. "I am protected by both the letter of the law and the spirit of justice. I demand that you lower that rifle!"

Maria didn't flinch. Nor did she lower the rifle. "Sam," she said, "I think I'm going to shoot this one."

Hearing the confidence in Dennison's voice and the calm resolve in Maria's, the Ranger stepped back from Frank Abbadele and half-turned toward Dennison, keeping one eye on Frank Abbadele and the rest of the outlaws. "You might know about the letter and the spirit," said the Ranger, "but right now you're meddling in enforcement. Who are you, mister, and what's your business here?" Sam asked.

"I am Parker Dennison, Esquire, sir. I am here serving as legal counsel for the Abbadeles and these other gentlemen." He started to sidestep Maria, but her rifle barrel pushed firmly into the soft flesh of his belly, holding him back. She looked to the Ranger and saw him give her a slight nod. Only then did she step aside grudgingly and let Dennison past her. "I'm afraid this is one time you have grievously misused the power of your office, Ranger."

"A lawyer?" The Ranger squinted at Frank Abbadele. "You have your own lawyer hired, just in case you get caught?"

Frank gave him a smug, mocking grin. "Doesn't everyone?" he said.

Hearing both men, Parker Dennison interjected. "It's the latest thing, Ranger. I would advise any ambitious man, regardless of his profession, to keep a personal attorney on retainer. You would do well to consider the idea yourself, given the offhanded manner in which you conduct your affairs."

"This rips it," the Ranger said. Then he turned back to Frank Abbadele and said to him in a lowered voice, "Play it your way, outlaw. When we're through seeing who can make the other jump the highest, I'll still mark your name off my list, looking down at the soles of your boots."

Frank Abbadele grinned. "I can hardly wait for you to try it, Ranger."

Stepping in closer, Parker Dennison said, "No more speaking with my client, Ranger. Anything you have to say to Frank or any of this group of gentlemen must be spoken to me on their behalf."

A hoot rose from among the outlaws. "Jerk a knot in his tail, lawyer!" said one of their voices. But at the back of the line, Lester Brooks said to his son, Kirby, "Stop laughing! This is pure foolishness, boy. We've got no business doing this."

"Relax, Pa," Kirby whispered. "Frank's just having a little fun."

"We ain't in the fun business," Lester hissed. "This is my and your livelihood we're playing with. Frank's showing off, and he's doing it at our expense. If I'd known this is what he had in mind coming here, we'd have pointed our boots toward Mexico."

The Ranger ignored the laughter and said to Sheriff Boggs, "Lawyer or not, they're going to jail, Boggs. Let's walk them in there."

Feeling better now that Parker Dennison was here, Boggs turned to the lawyer in expectation. "Is that all right, Mr. Dennison?"

"No, Sheriff," said Dennison. "On the contrary. I have to first question whether or not this jail is of an adequate size to accommodate this many prisoners."

The Ranger spun around and stared him hard in the eyes. "I'm not out to *accommodate* them. I'm out to jail them," he said, controlling his level of voice and temper. "Jails aren't supposed to be hotel rooms."

"I beg to differ with you, sir," said Dennison. "These men are innocent until proven guilty. The law has no right to subject an innocent man to inadequate living conditions. To do so is now considered to be in violation of the individual's rights as declared in the Constitution of the United States of America."

"I'm not torturing these snakes," said Sam. "I'm just confining them until a judge finds them guilty." He slid a glance at Frank Abbadele and the rest of the men, then looked back to the attorney. "That's more than I wanted to do. I had hoped they might want to settle up with me out of court."

"Sorry to disappoint you, Ranger," said Dennison, "but I'm afraid you won't be able to shed any innocent blood here today, nor will you be incarcerating innocent men." He proudly looked around at the faces of the outlaws as he continued. "I am waiting right now for a telegram from Circuit Judge Udall Henley. I have beseeched His Honor to grant these men bailment on their own resources as both property owners and citizens of this territory." He looked toward the telegraph office, where Sturgen had gone as soon as he'd stepped down from the buggy. "I'm sure he will grant my request based on these inadequate facilities."

"How can you call this jail inadequate?" the Ranger asked. "You haven't even taken a look inside it."

"I don't have to look inside," said Dennison. "The size of this jail alone is enough for me." He said to Sheriff Boggs, standing closer to him now, "Sheriff, how many cells does this jail have?"

"Two," said Boggs.

"And one is presently occupied by another prisoner," said Dennison in a curt voice. "Am I correct?"

"You are," Sheriff Boggs answered as if being questioned on a witness stand.

"And how many confinees is this jail designed to house?" Dennison inquired, appearing to already know the answer and the outcome as well.

"Confinees? Well" — Boggs scratched his head — "the cells have two cots in each of them, but I reckon that if a person needed to —"

"There, you see?" said Dennison, cutting Boggs off. "I explained to the judge what was about to happen here. I look forward to him agreeing with me." He pointed to the Abbadeles. "Besides, these men aren't going anywhere. They own one of the largest pieces of land on this side of the territory!"

"Maybe the Abbadeles do," said the Ranger. "But these other men don't have a thing holding them here."

A murmur of discontent rippled across the outlaws. "But not to worry," said Dennison, raising a hand and his voice. "I have asked the judge to allow the Abbadeles to post mortgage on their ranch to ensure that these men will not leave until the judge has arrived and found them all innocent."

A cheer rose from the outlaws. Dennison smiled in satisfaction. From the telegraph office, Sturgen came in a stiff trot, three sheets of telegram paper in his hand.

Big Shod had moved up beside the Ranger, keeping his hat brim lowered to hide his face from Parker Dennison. He pulled the Ranger a step to the side and said in a lowered voice, "Ranger, don't try to argue or match wits with this man. I've seen him in action. This is not your style. Don't let him make you step outside the law."

"That won't happen," the Ranger said guardedly. "But what about you? You've got a stake in this game, too."

"I'll make out," Shod whispered. Then he stepped away quietly, the sawed-off shotgun in his gloved hands.

When Sturgen arrived, coming to an abrupt halt in front of Parker Dennison, the lawyer snatched the papers from his hands, looked them over quickly, then said to Sam as he shoved the papers toward him, "Read them and weep, Ranger . . . to quote an old poker term."

Sam took the papers and read them quickly. He shoved them back to Parker Dennison and said in disgust, almost to himself, "The judge has given him everything he asked for. That includes releasing Dick Abbadele on bailment."

Cheers and laughter rose from the outlaws. Maria's shoulders slumped. She watched Sam level his hat brim and look around at the crowd of townsfolk. *Poor Sam,* she thought, seeing that most of the townsfolk seemed to be enjoying the fact that a band of killers and robbers had just managed to make a mockery of the law Sam Burrack had sworn to uphold.

Lester Brooks and his son, Kirby, stayed with the horses while the rest of the men followed Frank and Bob Abbadele and joined Parker Dennison in the street. "Stay here with me, boy," Lester said, taking Kirby by his forearm, keeping him from tagging along with the others. Lester's eyes shifted back and forth, taking in the Ranger, Maria and Big Shod warily.

"But, Pa, I want to hear what this man has to say!" Kirby protested.

"To hell with that lawyer," said Lester. "He's looking out for the man who's carrying the money. He don't give a damn about you or me, either one."

"You heard Frank say it, Pa. Parker Dennison represents all of us," said Kirby.

"If I thought you'd never get any smarter than you are right now, I believe I'd be doing you a favor by blowing your head off," said Lester, cuffing his son on the side of his head.

"Damn it, Pa!" Kirby flinched and straightened his disheveled hat. "What's bothering you, anyway?"

"Tell me this, boy," said Lester in a low voice. "Is there or is there not a warrant for you in the State of Texas?"

"Sure there is, Pa," said Kirby. "We both know that. What's it got to do with anything? That warrant is over a year old."

"Those two boys that robbed that store with you . . . the one they didn't hang?

160

Didn't he know your real name?"

"Yeah, so what?" said Kirby.

"I'll tell you so what," said Lester Brooks as he and Kirby stood partly hidden behind the horses. He grabbed Kirby by his jaw and turned his face toward where Big Shod stood next to the Ranger, the shotgun across his forearm. "See that colored man right there?"

"Yes, Pa! I see him," said Kirby. "Let me go!"

"That man is a bounty hunter — works mostly between here and Texas. Before this day is over, that man is going to throw somebody facedown over a saddle and haul them away from here. I don't want you to be that somebody."

Kirby gave his father a serous look, no longer questioning his judgment. "Pa," he whispered, "should I warn the others?"

"No," said Lester. "Let them look out for their own hides. Walk your horse away from here easy-like until you get around the corner. Then skin out of here."

"Where should I go, Pa?" Kirby asked.

"Just go," said Lester. "I'll be close behind you. Meet me at the bottom of the hills. Now go on. Get out of here." He gave his son a shove, then turned his gaze to Shod.

Across the street, watching while Parker Dennison and the Abbadele Gang stood in a close huddle in the dirt street, Maria said to the Ranger, "For all of his talk about fried chicken and beer, Frank Abbadele knew that he and his men weren't going to see the inside of a jail cell." She drew in a tight, angry breath. "It is a terrible thing when the Abbadeles of this world can make the law work for the lawless."

"The law works for everybody," said Shod, adjusting his spectacles with a long finger. "Today it's working for the Abbadeles because they think they have come up with something new, some clever gimmick that our judicial system has over-looked somehow. But that's nothing new. It happens every day."

"Every fool is his own undoing," the Ranger added. "I'm no lawyer or scholar, but I've lived long enough to learn that. Today, Frank Abbadele thinks he's beaten the world with the help of this man and his knowledge of the legal system, but Frank will soon run out his string. This isn't the first time you've seen it happen, Maria."

"*Sí,*" said Maria. "I have seen it happen many times. But right now I am angry, and I think I have earned the right to be. How is it that we can be so confident in the law of this country when we see how easily it can be misused?"

"What else have we got?" the Ranger said with finality.

A silence passed as the three stood in contemplation, watching the outlaws and their attorney in the dirt street. Then the Ranger said to Shod, "You and this Dennison must've locked horns somewhere along the way, huh?"

"Yes, you could say that," said Shod.

"I suppose that's why you didn't want him seeing you?" Sam asked.

"I've got nothing to hide from him," said Shod. "I just didn't want to have to speak to him or acknowledge him in any way."

"I understand," said the Ranger. "Sounds like he must've wiped up the floor with you — legally speaking, that is."

"Yes," said Shod, "that's an apt, albeit blunt, assessment." He reached up again with a finger and adjusted his spectacles on the bridge of his nose. "Parker Dennison has more twists and turns than a sack full of rattlesnakes."

"And can't care less if his client is guilty, I suppose," said the Ranger.

"Not in the least," said Shod. "But then, a lawyer can always justify that by the fact that everybody is entitled to legal representation, so what can you say?" He shrugged. "In spite of what we think about the misuse of the law, if lawyers refused to defend people like the Abbadeles, our justice system wouldn't work for any of us."

"I understand all that," said the Ranger. "But with a lawyer like Dennison, what it comes down to is that a man is only as innocent as he can afford to be."

"There's nothing new about that notion, either," said Shod. "It's been that way since somebody invented *round* and turned it into a coin. As much as I dislike Parker Dennison, I can't blame him for how far money tips the scales of justice."

"I know it," said Sam. "But he's the one throwing it in our faces today. I just hate seeing it up so close, where I'm forced to breathe the stink of it."

On his other side, Maria cut in, saying as she watched the outlaws file into the saloon, "They are on good behavior now, but wait until they get whiskey boiling their brains."

"That will be Boggs' problem," said Sam. "We're heading out of here. I've seen as much of this as I can stand for one day."

"But Sam," Maria said, "we can't leave these men free to do whatever they please to Sabre Ridge. We must be here when this town begins to see their other side."

"Don't worry, Maria, we will," said the Ranger. "We'll make camp outside of town and be ready for whatever this turns into." He looked at Shod. "You're welcome to camp with us, if it suits you."

"Much obliged," said the bounty hunter, "but I enjoy my solitude. Besides, I've still got business to take care of."

"What?" Sam asked, looking a bit surprised.

Shod pulled four wrinkled wanted posters from inside his shirt. "You're through here for now, right?"

"Yes," said the Ranger, "but —"

"No buts about it," said Shod, cutting him off. "I backed you up as far as I could. Now that we're finished doing our civic duty for the day, I've got four bounties to collect."

Chapter 10

Lester Brooks and his son, Kirby, left town so quietly and quickly that no one among the Abbadeles noticed they were gone until Big Bob looked all around and said, "Lester? Lester?" His visual search widened. Then he said, "Anybody seen Lester and Kirby?"

Across the street, the Ranger nudged Maria and brought her attention to the two streams of dust headed out of town. "It looks like somebody felt like they'd overstayed their welcome. I expect Shod's bounty number just fell from four to three." As he spoke, the Ranger and Maria moved from the hitch rail and took up a better position flanking the Abbadeles in case Shod needed help. The outlaws and Parker Dennison had turned and started for the door of the sheriff's office when Big Shod stepped out in front of them with the double-barreled shotgun cocked and pointed. Making sure the shotgun stayed aimed straight at Frank Abbadele's chest, from a distance of ten feet away he called out, "Not so fast, gentlemen. Four of you have bounties on you. Step to the side as you hear your name called."

The outlaws came to an abrupt halt behind Frank Abbadele, who stood between Big Bob and Parker Dennison. A short, nervous laugh rose up. "Go to hell!" an angry voice said.

"I've got picture posters on you," said Shod. "Don't make me pull them out and match them up to you. It'll start us off on a bad foot all the way to Texas."

"Who does he think he's kidding?" a voice said.

"Shut up back there! There's a damn shotgun pointing at me!" Frank shouted back over his shoulder. "Does that look like he's kidding to you?" Then, to Shod, Frank said, "Bounty hunter, you better make sure you know damn well what you're doing. We're unarmed now, but we won't be for long!"

Big Shod ignored Frank's words and called out, "Doyle Royal, Bennie Pearl, Otis Harpe, Billy Stone."

"What should we do, Boss?" Otis Harpe asked.

"Damn it all," Frank growled under his breath. He stared at the shotgun pointed at his chest, then said aloud to the men behind him, "Do like he says, boys. Don't give this bounty hunter any excuse to kill you. You won't be forgotten about — you have my word."

"Can't this lawyer do something?" Bennie Pearl asked.

Staring at Big Shod and recognizing him, Parker Dennison said, "Gentlemen, I will do what I can for you. But right now, Frank is advising you correctly. I know this man, and he is a cold-blooded killer. Don't allow yourselves to be gunned down like dogs!" He stared with contempt at Big Shod.

"You heard him," said Shod. "That might be the wisest advice he's ever given a person. Now all four of you, get over there."

Bennie Pearl stepped grudgingly to the side. A moment later, Otis Harpe did the same. The two stood slack-shouldered. Shod called out, "All right, gentlemen, don't be bashful. Where's Billy Stone and Doyle Royal?"

"These two are all you get, bounty hunter," said Frank. "Billy Stone got blown away in the storm. If you go look real close across the flatlands, you might see him stuck high up on the side a big ole cactus somewhere."

"What about Royal?" Shod asked, looking the faces over for any sign of deceit.

"We haven't seen him around," said Frank. "He might have also gotten blown away, as far as we know."

On the boardwalk, Sheriff Boggs stepped out of his office carrying the feed sack full of firearms, ready to give them back to their owners. Behind him came Dick Abbadele, wearing a big smile, happy to be released. But the Ranger motioned Boggs back inside. Boggs looked confused and frightened, seeing the outlaws wanting their firearms, yet under the Ranger's gaze he gave Frank Abbadele a sympathetic shrug, stepped back inside his office and bolted the door. Frank Abbadele seethed, giving the Ranger a hard stare. Seeing the tenseness of the situation, Dick Abbadele's smile faded. He walked cautiously along the boardwalk, then stepped down and joined the outlaws in the street.

"What's going on?" Dick asked in a lowered voice.

Without answering him, Frank gave a toss of his head, motioning for Dick to get behind him. Dick did so quickly.

Then Frank turned his attention back to Shod. "Good luck trying to get these men back to Texas, bounty hunter." He spit toward the ground at Shod's feet.

"Good luck?" said Otis Harpe in a shaky voice. "Damn it, Frank, what do you mean, wishing him good luck? You're supposed to be on our side —"

"For God sakes, Otis!" shouted Frank. "It's just a figure of speech! Of course I'm not really wishing him luck, you idiot! I told you we're not going to let him get away with this!"

But Otis wasn't through yet. "If you hadn't told us to ride in here, then to give up our guns, this wouldn't have happened! Now look at us! I'm going to jail! Pearl is going to jail! Way to go, Frank! Guess we need to get ourselves a good lawyer . . . like you did!"

Frank felt the sting of Otis' words, knowing that they were true. This had all been his idea. He thought he and Dennison had figured everything out. But they hadn't planned on a bounty hunter stepping forward and taking two of his men right out from under his nose. It made him look bad in front of the others. He said in a lowered tone to Parker Dennison, who stood beside him, "Are you sure there's nothing you can do to stop this right here and now?"

Staring coldly at Big Shod as he spoke, Parker Dennison said to Frank, "Believe me, sir, if there was anything I could do right at this moment, I already would have done so. I told you, I know this man. He's an animal."

"Keep it up, Dennison," said Shod. "You might get by talking that way to people in a courtroom. But all it'll get you here is a busted head. I'm doing my job. Don't keep trying to distract me."

Even as Shod spoke to the lawyer, Otis Harpe eased his hand around inside his back pocket, brought out a small pistol and held it down his side, concealed by his hand. He whispered sidelong to Bennie Pearl, "Get ready to make a run for it."

Giving only a slight nod, Bennie Pearl stood in silence, poised and ready. His eyes darted back and forth along the street until they came upon a horse standing at a hitch rail in front of the bridle shop. A rifle butt stuck up from a saddle scabbard as if beckoning him.

"Now!" Otis Harpe shouted. He raised the pistol to arm's length and got two shots off toward Big Shod. The first shot went wild; the second lifted the bounty hunter's hat from his head and sent it spinning in the air. But before Otis could get the third shot off, he saw that he had made a deadly mistake.

Shod swung the shotgun into his left hand, still cocked, still covering the other outlaws. His right hand went to the big Colt on his hip and brought it up before his hat had hit the ground. Otis Harpe tried to crouch and fire, but the bounty hunter's bullet hit him dead center in his chest, lifted him backward and dropped him beneath a thick spray of blood.

Moving quickly, the Ranger and Maria covered the outlaws with their drawn Colts, letting them know better than to make a move and rush Shod, in case the shotgun in his hand wasn't reason enough. Shod kept an eye on the rest of the outlaws and called out to Bennie Pearl as he made a dash toward the horse and rifle. "Stop right there, Pearl, or I'll shoot!" Out of the corner of his eye, Shod saw Pip Richards flee from his shady spot and dive for cover behind a water trough.

Bennie Pearl wasn't about to stop. He made it as far as the horse. There was an instant where it looked like he might grab the reins instead of the rifle. The Ranger wondered what Shod would do if the fleeing outlaw made a run instead of a stand. Would the bounty hunter shoot him in the back? The Ranger didn't have to wonder long. Instead of snatching the reins, at the last second Pearl grabbed the rifle and levered it as he turned around to face Shod. "Come and get me, bounty hunt—"

Shod stood with his pistol already aimed and cocked. Seeing the rifle come up into play, he squeezed the trigger. The explosion resounded along the street. The outlaws flinched, seeing the shot pitch Bennie Pearl up onto the boardwalk and backward through the large window of the harness shop. Shards of glass rained across the boardwalk. The horse at the hitch rail went crazy, bucking and jerking on its reins.

"You murdering heathen," Parker Dennison said. Behind him, the enraged outlaws seemed on the verge of lunging forward toward Shod, but Frank and Dennison stopped them with their arms spread.

"Everybody stay put," said Frank. "Don't give him cause to kill you, too. Our time is coming, you can count on it."

"Give us our guns!" shouted Terrence Knox. "Our time will be right now!"

"Ye-yea-yea, gi-giv-give us, our gu-gu-gun-uns," Hirsh Knox stammered in his rage.

"No, both of you listen to me!" said Frank, turning to face the men. "That's what the Ranger and this bounty hunter want you to do!" He pointed at Otis Harpe's body lying flat on its back in the dirt street. "You think these two didn't have it all planned to work out this way? That bounty hunter couldn't be happier! Now he doesn't have to feed them all the way back to Texas."

Earlier, the townsfolk had drawn back away from the scene in the street. But now that the shooting had stopped, they ventured forward again. It was plain to see that most of them sympathized with the Abbadeles. They gave Shod a stern look as Frank Abbadele pointed a finger and denounced him for killing the two outlaws. It didn't seem to matter that the two were wanted for crimes in Texas. Here in Sabre Ridge the Abbadeles and their friends had kept their noses clean and spent their money. From the Hung Dog Saloon to the mercantile store to the town barbershop, the Abbadeles were known for their generosity. Now two of their men lay dead.

Seeing the townsfolk draw closer in the street, Frank Abbadele raised an accusing finger toward Big Shod. "Sabre Ridge better decide who its friends are, folks," he said, loud enough for everyone to hear. "All the time my brothers and our men have been coming to this town, there has never been anything like this happen! Now that *outsiders* come to town, wanting to enforce the law on us, look what we wind up with on our streets!"

While Frank Abbadele continued talking, Shod took the wanted posters from his shirt pocket, walked over to Otis Harpe's corpse and rolled the dead face from side to side with his boot, looking at it closely. Onlookers appeared enraged by his action. A slight smile of satisfaction came to Parker Dennison's face. The Ranger saw Dennison's expression and said to Maria as he stepped away from her and toward the gathering crowd of onlookers, "Mr. Shod doesn't pay much mind to public opinion, I see."

Maria only nodded, keeping her rifle pointed toward the outlaws and their lawyer.

To shift attention away from Shod, the Ranger stepped around between him and the townsfolk and said to the angry faces, "This man has a right to apprehend criminals who are on the run and wanted by the law in other parts of this country. You might not like how this happened, but he

175

wasn't the one who put this outcome into motion. It was these two when they decided they'd rather kill him than obey the law."

"He killed them!" shouted a voice. "That's all we know, Ranger. They might be wanted in Texas, but they haven't broke no laws here."

"If it was the other way around," said the Ranger, "would you want men who've broken the law here to be able to go to Texas and go unpunished?"

The townsfolk didn't seem to hear that question. The Ranger looked around, saw the smug look on Frank Abbadele and Parker Dennison's faces, then saw Shod walking toward the broken window where the dead outlaw lay with his feet sticking out. "He's doing his job, folks," the Ranger said. "Nobody ever said law work was pleasant to watch. You'd do us a favor by going on about your business and letting us take care of ours."

"What the hell is everybody afraid to say here?" said a raised voice. From among the townsfolk, a tall man stepped forward wearing a clerk's apron and pointed at Shod. "We all know that every time one of *his kind* comes along, there's trouble!"

Shod stopped in his tracks in the dirt

street and turned facing the man. The Ranger decided not to step between Shod and the townsman. Instead, he took a step to the side and kept an eye on the outlaw and the lawyer as he spoke to the clerk. "By *his* kind, you do mean bounty hunters, don't you?"

A deathlike silence had fallen over the street as Shod turned and stood facing the clerk. The clerk swallowed a knot in his throat and seemed to consider the Ranger's question for a second. Then he said in a tight, nervous voice, "Yes, of course! That's what I meant. *Bounty hunters.*"

At the first sound of gunfire, Toot Abbadele had handed April the baby and hurried to the hotel window. He'd seen Otis Harpe lying dead in the dirt, then had watched as the bounty hunter's shot hurled Bennie Pearl backward through the window. Toot's first instinct had been to slap a hand to his hip, before realizing his holster was empty. "I better get down there," he'd said.

"Toot!" said April. "What about us, the baby and me? You just said we were going to be a family!"

"We are, April," Toot said, hearing the fear in her voice as he watched the street.

"Just calm down and let me think!" He raised a hand and rubbed his forehead, feeling torn between his woman and baby and his loyalty to his brothers and friends. In a moment, upon seeing that the shooting had stopped and that his two brothers stood safely with the lawyer, he let out a breath of relief and continued watching as the bounty hunter turned away from facing the clerk in the street and walked over to the shattered window of the harness shop.

"I think we need to get out of here," April said, sitting in a chair beside the bed, holding the baby to her breast. "As long as you're around your brothers, you're going to be a part of whatever they're involved in."

Toot turned from the window, came to her and kneeled beside her chair. "I don't mean for it to be that way, April. It just happens. It's hard to turn away from the people I've been with my whole life. Even though Frank and I are always ready to argue at the drop of a hat, he's still my brother." Toot glanced toward the window. April saw that he was anxious to get down there in the street with his brothers.

"I know it's not easy for you, Toot," said April. "But if we're ever going to be a family of our own, you have to break away from your brothers. They're outlaws. I won't be an outlaw's wife."

"I wouldn't ask that of you, April," said Toot. He brushed her hair from her cheek, looking down at the sleeping baby. "And I don't want to lose you and the baby. When I got separated from you in the storm, I thought I was going to lose my mind. Then later, when I got myself a horse and got on your trail, I came to the mining shack and found dead *comadrejas* lying everywhere. Saw there had been a battle there." He shook his head and grimaced just thinking about it. "My first thought was that you had been taken captive by those desert weasels and that I'd never see you again."

"We have the Ranger and his woman, Maria, to thank for me and the baby being alive," said April. "The Ranger even took my word that you were with me when your brothers robbed the bank in Riley. That's why you're not standing down there in the street right now." She turned her eyes from the baby up to his.

"I know," said Toot, hanging his head, feeling more and more pressured. "But they're still my brothers. What can I tell you?"

"You can tell me where you and I stand

179

if your brothers and the gang go up against the Ranger and Maria." April said pointedly.

A silence passed as Toot seemed to gravely contemplate the matter. Then he said, "I don't know, April. That's as honest as I can be about it."

She looked at him closely. "Did you really go back looking for me, Toot?"

"For God sakes, April! *Yes,* I went back looking for you! I would be looking for you right now if . . ." His words trailed.

But April picked them up for him. "You mean if Frank and the others hadn't stopped you?" she asked.

"No," said Toot, "that's not what I meant. I mean, I would have gotten myself outfitted and gone searching for you . . . thinking the *comadrejas* had taken you. That's the God's honest truth, April." He studied her dark eyes, then asked, "Why are you talking like this? Don't you believe me? Don't you believe that I love you? That I meant what I said about you and me and the baby?"

"I believed you until I saw how you acted a while ago when you thought your brothers might be in a shoot-out with the law," April said. "Now I'm not sure what I believe. You said you wanted us to be a family . . . Well, here we are, Toot. Now what?"

"Now we get ourselves a place and get settled in," said Toot. "We don't have to go halfway across the country. There's plenty of room right here. A few acres of land, a few head of our own cattle; we can —"

"Stop it, Toot. You know better," April said, not letting him finish his wishful thinking. "If we make our home here, near your brothers, what do you think will ever change?" She took a deep breath, then asked, "Did you even dare tell Frank about the baby?"

"Sure, Frank knows all about the baby," said Toot, ducking the intent of the question.

But April caught the way he said. "*You* told Frank about the baby?"

"No," said Toot, seeing she was on to him. "The Ranger told him before I got a chance. But what's the difference? Frank knows."

"The difference is that you said *you* would tell him," said April. "Not the Ranger."

"All right," said Toot. "Things didn't work out the way I planned them, but I would have told Frank. That's the truth." Again Toot glanced toward the window. "I better go see what's going on down there. I'll only be a minute."

"And what did Frank have to say when the Ranger told him?" April asked, ignoring his comment about wanting to go down to the street. "I'm sure he wasn't exactly delighted at the prospect, was he?"

"No, he got pretty upset, April, to be honest," Toot admitted. "But, damn it, so what? He's not going to be running our lives. Who cares what he thinks?"

"You must care, Toot," April said, "since you're having such a hard time breaking loose from him." She turned her eyes away from him. "Are you ashamed of me and this baby, Toot? Is that it? Are you ashamed of us?"

"God, no!" said Toot. "I love you . . . both of you. We've just got things that need to be straightened out. When the time comes, April, you'll see I'm not tied to my brothers," Toot said. "But right now, I better go make sure everything is all right."

"The time *has* come, Toot," April said with finality. "You have to decide right now. Is your life here with us or down there in the street with your outlaw brothers?"

"I can't do this right now, April," Toot

pleaded. "Can't you see the spot I'm on?"

"Yes," April said, "I see what a spot you're on. But all you have to do is step off of that spot one way or another. If you leave us now and go join your brothers, that's one way of getting off the spot."

"What do you mean, April?" Toot asked.

"I mean, this baby and I could have died out there in the badlands if it hadn't been for Maria and the Ranger. God sent them along to give me a second chance at life. I'm not going to waste time on a man who doesn't know if he wants me or not. Whatever I do now, I do it for this baby and me. If you want us, stay with us. If you want to stay with your brothers, I won't try to stop you. When the stage from Circle Wells comes tomorrow, the baby and I will be leaving on it."

Chapter 11

Sam and Maria kept a close eye on the Abbadeles and their lawyer while Shod dragged the bodies of Otis Harpe and Bennie Pearl to the boardwalk out front of the sheriff's office and laid them there, their heads leaning against the front of the building. Moments later, the town photographer arrived, hurriedly set up his equipment, took pictures and disappeared, but not before he handed Shod his business card and caught the gold piece Shod flipped to him.

The Abbadeles stood seething, waiting until Shod walked to his horse, stepped up into his saddle and nudged it over to the Ranger. "Are you two going to be all right here?" Shod asked, looking down at them through his thick spectacles.

"We'll manage," said the Ranger. "I suppose you're going after the two who weren't here?"

"Might as well, while the trail is still clear," said the big bounty hunter, giving a glance around the street, then out toward the badlands. A stream of dust left behind Lester and Kirby Brooks' horses stood high on the hot air. "I can't make the Abbadeles or these townsfolk any madder than they are already."

"That's a fact," said the Ranger. "I'll check on how your photo plates are coming along. It could take a couple of weeks or longer before you get the photos sent back to Texas and get yourself paid. I'll sign an affidavit attesting to who they are."

"Much obliged," said Shod. Then, turning to Maria, he touched his gloved fingers to his battered hat brim. "Ma'am, Ranger. It's been interesting, to say the least."

Riding away slowly, the bounty hunter felt the harsh stares of outlaws and towns-folk alike, but he ignored them and rode on.

Sam said quietly to Maria, "I kept telling myself he could have handled things a little more delicately, but I can't really say how."

"I know," said Maria. "He hunts wanted men for a living, and we've just seen the way he does it. Perhaps it is difficult for us to witness this, when we are used to being the ones standing in the gun sights."

"Maybe that's it," said the Ranger. He

looked out across the street at the outlaws. "We just got a reminder of what a dirty, gruesome business this is."

"*Sí*," said Maria. She stared at the outlaws with him. "What do we do now about these men? Must we wait here for a judge, then go through a whole trial process?"

"If that's the way they've decided to play it," Sam said, nodding slightly at Frank Abbadele and Parker Dennison, "we have no choice. I don't like the idea of bailment, but it's been around a lot longer than most folks realize. It takes some slick lawyer like Dennison to request it. If the law worked this way all the time, the criminals would soon overfill the courthouses."

"Not if Mr. Shod can help it," said Maria, looking over at the two dead outlaws on the boardwalk.

As they talked quietly between themselves, Toot Abbadele came out of the hotel and walked quickly to join his brothers in the middle of the street. "That's one conversation I'd like to hear," Maria said softly to the Ranger. Sam only nodded in reply.

In the street, Frank Abbadele walked forward a few steps to meet his brother before Toot made it all the way over to where the men stood closely surrounding Parker

Dennison. "What the hell was that ranger talking about, that colored girl having a baby?" Frank growled low, keeping the others from hearing him.

"All right, Frank, calm down," said Toot, coming to a halt, seeing Big Bob come forward to join them. "Yes, it's true. April and I have a baby girl." As he spoke, Toot took a careful step back as Frank advanced on him. "Are you going to settle down and listen to what I've got to say or start acting like a damn fool, Frank?" He looked at Big Bob and Dick, then said as the two of them stopped beside Frank, "All three of you listen to me for a second. This ain't what you two think it is."

"You kept poking that little gal after I told you to get shed of her," Frank said, "and you ended up siring yourself a spotted calf! If this ain't what we think it is, you tell us right now just what the hell *is it?*"

"All right, I care some about the girl," said Toot, sounding a little weak in the throat. "What's the harm in it?"

"You care *some* about her?" said Frank with a sarcastic snap to his voice. "Well, you just better see to it that you *stop* caring some about her. And I mean you better stop caring some about her right now! We need to make a strong showing. We can't do it with you pumping up the belly of any stray nigra who happens past your window!"

Big Bob cut in. "This is no time to be taking a stand against the rest of us, Toot, damn it. Frank's right."

"Family has to stick together," said Dick, happy to be out of the cramped jail cell. "Look where I would be sitting right now if it hadn't been for Frank and the rest of you."

"Oh yeah, Dick? Stick together, huh?" Toot looked up and down the street, making a show of searching for someone. "You mean the way Tillis is doing? Has anybody seen him since things started turning tight with the law?"

"Tillis?" Frank growled. He lowered his voice and said between the two of them, "Dick just told me a while ago that Tillis is carrying the money from the Riley bank. So don't worry about Tillis doing his part. He's doing it. Now, you get yourself rid of that colored gal and her half-breed baby. I don't want to see them. I don't even want to hear about them again. Do you understand me, Toot?"

"If I don't," Toot said wryly, "I bet you'll be kind enough to remind me again."

"Stop fooling around, little brother," Big

Bob warned. "We've got that blasted ranger and his woman down our shirts . . . in case you don't realize it."

Toot turned his gaze toward the Ranger and Maria, who stood thirty yards away, looking back at him. "April said those two saved her and the baby from a bunch of *comadrejas*," Toot said absently to Dick and Big Bob.

"Well, bless their little lawdog hearts," Dick said with sarcasm.

"Yeah. Maybe you'd like to go over and thank them. Shake their hands, buy them both a drink?" said Bob, also looking over at the Ranger and Maria.

Frank said with anger and contempt, "That's just one more reason to kill them both." He turned and walked back to where Parker Dennison stood with the others.

"You've got him fit to be tied," Bob said to Toot as soon as Frank walked away.

"Damn it, Toot," said Dick. "I knew something was going on when you split off and didn't ride to Riley with us. Sometimes it looks like you go out of your way to goad Frank."

"I don't have to goad him," said Toot. He spit and ran his hand across his mouth, watching Frank walk away. "Him and me never have got along, and we never will."

When Frank stopped in front of Parker Dennison and turned facing his brothers, the lawyer asked, "Is everything all right, Frank?"

"Yes, everything's fine," said Frank. "My brother Toot just has his head on a little crooked right now. Don't worry. I'll jerk his tail hard enough to straighten him out."

"Let's hope so," said Dennison. "Unity is of the utmost importance to us. We want to have ourselves a good, strong legal defense prepared when the judge gets to town."

"That's your job, Dennison," said Frank. "Just lead the way."

"First things first, of course," said Dennison, looking around at the men. "Do you suppose these gentlemen have cooled their tempers enough to be trusted with their guns?"

"They'll do like I tell them," said Frank. "As long as nobody jerks iron on them first, they'll keep their guns holstered."

"Very good then," said Dennison. Gesturing a manicured hand toward the sheriff's office, he said, "Shall we . . . ?"

"Sure, why not?" Frank Abbadele motioned for the men to follow him to the sheriff's office. Stepping up onto the boardwalk, Frank looked down at the two dead outlaws and said, "A couple of you better get these boys off the planks and over to the undertaker. Flies are starting to swarm." He brushed a hand back and forth in front of his face. "The rest of you wait out here. And remember what I said: *no trouble.*" He stepped inside the sheriff's office, followed by Toot, Big Bob, and Parker Dennison, who closed the door behind him. The outlaws stopped abruptly and looked at one another.

"Kurt," said Lenbow Decker to Kurt Jones, "since you and Otis knew each other from before you joined up with us, I reckon it ought to be you who hauls him and Bennie away from here."

"Like hell," said Jones. "I mighta known Otis before, but I don't owe him or Pearl a damn thing." He spit, then looked down at the two corpses. A large blow fly walked across Otis' pale dead face. "And to be honest, I never did like this rotten son of a bitch. Let me tell you what I caught him doing one night out along the Brazos."

Terrence Knox cut in, giving Kurt Jones a hard stare. "This ain't the time to belittle a man. You never said nothing about it to his face when he was alive, so kindly keep your mouth shut now."

"Ye-yea-yeah, Jone-Ja-Jo-Ja—" Beside Terrence, his brother Hirsh tried to join in, but his words twisted and tangled into meaningless stammering.

"Jesus!" Jones said to Terrence while he looked Hirsh up and down in bemusement. "Stop him before he swallows his tongue!"

"Never mind about Hirsh's tongue," said Terrence. "See to it you keep yours in check." His hand slid instinctively to the empty holster on his hip.

But Jones got the message all the same. "All right. Damn! Don't take it so serious," he said. "I meant no harm to your brother or this dead son of a bitch, either one." He nodded down at Otis Harpe's body. "If that glass-eyed bounty hunter was here, for two cents I'd smack the cold yeller piss out of him, make him haul these boys to the undertaker himself."

"Ha!" Hirsh Knox scoffed. "I'd like to see-sa-see ya-you-ya-ho try-tr-try —"

"Hush up, Hirsh!" said Terrence Knox, stopping his brother's garbled dissertation.

"Damn!" said Kurt Jones, shaking his head. "No offense. But that boy can't say shit, can he?"

Both Hirsh and Terrence Knox reddened with anger. But before either could say any more, the door to the sheriff's office swung open and Sheriff Boggs stepped out onto the boardwalk carrying the sack full of weapons. Stepping out behind the sheriff, Frank Abbadele said, "I'm going to say it one more time: Everybody keep a tight rein on your tempers." His eyes went to the Ranger and Maria, still standing in the street. "Don't let anybody goad you into breaking any laws while we're here." He looked down at the two bodies, then said, "As soon as you get these boys moved, come on over to the saloon. Drink yourselves some whiskey, play some poker, twirl a whore or two, whatever you like. Just watch your step. Once the judge gets here, Parker Dennison will show us how to go about skinning a ranger and salting his hide." A cheer went up from the outlaws.

"He means figuratively speaking of course!" Parker Dennison said, shooting the Ranger a glance then raising a hand, acknowledging the outlaws.

From the street, the Ranger and Maria watched the men step down from the boardwalk out front of the sheriff's office. Frank, Toot and Bob Abbadele walked with Parker Dennison toward the Hung Dog Saloon. Decker and Walsh picked up

Harpe's body, and the Knox brothers picked up Pearl's. Kurt Jones tagged along behind them as they carried the bodies away.

Maria said to the Ranger, "Poor April. It looks as if Toot Abbadele is having a hard time deciding who to stick with, the woman he loves or his outlaw brothers."

"Yes, it looks like it," said the Ranger with a sigh of exasperation. "But he better decide pretty quick. He might get by with stringing that poor girl along for a while, but if he tries it on these men, brothers or not, it'll get him killed graveyard dead."

Inside the Hung Dog Saloon, the bar owner, Sydney Pine, worked hard keeping glasses filled and spills wiped up. He lit cigars, laid out trays of cold cut beef and sliced bread, and kept the beer tap working, allowing more than an ordinary head of foam to rise up and spill over the edge of the tall, thick beer mugs. He sent the frothing mugs sliding down along the inside edge of the bar to eagerly waiting hands. At the same time, he tipped a bottle of rye bar whiskey above what seemed like an endless line of shot glasses. Now that the Abbadeles were back, they drew with them the rest of the town drinkers, most of whom were angry at the law and welcomed a chance to say so over a glass of fiery liquor.

At the end of the bar, Tommy Walsh looked at an aging painted whore named Delphia who was working her way skillfully from drinker to drinker. "I swear," Walsh said to Lenbow Decker, who stood beside him, "when I first got here, Delphia reminded me of my beat-up old grandma. Now, the more I look at her, the more she reminds me of my sweet young cousin Ilene."

"Do what suits you," said Lenbow Decker, wiping beer foam from his upper lip. "I'm saving my money till Swan and Clare-Annette get back to town. Delphia will cause you bad dreams from now till Christmas."

Walsh grinned. "Sometimes bad dreams beat the hell out of no dreams at all." He drained his whiskey glass, belched, and walked down to where Delphia stood sipping whiskey and rubbing a jeweled hand in the small of Kurt Jones' back. "Come with me, sweet thing," said Walsh. "Tell me how it was when this all belonged to Mexico."

Big Bob stood at the bar and watched his younger brother toss back shot after shot of rye. At the end of each drink, Toot would rap his shot glass on the bar, demanding a refill. Finally, Sydney stood a new bottle in front of Toot and left it. "Help yourself," he said. "I know a hair-trigger elbow when I see one."

"You best slow down, Toot," said Big Bob, "unless you want to find yourself sleeping facedown on a poker table."

"Mind your own business," Toot snapped. He turned and walked restlessly to the batwing doors and looked out above them at the upper windows of the Miller Hotel. "Damn it to hell," he said. Then he turned, walked back to the bar and poured himself another shot of rye. He tossed it back, let out a slight whiskey hiss, then said, "Where's those whores? Swan and the other one, what's her name?"

"Clare-Annette," said Sydney Pine, wiping a damp rag back and forth on the bar top through a spill of beer foam. "I wired Circle Wells earlier today. They should be back on the stage tomorrow." He nodded toward Delphia and Tommy Walsh as the two climbed a steep set of stairs, laughing and slapping at one another like schoolkids. "Of course, there's always Delphia. Experiencewise, she's like getting four whores for the price of one."

"Get away from me, Sydney," Toot sneered, "before I pistol-whip you to the floor."

"Yes, sir, Mr. Abbadele. Right away!" The frightened bar owner snatched up a handful of shot glasses and a bottle of rye and hurriedly moved to a spot farther down the bar.

"What the hell got into you, Toot?" Bob asked. "Sydney meant no harm. He was just trying to be hospitable."

"He can grab his *hospitable* with both hands and shove it," Toot grumbled, spilling some of the rye from the bottle as he sloppily refilled his shot glass.

From the far end of the bar, Frank and Dick Abbadele watched Toot drunkenly raise the glass to his lips. Beside Frank and Dick stood Parker Dennison, working on a black cigar, silently appraising Toot's behavior. On the other side of Dennison stood Sturgen, looking stiff and uncomfortable with a full shot glass standing on the bar in front of his folded hands.

Big Bob shot a glance at Frank and Dick and saw the dark expression on Frank's face. "Damn it, Toot," Bob said. "Have you let that little colored gal drive you *loco?*"

"Get off me, Bob," Toot warned. "You're

my brother, but I don't have to answer to you for any damn thing."

"That's right, you don't," said Bob. "But that ain't going to stop me from telling you what I think. And I think if you don't get a grip on yourself, you're headed for a mighty big downfall. Look at yourself, drinking whiskey with both hands. This ain't no way for a man to act."

Toot stood silent for a moment, his right hand around his shot glass, his left hand around the bottle of rye. He'd already filled his glass, but before drinking, he slid the bottle away from him and stared down at his waiting drink. Settling down, he shook his head slowly and said, "Damn it all, Bob, what would be so wrong if I decided me and April ought to take up with one another, try to raise our baby?"

Big Bob looked him up and down, registering his surprise, as if finally realizing his brother's condition for the first time. "So that's how it is. You've gone and let yourself fall ass-over-elbows for that little gal! You're really wanting to keep her?"

Toot scowled. "We're not talking about a stray calf, Bob. Her and I have been seeing each other for quite a while . . . ever since she arrived at the colored settlement over near Bentley."

Bob said, "The colored settlement? What the hell were you doing there?"

"What difference does it make what I was doing there?" Toot replied, trying to keep himself settled. "That's where I met her."

"It makes all the difference in the world," said Big Bob. "A white man has no business fooling around there. They're not our kind."

"Jesus, Bob," said Toot. "I'm so sick of hearing who is or ain't *our kind*." He stopped talking long enough to toss back the shot of rye and let out a hiss. "What exactly is *our kind*, Bob? Can you tell me that?"

"I don't think you need that explained to you, Toot," said Bob. "If you do, you might be too stupid to be an Abbadele."

"I ain't sure that's possible, Bob," Toot said with a sarcastic twist and a wry smile. Looking down at the empty shot glass, he instinctively pulled the bottle back across the bar and refilled it as he spoke. "But aside from who is or ain't our kind, what's wrong with a man and woman being together if they both care about one another?"

"It's already past whether there's anything wrong with it or not, little brother," said Big Bob. "The fact is that Frank told you long before this not to get tangled up with that young woman, and you went right on ahead and did it anyway." He shrugged his broad shoulders and added, "Frank's the oldest. He's the boss. You knew how he'd act before you got involved with that woman."

"Listen to yourself, Bob." Toot shook his head as he studied his drink again. "We've got to worry about who's *our kind*. Frank's the oldest, so *he's the boss*. We're outlaws, Bob. We're men who live by our own rules. How'd we ever let ourselves get so boxed in by what's right or wrong?" He raised the glass to his lips, this time only taking a sip, feeling himself grow a little more calm inside. He wasn't sure if it was the rye or his attempt to expound reasoning to his brother that seemed to help him straighten out his own thinking. "Are we afraid somebody's going to reach out and smack our hands for something?"

Bob only stared at him.

"Besides," Toot said with a note of finality, "I never said for sure that I was going to *keep her*. I only asked what would be wrong if I did." He paused, then said with a tone of regret, "So far, all I've heard from you is the kind of reasons old-timers

200

use when they tell you why their life went straight to hell on them somewhere along the way."

"First of all, little brother," said Bob, "I ain't exactly an old-timer. Second of all, I've got no complaints about my life. I do what I do because it suits me. If I didn't want to be a part of this bunch, I'd cut out and do as I damn well please. I've got choices." He tapped a thick thumb on his chest. "So do you. But you best quit pussy-footing around and playing both ends against the middle. This is serious business we're in. You best go look at Otis Harpe and Bennie Pearl if you think otherwise."

Toot Abbadele started to reply, but the sound of the batwing doors opening slowly caused him and the rest of the drinkers to fall silent and cast a glance over their shoulders. Standing with a hand on either door, spreading them open, stood a thin, elderly black man wearing a clergy collar. He wore a black linen suit beneath a ragged riding duster. In his right hand, he held a frayed-edged Bible pressed against the batwing saloon door.

"Well, now," Parker Dennison said quietly to Frank Abbadele beside him. "What have we here?"

A battered Bledso horse pistol stood in

the clergyman's waist belt, its butt turned to his left. Seeing the eyes turn toward him as silence spread along the bar, the man said in a stiff but resonating voice, "I am looking for a Mr. Toot Abbadele. I require his presence in the street." His dark, faded eyes moved back and forth along the bar. Toot Abbadele started to step forward, but Big Bob stopped him with a slight nudge.

"Oh, do you now?" Frank Abbadele said, offering a mock show of courtesy and a flat trace of a smile. "I'm Toot Abbadele's brother Frank. Maybe you better tell me *why* you *require* my brother's presence in the street, preacher."

"Very well, sir," said the aging clergyman. He swallowed a dry knot in his throat and stepped forward, letting the batwing doors flap to a halt behind him. "I propose to kill him . . . may God forgive me."

Chapter 12

Sam had seen the clergyman ride in on a sweat-streaked mule and hitch the animal in the alley alongside the Hung Dog Saloon. As the man stepped onto the boardwalk and walked toward the batwing doors, Sam had noted the well-worn Bible in his hand. He'd also caught a glimpse of the big horse pistol in his belt. Sam took a searching look at the window of the hotel, where only moments before Maria had gone to check on April and the baby. Then he adjusted the Colt in his holster and walked to the saloon. Stepping quietly onto the boardwalk, he took a position beside the doors where he could listen without being seen. As soon as he heard the preacher express his intention to kill Toot Abbadele, the Ranger prepared himself to move quickly and silently at the right second.

Inside the saloon, Toot Abbadele had taken a step forward, determined not to let his brother Frank speak for him. "I'm Toot Abbadele," he said. "And I know who you are. You're Reverend Oridine Bullard, April's grandfather."

"That's correct, sir," said the elderly minister. "Except today, I'm afraid I cannot honor the title of *Reverend*." He reached up, untied the white clerical collar with his left hand, took it off and gently pushed it down into his suit coat pocket. "Many times I implored my granddaughter to introduce us, but she always made excuses for you not to do so. I suppose you refused to waste your time meeting the family of a colored girl?"

"Now, that's not true, Reverend," said Toot. "The fact is, I asked April to introduce me to you and her grandmother. She said you wouldn't hear of it!"

"Jesus," said Frank Abbadele, looking disgusted. "I can't believe my ears."

"Our own brother," said Dick, "browbeaten by a young —"

"Both of you stay out of this," Toot warned. The rest of the men looked dumbfounded.

"April told you it was *I* who refused to be introduced?" Reverend Bullard cocked his head slightly, contemplating Toot's words, as if realizing that perhaps his granddaughter had not been completely honest with her family.

"That's the fact of the matter," said Toot. "I would have met you had it been up to me. You can believe that or not." His hand rested on his pistol butt.

The minister let out a sigh. "Either way. That doesn't pardon what you've done to that poor girl. I still have to kill you to set things right." He gestured his Bible toward the street. Without noticing the faces of the men perking up at the sight of the Ranger slipping silently through the doors, Reverend Bullard continued to speak. "My wife and I raised April from an infant after she lost her mother and father in a train accident in Illinois. When you wronged her, you —"

His words stopped short when he felt the hand reach around from behind and slickly lift the big pistol from his waist. He spun in time to see the Ranger step to the side, keeping the Bledso horse pistol pointed at his chest, his own pistol in his other hand, cocked and pointed at the outlaws. "Easy, Reverend," the Ranger said. "I'm an Arizona Ranger. I know you don't really want to kill anybody. You back out of here with me before this thing gets out of hand."

"Give him his gun back, Ranger," said Frank. "Every man has a right to decide how he wants to die. Ain't that right, preacher?" he asked Reverend Bullard. He stepped from around the far corner of the bar with his hand poised near his pistol butt.

"And that's what *you're* deciding right now, Abbadele," said the Ranger, honing an aim on him. "I hope you make the mistake of thinking I won't drop you dead in your tracks."

Frank stopped cold. "You're just about crazy enough to shoot me, Ranger, even though my men will splatter you all over the wall."

Keeping his eyes on Frank, the Ranger said to Toot Abbadele, "Is this what you want to see happen, Toot? Want to see your brother gun down April's grandfather?"

Toot spoke up. "Frank, this is my business. Stand down."

Frank released a sigh of whiskey and exasperation but eased back a step. "Toot, I don't know what the hell goes on inside that hard head of yours."

"You don't need to know," said Toot. "Just give me room to handle my own business." He turned his gaze back to Reverend Bullard. "Sir, I don't want you and me killing one another. No matter what the outcome, it's going to be awfully hard on April. I might be every bit as no-good as you think I am, but that won't make it any easier on her."

"Better listen to him, Reverend," Sam said quietly, standing close behind Bullard. "He's the only one here making any sense right now."

"There comes a time when making sense doesn't matter, Ranger," said Reverend Bullard. "April ran away. She ran away to be with him. Now she's missing. I don't know if he killed her, or the storm, but he's responsible. Now my wife and I are never going to see our poor grandchild again."

Before the Ranger could speak, Hirsh Knox took a step forward from the bar. Shaking his head, he pointed at the Ranger. "Reverend, that ain't so — sa-so — He — He — He-eee, ta-ta-te-too—"

At the bar, Terrence Knox pulled his brother back by his shirt. "Let it go, Hirsh," he said. "It's their business."

The Reverend Bullard gave Hirsh Knox a strange look and whispered something under his breath. For a moment, the old clergyman's and Hirsh Knox's eyes seemed locked on one another across the barroom floor. Something strange had just clicked between the old clergyman and the young, speech-impaired outlaw. Whatever it was, the Ranger saw it, but he had no time to

207

question it. "Reverend Bullard," he said. "What that man tried to say is that your granddaughter April is alive and well."

"What?" Reverend Bullard's dark, faded eyes pulled free of Hirsh Knox and searched the Ranger's. "Do I dare believe him, sir?"

"You can believe me," said the Ranger. "My partner and I found April out in the badlands and brought her here. She's at the hotel right across the street. Would you like to go see her, or would you rather stick around here until somebody ends up dead?"

"Oh my Lord, my Lord, thanks be to you, sweet Jesus, that poor child is alive!" Tears streamed down his face. He clutched the Bible to his chest and muttered something unintelligible. His thirst for vengeance seemed to have vanished with the news of April being alive.

Sam stared at Frank Abbadele with his big Colt still pointed and ready to fire. Frank saw the Ranger's expression and said with a wave of disgust, "Yeah, go on. Get that old crow out of here before he goes double-dog nuts with that spiritual babbling."

"Come on, Reverend," Sam said almost in a whisper, still keeping his eyes on

Frank and the others. "Let's back out of here now."

"Oh Lord, what have I done," said the old minister, looking at his old Bledso revolver in the Ranger's hand.

The Ranger moved around in front of Reverend Bullard and, with both pistols cocked at arm's length, pressed him back through the batwing doors. On the boardwalk, Reverend Bullard sighed and tried to stop as the Ranger half-turned toward him, still keeping an eye on the saloon. "Not yet, Reverend," the Ranger said. "Not until we reach the alley. These men are as unpredictable as scorpions."

No sooner had the Ranger spoken than Hirsh Knox stepped out onto the boardwalk and stood looking at the minister as if dumbfounded. But only for a second. When the Ranger raised a pistol toward him, Hirsh raised his hands chest high in a show of peace.

"Don't shoot, Ranger, please," said Bullard. "This man means me no harm. That much I can safely promise you."

"Then back off," Sam warned Hirsh, staring hard at him from behind his big Colt. With a confused, lingering gaze at the aging black minister, Hirsh stepped back inside the Hung Dog Saloon.

"That poor man," the reverend whispered.

The Ranger looked at him questioningly for a second, then motioned him toward the mule waiting in the alley. "Let's not worry about him right now. Let's get your animal and get over to the hotel."

"Of course," said Reverend Bullard. "You'll have to pardon me, Ranger. I am at the service of the Lord. When one of the afflicted stand before me, I can do no less than the Lord has ordained me to do." Even as he stepped down to the mule, Reverend Bullard gripped the Bible tightly to his chest. "Heavenly father forgive me," he recited upward to the stripe of sky above the alleyway, "for I came here seeking blood in vengeance. Yet even in the midst of my dark evil endeavor, I see now your purpose in leading me here."

"Uh, Reverend," the Ranger said respectfully yet firmly. "This is not the best place to stop for prayer. These are evil men. They can't be trusted."

Reverend Bullard gave him a soulful gaze. "What better place is there to pray than among evil?"

"Amen to that, Reverend," said the Ranger, coaxing him closer to the sweat-streaked mule as he spoke. "But your granddaughter is so close, I know you want to get to her as quick as you can."

"That is true indeed, sir," said Reverend Bullard, unhitching the mule's reins. "Let us see what else the Lord has in store for us on this glorious" — he tossed another glance upward, this time squinting at the sun's glare — "although terribly hot afternoon."

Big Shod stared down from the edge of a long plateau where it appeared that the rest of the world had split away and dropped three hundred feet to a lower level. On the far side of that broad flatland beneath him stood a stretch of low foothills. The badlands, he said to himself, as if in warning. A few moments earlier, he'd heard the report of rifle and pistol fire and had hurried the big gray forward. Now, at the far left end of the foothills, he saw a stagecoach come into view, a high wake of dust spreading behind it. Farther back along the trail, he saw many riders coming fast, obscured by the dust and firing heavily on the fleeing coach.

Without a second thought, the bounty hunter reined his horse left along the edge until he came to a steep switchback path leading downward. He let the animal find its own way until, after a few sliding, backpedaling moments, the horse leveled onto the flatlands. Shod batted his boots to its sides, pointing it toward the harried stagecoach. As the big gray shot forward and stretched out into a hard run, Shod drew his rifle from its scabbard, keeping an eye on the foothills to his right, not forgetting for a second that he had trouble of his own waiting out there. He levered a round into his rifle and sped forward, seeing return gunfire explode red-orange in the dust from the side door of the coach.

Inside the coach, Swan Hendricks fired another shot back through the thick dust at the *comadrejas*, then pulled her head inside and looked at Clare-Annette and Judge Udall Henley, who sat huddled together on the cloth-covered seat. "It's no use," said Swan above the roar of the coach, the horses' hooves and the constant gunfire. "I'm not able to hit anything in all this dust." She gestured the gun barrel toward the flatlands. "But I think I just saw a rider coming across there. It looked like he was firing on the *comadrejas*." Swan's hair and forehead were smeared with blood. It wasn't her own blood, but rather the blood of the man lying dead at her feet.

"Hear that, Judge Henley?" said Clare-

Annette, her voice also raised. "Don't you die on me. Swan says we've got some help coming." She held the judge's bloody head against her bosom, a blood-soaked handkerchief pressed to his terrible head wound.

"I'm fine; I'm good; I just can't see anything," the judge babbled, rolling his sightless, blood-filled eyes. "But my poor shoes aren't mates, are they? Dear God, it's gotten awfully hot in here!"

Looking at Clare-Annette, Swan shook her head slowly, referring to the judge's condition as she opened the big revolver to reload. "Your shoes are fine, Judge," said Swan. "So sit still and let your head stop bleeding before your brains spill out on Clare's new traveling dress."

"Swan, please!" Clare-Annette whispered harshly, a tear forming in her eye. "Don't tease him, not now. Look at him."

"No brains spilling here," the judge said, probing the side of his head with his bloody fingertips. "Everything sure feels wet and soft up there."

"Stop it, Judge," said Clare-Annette, the tear trickling down her dusty cheek. She brushed the judge's hand down and kept him pressed against her, his blood beginning to cake thick and dark on her cleavage. She sobbed, "See what I was telling you before we left? I never travel well by stagecoach. Never in my life."

"So far the trip's gone better for you than it has for this poor man," said Swan, reaching down with her bare foot and rolling the body of Bradford Coolidge over enough to reach the bullets in his gun belt lying on the floor beneath him. She popped out six fresh cartridges and let the body flop back into place. The dead man's head lay facedown on Swan's discarded bloomers, which lay where she'd thrown them earlier before the *comadrejas* had swooped down and interrupted their private foursome. Coolidge's trousers were down around his knees; a fly walked busily back and forth on his naked behind.

"At least he went away satisfied," said Clare-Annette tearfully. "I'm glad you were here for him, Swan. I think that was good, don't you?"

Swan shrugged, reloading the pistol. "He got his money's worth, I reckon. That's all the warranty I ever give." Above them, the shotgun rider lay prone, levering shot after shot from a big Henry rifle. Swan quickly stuck the last bullet into the revolver's cylinder and slapped it shut. "Keep the judge comfortable, Clare. If this thing goes badly, I'm keeping you and me a bullet apiece here." She shook the pistol to show Clare-Annette what she meant. Then she stuck her head out of the coach and began firing.

A *comadreja* flew from his saddle beneath a shot from Big Shod's Winchester rifle. Shod rode hard, closing the gap between himself and the harried stagecoach as the *comadrejas* began to see that they had more than just the stage crew and passengers to worry about. Another shot from Shod's rifle took another rider from his saddle, this time causing the horse to stumble and roll end-over-end, bringing down two more riders in the swirl of dust. Shod saw the return fire from the stagecoach and reined his horse around, running parallel alongside it less than thirty yards away. Riding hands-free, Indian style, the bounty hunter quickly turned the *comadrejas* into vulnerable targets at this close range. Several of the riders fired at him, but their own dust kept them at a disadvantage. Before the stage had continued another hundred yards, Shod saw the riders falling back, giving up ground until at length they turned and disappeared toward the foothills.

Inside the coach, Swan Hendricks

shouted out the window. "Take that, you weasel sonsabitches!" She peeled off one last shot, feeling the coach begin to slow down.

"Are they stopping us?" Clare-Annette asked, clutching the judge against her blood-soaked breast.

"Hell, no! Whoever's out there, we've whooped them!" Swan cried out in excitement. Still waving the big pistol, her hair plastered to her forehead by Bradford Coolidge's drying blood, Swan hurled herself forward with a loud shriek of joy, throwing her arms around Clare-Annette and the wounded judge. "We are a couple of tough whores, you and me!" she exclaimed.

"Careful about my head now," said the judge, his voice muffled against Clare-Annette's supple flesh, slick with his blood. "It's gone numb on me. I can't feel nothing up there."

"Don't worry, Judge, I'm careful, you poor darling, you," said Swan, stroking the judge's shoulder as she pulled away, feeling the coach slowing to a halt. Through the door window, she saw the black bounty hunter riding close beside them in the haze of dust.

"Everybody all right in there?" Shod

216

called out, his rifle still in hand as his eyes looked back, searching the trail behind them.

"We are now, big fellow," said Swan, sizing him up as the coach rocked to a halt. She raised her fingertips to the side of her hair to straighten it, but then stopped when she realized how futile her efforts were with blood all over her head. "Say, I remember you!" she said, getting a better look at Shod. She threw open the door. "Look Clare! It's our friend from the Hung Dog!"

As Swan spilled out of the coach barefoot, the weight of the big pistol seeming to keep her off-balance, Shod called out to the shotgun rider, "You two all right up there?"

"The driver's dead," a voice said bluntly. "I'm wounded pretty good. But I'm still game as a fighting cock."

Stepping down from his horse to help the shotgun rider down, Shod saw all the blood on Swan Hendricks, and behind her, still inside the coach, he saw Clare-Annette and Judge Henley, both of them covered with the judge's blood. "We can't stay here long," Shod said. "The *comadrejas* might be regrouping right now."

"What is it with those desert weasels anyway?" Swan said, looking back through the settling dust. "I've never heard of that many riding together. I've never heard of them attacking an armed stagecoach."

"They will attack anything they think they have outnumbered," said Shod, reaching a hand up to the shotgun rider, supporting him as the stocky, gruff-looking man stepped down, one gloved hand pressed to his bleeding chest.

"You don't look so good, Arnold," said Swan to the shotgun rider.

"I'm not so good," Arnold Rowe replied. "But I've got time to kill a couple more of those bastards before I cash in."

"You're not going to be able to drive this stage," said Shod.

"No, I reckon not," said Rowe. "But there's been a dead man driving it the last couple of miles. Surely I can do as well as he did."

When Shod cast a longer look inside the stagecoach, Swan Hendricks said, "That's Judge Udall Henley. You can see he's not going to be any help. I doubt if he's going to last as far as Sabre Ridge."

"Do what you can for him," said Shod. He nodded at the shotgun rider. "Let's get this man's wound dressed and get this rig moving before we get more weasels down our shirts."

"Well, yes, sir," said Swan, giving the bounty hunter a mock salute.

Noting the commanding tone of his own voice, Shod settled down and said, "That was quite a fight you two ladies were putting up back there. Good work."

"I didn't do nothing, really," said Clare-Annette, holding the judge as if he were a suckling child.

"Shut up, Clare," Swan said with a slight smile. "Can't you see he's trying to give you a compliment?"

"Oh," said Clare-Annette. "In that case, thank you, kind sir."

"You're welcome, ma'am," said Shod.

While Shod helped dress Arnold Rowe's chest wound and Swan Hendricks and Clare-Annette applied torn strips of white petticoat to the judge's bleeding head, two hundred yards away, atop a rise of broken boulders, Lester Brooks stared at them through a brass-trimmed telescope. "One good, clean shot from here, Kirby, and our troubles are all over with this man."

"Want me to go get your rifle from the saddle?" Kirby asked.

Lester considered it for a second, lowering the telescope and looking back with his naked eye toward the trail the *comadrejas* had used to escape the bounty hunter's deadly rifle fire. "Let's stick back aways and see how things go. Like as not, those desert weasels will do our work for us."

"That's those two doves from Sabre Ridge, ain't it?" Kirby asked, nodding in the direction of the stagecoach.

"Yes, it is," said Lester. "What of it?"

"Nothing," said Kirby. "Just seems a shame to leave them to the *comadrejas*. I hate them dirty weasel sonsabitches." He spit as if to rid himself of a bad taste.

"So do I," said Lester. "But if they can kill that bounty hunter, I'm all for it."

"Me, too, I reckon," said Kirby, but his voice lacked any conviction on the matter.

They lay in silence for a moment, Lester putting the telescope back to his eye and spotting a small band of mounted *comadrejas* forming back along the trail. Lowering the lens again, Lester's brow furrowed in deep thought for a moment. Then he said, "Them two are some awfully fun whores, though, ain't they?"

"They always did right by me," said Kirby. "Leastwise, well enough that I hate seeing them killed by a bunch of lousy *comadrejas*."

"I feel the same way," said Lester. "But it's a tough ole world for whores, outlaws and bounty hunters alike. If they die and in the course of it we shake that bounty man off our tails, I reckon that's a good day for us, ain't it?"

"Maybe so," said Kirby. "But it sure doesn't feel like it to me." Staring back toward the *comadrejas,* he spit and ran a hand across his lips. "I just hate them dirty weasel bastards something awful," he said.

Chapter 13

As soon as the stagecoach had gotten under way, Shod looked back from the driver's seat and saw the large party of *comadrejas* swing down off the trail leading from the foothills. "Get ready," said Arnold Rowe, sitting beside Shod. "Here they come again."

"I've never seen so many *comadrejas* in my life," said Shod, slapping the long reins to the backs of the coach horses. The coach jolted forward.

"Me, neither," said Rowe, stifling a painful cough inside his shattered chest. Above the sound of the horses and the creaking of the coach, he added, "But I want to kill as many of them as I can before I die." Pulling himself up from the seat, he stretched out atop the luggage compartment, taking a prone shooting position. The bandage on his chest had become saturated quickly. Within seconds he lay in a warm, dark pool of his own blood. Yet Shod noted that Arnold Rowe didn't seem bothered by his condition. Except for the blood and a deep wheezing in his chest, the shotgun rider hardly appeared wounded.

By the time the first rifle fire came upon them, Shod had the coach horses coaxed into a full run, pulling hard along the smooth dirt trail. His own horse ran alongside the horses, its reins tied to their traces. At the first sound of gunfire, Swan Hendricks stuck her head out the left door window and balanced Shod's Winchester rifle on the door frame. "What?" she called out at the sight of the *comadrejas*. "These turds still haven't learned their lesson?"

On the right side of the coach, Clare-Annette held Coolidge's big pistol out the window with both blood-streaked hands. She had tried to lay the judge down on the seat so she could shoot, but in his addled state, the judge would have none of it. He crawled up to her side, nestling his thickly bandaged head against her breast. "Lord, Judge, what am I going to do with you?" she said with a whore's patience. "All right, come on then." Without turning loose of the pistol, she spread her arms open enough to let him slip his head in and rest his bloody cheek on her cleavage. "Just don't get in the way of me fighting," she said.

"I won't," said the judge, whimpering slightly.

Outside, Clare-Annette saw four *comadrejas* appear as if out of nowhere fifty yards away, riding parallel to the coach. As she pointed the big pistol in their direction, she heard pistol shots from atop the coach as Shod caught sight of them. One of the riders fell from his saddle and rolled in a red spray of blood. Clare-Annette cocked the pistol and screamed when she pulled the trigger and felt the recoil of the explosion. "My God, Swan," she shouted. "It almost flew out of my hand!"

"Keep shooting!" Swan Hendricks demanded. She levered another round into the rifle chamber and took aim back into the thick dust behind them where blue-orange gunshots blossomed then vanished.

Clare-Annette recocked the pistol and fired again, still hitting nothing but causing the remaining three riders to veer away and add some distance between themselves and the pistol fire.

Behind Shod, Arnold Rowe struggled to reload his rifle, his wound sapping his strength, his fingers having a hard time shoving the bullets into the magazine. Shod kept the horses running at a dangerous pace, the long reins in one hand, his other hand firing out at the three *comadrejas* flanking them. Another one flew from his saddle, causing the other two to break away and drop back behind the coach.

The frightened women were holding their own; so was the dying shotgun rider. But Shod knew it wasn't going to last. Judging by what he'd seen earlier and the amount of gunfire coming from behind them, there could be as many as thirty *comadrejas* in pursuit. There was no possibility that the four already-tired team horses pulling the heavy Studebaker coach could outlast the horses on their trail. The big bounty hunter knew it was only a matter of time before this fight took a turn for the worse. Up ahead, he spotted a trail splitting off and turning upward into the rocky cover of the foothills. It was a poor refuge at best. But Shod saw no other choice.

"What's going on up there?" Swan Hendricks called out from the window.

The bounty hunter didn't answer; but hearing her voice and at the same time realizing that the firing behind them had grown more intense while the shotgun rider's rifle had fallen silent, he took a quick glance over his shoulder and saw

Arnold Rowe lying facedown, a streak of blood and brain matter down the back of his head. The rifle lay beside him, crawling away slowly with the vibration of the coach.

Shod leaned back, grabbed the rifle and stuck it down into the seat well. Then he picked up his pistol from where he'd laid it on the seat, cocked it and half-turning around, aimed it back at the blossoming gunfire. He fired two shots, leaving only one more bullet in the pistol. Then he felt a bullet slice across his thick chest like the bite of a bullwhip. He clenched his teeth, but had no time to even glance at his wound. He fired the last bullet and heard a scream from within the cloud of dust. He shoved the empty pistol down into his holster, knowing he had no time to reload. He saw the first two *comadrejas* emerge like raging demons out of the thick dust only a few short yards from overtaking the coach.

"They're all over us!" Clare-Annette shrieked, firing a wild shot back into the dust. The judge buried his face against her bosom and wept quietly, his eyes blinded by his own blood.

"Keep on fighting, Clare, damn it!" shouted Swan Hendricks. "Kill all these dirty sonsabitches!"

226

Shod managed to lever a round into the rifle he'd taken from beside Arnold Rowe's body. Knowing the odds of hitting anything this way were long against him, he aimed down alongside the coach as one of the *comadrejas* began to leap from his horse toward the side of the coach. But Swan Hendricks had just reloaded the Winchester rifle. She swung it up into play at just the right second. The shot nailed the *comadreja* in his chest and sent him flying away from the coach window. Shod swung his rifle barrel one-handed toward the other rider, but before he could get off a shot, a rifle exploded somewhere out on the flatlands beyond the dust.

The rider spilled off the side of his horse and rolled beneath the wheels of the coach. The cumbersome stagecoach rose high on one side as the body crunched beneath its wheels. A scream resounded from inside the coach. Shod leaned with the dangerous, bouncing sway, half-rising from the seat, balancing himself with the reins in one hand and the rifle in his other like some circus performer in a stunt gone awry. Slamming back down onto the wooden seat, he wasted no time looking around to see who had come to their aid. All he saw was the thick dust, the blossoms of gunfire. But above the rumble of the coach and the gunfire behind him, he heard rifle fire from the flatlands on their right, and he knew it wasn't *comadrejas*.

"Are you all right up there?" Swan Hendricks called out from below.

"Yes," Shod shouted in reply. "How about you?"

"We're still in the fight," she replied above the rumble of hooves and the roar of pursuing gunfire.

Behind him came a scream of pain at the end of a rifle shot. *The army?* Shod wondered. He hoped so. As many desert weasels as he had on his tail, it would be good to see an army patrol.

"Who's shooting at those bastards from out there?" Swan asked.

"I don't know, but they've got my full support," Shod called out to her. Drawing closer to where the trail split up into the foothills, Shod said, "Hang on — it's going to get a little rockier in a minute!" Behind them, the *comadrejas* seemed to have fallen farther back, the rifle fire from the flatlands having caught them by surprise. As Shod swung the coach upward onto the foothill trail, he managed to look back now at an angle that allowed him to see past the thickest part of the long wake of dust. He saw the riders bunching up in bewilderment. Rifle fire pelted them from the flatlands.

"Give them hell, cowboy," shouted Swan Hendricks, "whoever you are!" Hanging halfway out the door window, she waved the Winchester rifle back and forth, the weight of the gun almost tearing it from her grip.

"Better sit down, ma'am," said Shod, admiring Swan's courage. "I don't want to bounce you out of there."

"Don't worry about me, big fellow," Swan called out to him. "You wouldn't believe the bouncing I can take!"

"Yes, ma'am," said Shod, slapping the reins to the horses' backs. Looking out across the flatlands, he saw a single deadfall of white, sun-bleached piñon, the only likely spot for the shots to have come from. He breathed a sigh of relief. But he wasn't going to kid himself. The women, the judge and he were still in dire straits. "You best get everything reloaded now while we can. They'll be back upon us pretty soon."

"I've already seen to it, sir!" said Swan in mock-military fashion.

Shod allowed himself a smile, slowing the horses and guiding them toward a bed of upward-reaching rocks that ended against a sheer stone wall. Looking around, Shod could see no more perfect place to make a stand, nor could he see a place more difficult to get out of when it came time to flee. This was a stand of desperation, and he knew it. From this point, they lived or died with their backs against the wall. Arriving at the rock bed, Shod stopped the coach and jumped down to help Swan and Clare-Annette with the wounded judge.

Stepping down with the Winchester cradled to her chest, Swan looked around and saw the severity of their situation. "My, what a charming place," she said critically. "Do you suppose we'll be staying here long?" she asked, giving Shod a look that was intended to exclude Clare-Annette from hearing anything that might frighten her any worse.

"Don't start that kind of talk with me," said Clare-Annette, Coolidge's gun belt hanging from her shoulder. "I'm no idiot. I see what's going on. You don't have to soften anything with humor on my account." She came out close behind Swan, helping the judge as Swan turned around to assist her.

"Oh, I'm sorry, Clare," said Swan. "But

I know how you get nervous and silly-acting sometimes."

"Silly-acting, ha!" said Clare-Annette. "I guess you didn't see me shooting at all those peckerwoods back there." Easing the judge to the ground, they leaned him back against the side of the coach.

"All right, Clare, I apologize. Can we please not fuss?" As Swan spoke, she stooped down and checked the judge, taking his chin in her hand and moving his half-conscious head back and forth carefully.

"Gosh, that poor, dear man," said Swan, looking on. "That has to hurt. I wish there was something we could do for him."

Looking out upon the trail they'd just left, Shod leaned down and effortlessly scooped the judge into his powerful arms. "Let's get him into the rocks — looks like we've got company coming," he said.

Moving quickly, Swan and Clare-Annette hurried along, hiking their hemlines up to assist them in walking barefoot across the rocky ground. "Why didn't I grab my shoes?" Clare-Annette said, sounding annoyed at herself. "I should have known we'd end up running barefoot over hot rocks. I swear, traveling never goes right for me."

Standing with the judge in his arms, Shod paused and looked back along the trail. "Hold on, ladies. Looks like you've got time to go back and get your shoes." He nodded toward the *comadrejas,* who had turned off the trail and were now headed out toward the rifle fire coming from the deadfall of piñon. "Take a look back there."

"What on earth?" said Swan. "They've left us and gone after our friend out there."

"That's right," said Shod, hurrying with the judge, looking for a slice of dark shade against a rock. He found one and quickly set the judge down. "Let's get back to the coach and see if we can return the favor."

At the coach, Shod untied his gray from the team of horses and gave his reins to Clare-Annette while Swan rummaged inside the coach, found their shoes and brought them out. "Here," said Swan. "Let's not forget them again. This is hard ground on the feet." Then, turning to Clare-Annette, he said, "Take the horse and get back there with the judge."

"I can shoot, too," said Clare-Annette, holding the gray's reins as she stepped into one shoe, then the other, adjusting them on her feet.

"I know," said Shod. "But that pistol is useless from here. Watch out for the judge.

We'll do what we can with these rifles."

"All right," said Clare-Annette, understanding the logic of it. She turned and hurriedly led Shod's horse away.

"Have you ever fired a rifle long-range?" Shod asked Swan Hendricks as Clare-Annette made her way into the rocks.

"No, but I've always wanted to learn," Swan said wryly.

Shod took the Winchester from her and handed her Arnold Rowe's Henry rifle while he flipped up the long-range sight and adjusted it for a two-hundred-yard shot. "Take your time; stop breathing just before you squeeze the trigger." He handed the Winchester back to her, taking the Henry again in turn. "Be sure to squeeze slow and steadily; let the sound of the shot be a surprise to you. That way you won't flinch and throw off your aim."

"I think I can do that," said Swan, looking the rifle over. Squatting down and leveling the rifle across the rear bracing of the coach, she wet her thumb and tweaked it across the tip of the front rifle sight. "In fact, a dollar says I can knock one off. What do you say, big fellow?"

"Sure. Just do the best you can," said Shod, dismissing her notion. "If you don't hit anything, at least you'll get close enough to scare them back."

He kneeled beside her, raised and adjusted the long-range sight on the Henry rifle and settled the butt of it against his shoulder. Watching closely, Swan made the same move, getting the rifle butt comfortably in place. Shod drew a careful aim on the front rider as the group rode across the flatlands right to left in front of him. He aimed the Henry rifle just in front of his moving target and slightly higher, allowing for the drop of his bullet. He squeezed the trigger just as he'd instructed Swan to do. She noticed his eye didn't so much as flicker at the sound of the loud explosion. The front rider, horse and all, spilled forward, rolling in a tangle of hooves and limbs, causing the other riders to scatter, being fired on now from the deadfall of piñon and the stagecoach as well.

"There," said Shod, turning to Swan as he levered a round into the Henry rifle. "Take your time —"

His words cut short beneath an explosion from the Winchester rifle close beside him. As Swan looked up from the rifle stock, Shod saw one of the *comadrejas* hasten his pace, batting his bare heels hard to his horse's sides as the shot picked his hat off his head and sent it sailing away.

"Sort of like that?" Swan asked. "Except a tiny bit lower?"

"Yes, indeed," said Shod. "Like that . . . except a *tiny bit* lower."

For over an hour, the *comadrejas* were unable to get the upper hand in the battle. When they turned from the rifle fire behind the deadfall of piñon and tried to attack the coach, they were still under heavy rifle fire from two directions. Finally, after watching the last two riders disappear back along the trail bordering the edge of the foothills, Shod gazed out across the flatlands at the deadfall of piñon and counted six dead *comadrejas* strewn about, their horses milling aimlessly, grazing on clumps of wild grass. "Horses mean a lot to the desert weasels," said Shod to Swan. She sat beside him, leaning against the coach wheel. "They wouldn't even risk rounding up those loose ones. I'd say they've backed off and called it a day."

"You — you mean we've licked them?" asked Swan in astonishment.

"They've seen we're not easy game," said Shod. "Could be they've got other things on their minds. They're up to something, with this many of them banded together. But if that means we've *licked* them . . .

Yes. You could say that." He gave her a brief smile, then looked back out across the flatlands, adjusting his spectacles.

"Whoooie!" said Swan. She turned her head toward the rocks and called out, "Clare-Annette, we've whipped them rotten weasels!"

"What?" Clare-Annette called back to her. "I can't hear you."

"Never mind," said Swan. "I'm coming back there. I'll tell you then." Swan looked at Shod as she stood up, dusting the seat of her soiled, tattered dress. "I shot one. I don't know if you noticed it or not."

"Yes, I did," said Shod. "Good work."

"So . . ." Swan rubbed her thumb and finger together in the universal sign of greed.

"So what?" asked Shod.

"So, give me my dollar, remember?" Swan beamed.

"I remember." Shod shook his head but reached inside his shirt pocket, took out a dollar and gave it to her. "Hurry back," he said. "They could surprise us and pull another attack before nightfall."

"Sure," said Swan, tightly clutching the dollar he'd given her. "Wait till I tell Clare what I did out there — shooting that sucker dead!"

Shod stared off toward the deadfall of

piñon as Swan hurried back to where Clare-Annette sat holding the judge against her. "Jesus, Clare," said Swan. "Has he gotten stuck to you?"

"I feel like it," Clare-Annette replied, keeping her voice low, as if careful not to awaken the judge. "Every time I move him, he wakes up and starts whining, the poor thing. But he's really starting to get on my nerves."

Swan looked the wounded judge up and down. "Bill him for your time, if he lives through this," she said.

"Believe I would, but I don't think he's going to make it," said Clare-Annette, softly patting the judge's shoulder.

Standing beside the stagecoach, Shod watched two distant figures ride out from behind the deadfall and start toward him. "No, stay away," he said, talking to them under his breath. "Don't ride over here. Keep some space between us; they might come back."

The two riders rode closer until they reached a point twenty yards away, where one stopped and the other continued coming cautiously forward. Shod was relieved to see that they were battle savvy enough not to get too close and give up the crossfire strategy that had kept everybody alive so far. But as soon as the rider stopped and turned his horse sidelong to him, Shod realized why they hadn't come any closer. "*Hola,* bounty hunter," Lester Brooks called out to him. "Remember me from town? Me and my boy?"

Shod paused for a second, then called out, "Kirby Brooks? Wanted in Texas for robbery? Is that who you're talking about?"

"Yep, I won't deny it. That's my boy, all right. We're the ones you've been trailing. We cut out of Sabre Ridge when we saw Frank Abbadele acting a fool with that lawyer and such."

Shod thought about it for a second, then asked, "What is he trying to prove, bringing in a man like Parker Dennison?"

"Frank Abbadele is a puzzle to me," said Lester Brooks. "I don't reckon he has any reason for anything he does. None that I would understand, anyway."

A silence passed as they eyed one another. Then Shod motioned for him to come closer. Lester heeled his horse to within fifteen feet, then stopped with his hand on his pistol, his rifle lying cocked across his lap. "Anyway, I'm just one more gun riding for the Abbadeles. I don't have no say in decisionmaking."

"Much obliged to you for helping me

with the *comadrejas*," said Shod, dismissing the Abbadeles.

Lester waved it away. "I'd lend anybody a hand with those weasels. Besides, we did it mostly for those two whores. How are they, anyway?"

"They're fine," said Shod, glancing back, seeing that Swan and Clare-Annette stood watching from behind a rock. "The judge looks bad, but he could pull through, I suppose."

"The judge?" said Lester.

"Yes," said Shod. "That's Judge Udall Henley. He was on his way to Sabre Ridge."

"To try the Abbadeles?" Lester asked.

"That would be my guess," said Shod.

"I'll be double damned," said Lester. "I just helped the man who's going there to sit in judgment of all my friends. Don't that just tear it?" He offered a crooked, mirthless grin.

"It's been a strange day all the way around," said Shod. "If it hadn't been for you and your boy, I think we'd all be dead." He gestured back toward the women. "They're tending to the judge. If we can get him to town, maybe he'll live."

"Well, whether he does or not, I expect the Abbadeles will beat the charge anyway, all the money they're putting out for that lawyer. If he loses this case, he better know a big rock to hide under somewhere."

"We'll see," said Shod. "Now, what about that boy of yours?"

"What about him?" Lester asked.

"Do you figure I owe you for saving us?" Shod asked.

"If I did, I wouldn't know how to go about saying it," said Lester. "I've been at odds with anybody connected to the law my whole life. I raised Kirby to be the same way. Fighting them desert weasels don't cut nothing one way or the other far as we're concerned. Does that sound about right to you?"

"Yes," said Shod. "I feel the same way." He gazed out past Lester to where Kirby sat with his rifle standing up from his lap, his hand in position, ready for any move Shod might make. "The *comadrejas* could come back before nightfall."

"They could, but I don't think they will," said Lester. "Anyway, get the judge on in to town if he's hurt that bad. Kirby and me will stick back here for a while, keep your back trail clean for you."

"Obliged again," said Shod.

Lester grinned flatly. "If the Abbadeles should ask, be sure and tell them we only did it for the womenfolk." He nodded past Shod at Swan and Clare-Annette. "Them two has been a pure joy to anybody who ever knew them, and I ain't even talking about the whoring part. They're just good people, if you know what I mean."

"I understand," said Shod. "I'll tell them both you asked about them. They'll be happy to hear it, I'm sure."

"Well, I reckon you best get started then," said Lester.

"Yes. You, too, I suppose," said Shod. He took a step back but didn't turn and walk away. Instead, he kept a hand on his pistol, the same way Lester did.

"Yep, me, too," said Lester. Yet he made no effort toward turning his horse to ride away. Instead, he sat staring at Shod as if waiting for him to make the first move.

Finally, Shod said in a flat tone, "How long does it take a person to starve to death?"

"Huh?" It took Lester a second to get Shod's meaning. Then he spread another grin. This time it looked more genuine. "Oh, well . . . *Adios* then, bounty hunter." He backed his horse a good ten feet before half-turning it and cantering quarterwise another five yards farther before turning it again and making a dash back to where Kirby sat waiting.

Shod stood watching, his hand still on his gun butt until he saw Lester and his son talking back and forth, still staring toward him. Then Shod shook his head and walked backward a few steps. "Outlaws," he said under his breath, turning and walking back to where the women stood watching.

"What was that all about?" Swan asked. Before Shod could answer, she asked, "Wasn't that old Lester Brooks? Why didn't they come on in and say howdy?"

"Kirby is the one I was hunting," said Shod. "Lester said to tell you both hello. I take it all of you know one another."

"Oh, of course, we both know Lester and his son." Clare-Annette beamed, looking out in their direction.

"Well, isn't that just the sweetest thing ever," said Swan, also looking out for them, raising a hand to her brow to shield her eyes from the sun's glare. "Here they are being hunted themselves and still they took time to help us."

"I'm not going to forget that," said Clare-Annette, both of them raising a hand and waving back and forth until Lester and Kirby did the same.

Chapter 14

Santaglio sat atop the stolen silver gelding and looked down on the six bodies of his *comadrejas* lying dead in the hot sun. This hadn't gone as well as he had expected; or, more specifically, it hadn't gone as well as he had *needed* it to go. What he needed was some sort of victory to dangle in front of his followers. Ever since the night the white man, Ramoul and he had tried to overrun the shack on their own, Santaglio had become the new leader of the *comadrejas*. He'd told of how he'd courageously tried to save the white man and Ramoul, but the odds were too heavily stacked against him. After returning to the shack and being beaten back by only two rifles, one inside the shack and one outside, the *comadrejas*, rather than admit that they couldn't outfight two rifles, found it easy to believe that they, too, had been greatly outnumbered.

Santaglio smiled to himself, liking the way these fools could be led to believe anything he told them. Still, he needed something to embolden them. The stagecoach should have been it. But it wasn't. *Now what?* Looking away from the bodies on the flatlands as if to purge today's events from his memory, he stared off to the east, where two of his riders came riding in from a long ways off, escorting a buckboard wagon covered by a canvas tarpaulin. Their wake of dust drifted sidelong on a hot wind.

"Santaglio, why we don't go to Old *Medico*, steal some horses, something like dis?" asked the man beside him. "I think des *Americanos* are tougher din we thinks."

"*Americanos* are cowards and fools," said Santaglio, "and I am sick of stealing horses. I am not any longer a criminal, Merza," he said, puffing out his chest. "From now on, I fight to free our people."

"Free us from what?" Merza looked all around, scratching his head.

Santaglio didn't reply. "I despise this *America* and its people and their way of life. Stay beside me, Merza. We are small in numbers, but the time is right for us to defeat this beast. They are so busy fighting among themselves, a military leader like me can defeat them before they know what has hit them."

"Military leader?" said Merza, sounding

dubious. "I did not know dat you were ever de leader of a military."

"Of course you did not know," said Santaglio. "Because I never told you. But now that you know, stop asking me so many questions! Do you doubt what I tells you?"

Merza shrugged. "No, I think not."

"Good," said Santaglio, backing his horse. "Then follow me. I have something important to show you."

The two turned and rode through the gathered *comadrejas,* causing the whole party to turn behind them and follow closely. At the edge of a trail leading up from the flatlands, they met the buckboard and gathered breathlessly, watching as Santaglio rode to one corner of the wagon, loosened the tarpaulin and threw it back, exposing the wagon's contents. "There, Merza," said Santaglio. "Tell me how many Americans we can kill with this."

Merza stared at a Gatling gun lying on its side surrounded by wooden crates of ammunition and empty magazines stacked all around the sides of the wagon. "Santaglio!" he gasped. "Where did you get such a weapon as this?" Leaping down from his saddle, he reached a hand into the wagon and ran it along the gun's brass-trimmed handle, brushing a trace of dust from it. The rest of the *comadrejas* pressed close, coming down from their horses and shoving one another aside for a better position.

"I got it from zees old white horse trader we dealt with over near to the border. He got it from a stolen shipment of guns going to zees American army." Santaglio smiled with satisfaction. "With this, we can overthrow this pitiful country and make it ours."

Merza and the other *comadrejas* gave one another a look, then shrugged and turned their attention back to the big Gatling gun. "Quickly!" said Merza to the others. "We must get it set up and get the magazines loaded. We must fire it and make sure that it works!"

"Don't be a fool, Merza," said Santaglio. "Of course it works. Get it set up and loaded, but do not fire it until I say so. We save our bullets for these American pigs."

"Jou heard him!" Merza barked at the men standing around the wagon. "Get it off of there and get it cleaned and set up." He stepped back into his saddle as he gave them orders, then reined around beside Santaglio.

"What do jou say about it now, Merza?" said Santaglio, his wrists crossed proudly on his saddle horn.

"I say we are ready to go to war," said Merza. "Where do jou want to start? We could hit zees army camp along zees river. We can go attack a train as it comes back from zees —"

"No," said Santaglio, cutting him off. "There is only one place to start. We start by destroying Sabre Ridge."

"Why Sabre Ridge?" Merza asked.

"Because I happen to know that zees town is weak and its people they are *stupido*," said Santaglio. "The sheriff there, he is a drunkard and a weakling. The town is overrun by outlaws who care for nothing or no one but themselves." He shrugged. "Zees town will fall so quickly they will not know what has hitted them. Once they are on their trembling knees in the dirt, begging us to spare their lives, we will take everything they have: money, women, horses, guns. It will all be ours, eh, Merza?" He winked with a sly grin.

"I am at your service," said Merza, already picturing it in his mind.

At daylight, the drinking crowd at the Hung Dog Saloon finally wound down.

Behind the bar, the owner stood leaning on his elbows, his face in his hands, a damp, dirty bar towel slung over his shoulder. Drunken outlaws lay sprawled in chairs and on the floor. Bob and Dick Abbadele lay stretched out back-to-back on a billiard table. On the floor beside the table, Sturgen sat with his bony knees drawn up, his arms wrapped around them, his hat pulled down over his eyes.

Sheriff Boggs had excused himself and left shortly after midnight when the crowd showed signs of getting rowdy. But Deputy Fuller Wright had stayed, drinking with the outlaws, trying his best to match Parker Dennison drink for drink. That had been a mistake. Wright had gotten drunk so quickly, he'd sobered up by three in the morning and began drinking anew. From that point on, he'd become wild-eyed and belligerent, the whiskey no longer making him drunk, just keeping him in a jittery, unstable stupor. Before long, he'd begun to imagine himself a part of the Abbadele crowd.

"I've always thought, if I wasn't walking this side of the law, I'd make a damn good highwayman," he said to Parker Dennison and Frank Abbadele.

"Highwayman!" Parker Dennison chuckled.

"Now, there's a term I haven't heard used in a long while."

Fuller Wright became a bit surly, thinking Dennison was making fun of him. "Well, whatever term you want to use, I think I'd be good at it, Frank," he said, turning his attention away from Parker Dennison.

Frank liked the idea of standing there talking freely with a lawman, not having to deny the fact that he was an outlaw — in fact, feeling proud of it. He even sensed a little envy from the deputy. Throwing back his shot of rye, he said, "Oh yeah? How so, *Fuller?*" He gave a little sarcastic snap to the deputy's name, looking him up and down. It was the first time the deputy had called him by his first name instead of Mr. Abbadele.

"No disrespect intended, Mr. Abbadele," said Fuller Wright, checking himself down. "But I can ride, shoot and do about anything else as good as any man you've got working for you, and that's a fact."

"No kidding?" Frank grinned tightly. "Well, I'll take your word on the riding, but if you want to, we'll wake some of these boys up and tell them you think you can shoot their eyes out in a gunfight."

"Whoa now, that ain't how I meant it,"

said the deputy, raising a hand as if holding back trouble. "I'm just saying I can handle the work is all. Especially the shooting part . . . not that I want to tangle with any of these boys." He gestured a hand about the saloon, then tried a casual shrug and said, "Hell, these boys all seem like friends of mine."

"Lucky for them," Frank goaded. He sat his empty shot glass on the bar.

Parker Dennison filled his and Frank's glass from a bottle of rye. "Frank, it sounds to me like this young lawman is seeking a position with your high-venture enterprise."

Now it was Frank's turn to chuckle. "Yes, I guess it does." He looked back at Fuller Wright, this time deeper into his eyes. "Who have you ever shot, Deputy?"

"I've done my share of shooting," Wright said, giving a glance around as if to make sure it was safe talking about his past. "I wasn't always a lawman, you know. I did some long riding right after the war."

Frank feigned surprise, cocking an eyebrow. "No! I didn't know that. Did you ride with anybody I might have heard of?"

Wright couldn't tell if Frank was being sincere or mocking him, but he had to carry on the best he could. "No, I suppose not." He paused for only a second, then said, "You asked if I ever shot anybody. Yes, I have. And I'll tell you this: While Sheriff Boggs sits around getting broader in the shanks, I'm out there on the hot sand practicing with this baby." He patted his pistol butt as he spoke.

"And you're fast with it?" Frank asked.

"Yep," said Wright with confidence.

"And you hit what you aim at?" Frank asked.

"Yep." Again the confidence in Wright's voice.

Frank stared at him a moment longer, a dark thought beginning to form in his mind. Finally, noting Wright's unwavering expression, he said, "If you ever really want to ride with me and the boys, come talk to me. I'll see what I can do." Then he half-turned away from Fuller Wright as if to exclude him from any further conversation.

"That's what I'm trying to do right now, Mr. Abbadele, is talk to you," said Fuller Wright, not budging an inch, his expression the same.

"Oh . . ." Frank let his voice trail, turning back to Fuller Wright. "In that case . . ." He seemed to consider something for a second, then said, "The fact is, I can always use a damn good gunman.

Cutting through all the rye and hot air and *highwayman* talk, just how good are you with that gun?"

"I told you, I'm good," said Wright. "You point something out in here, and I'll nail it for you, dead center."

The saloonkeeper looked up with apprehension.

Frank gave him a gesture of reassurance, then said to Wright, "It's one thing to talk about being fast and good with a gun; it's another thing to back it up." He looked Wright up and down again as if still considering something. "Let me just ask you flat out: Can you stand toe-to-toe in a fair fight and take down the Ranger?"

A tight silence set in. Then Parker Dennison picked his derby hat up from the bar, cleared his throat and said, "Gentlemen, I afraid this rye is running straight through me. Excuse me while I go out back and relieve myself." He adjusted the derby hat and added, "I trust you'll have ended this conversation by the time I return, knowing that, as an officer of the court, I cannot hear such conspirations, although I know they are only speculative." He quickly left.

"What did he say?" asked Fuller Wright.

"I don't know," said Frank, giving a

252

slight shrug. "I think he makes up about half of his big words." He gave a glance along the empty bar, then said, "You got awfully quiet when I mentioned the Ranger." He picked up the bottle of rye, reached and filled the shot glass in Wright's hand. "I reckon you'd have to go back out on the hot sand a while longer, shoot some more sticks and tins, before you'd be ready to cut a chunk off the Ranger." He stared flatly into the deputy's bloodshot eyes.

Fuller Wright's jaws tightened. "I'm more than a match for the Ranger," he said. "I just hadn't given him any thought is all." He tossed back the rye, emptying the shot glass in one long drink. "Far as I care, I'll take him on anytime, anyplace." He wiped a hand across his lips.

"This is the time; this is the place," said Frank with finality.

Fuller Wright looked nervous and gave a glance at the bottle in Frank's hand. "Let me think about it some. Just get my head clear on it."

"Yeah, Deputy, by all means," said Frank. He stuck the bottle of rye out, poking the bottom end of it into Wright's stomach, forcing him to take hold of it. "Here, maybe you'll think better with this." He turned, dismissing the deputy. "If you can handle the Ranger, I'll soon know it for myself. If you can't . . . Well, I reckon I'll know that, too."

Frank watched Fuller Wright in the mirror behind the bar. Wright walked away dejectedly to a dusty front window where he wiped a round circle with his shirtsleeve and stared out at the empty darkness, drinking straight from the bottle. Returning from his trip out back, Parker Dennison saw Wright's hollow eyes staring mindlessly past him as he walked along the boardwalk. Once inside the saloon, standing beside Frank Abbadele, Dennison jerked his thumb toward the deputy. "Looks like someone just pissed in his breakfast gravy. I take it things didn't go to suit him?"

Frank smiled flatly, shoving a fresh shot glass in front of the lawyer. "I showed him what he didn't want to be. Now he's got to decide whether or not he wants to change it."

Filling his shot glass, Parker Dennison said, raising a cautious hand, "That's enough. I don't need to hear any more than that."

Across the street at the hotel, the Ranger eased up from the feather bed and dressed quietly in the dark to keep from waking Maria. Buckling his gun belt around his waist, he stepped softly to the door adjoining the two rooms, opened it an inch and looked in just long enough to check on April and the baby. They lay asleep, the baby nestled in the crook of its mother's arm. On the floor a few feet away lay Reverend Bullard, snoring peacefully on a quilt pallet, an Indian blanket wrapped around him. Sam smiled to himself and gently closed the door. He left the room and made his way through the sleeping hotel until he stepped out on the porch. In the east, a thin mantle of sunlight lay on the horizon.

On his way to a restaurant where a lantern glowed in the front window, Sam looked across the street at the Hung Dog Saloon. Seeing the Ranger look his way, Deputy Fuller Wright stepped back from the window. He stood brooding, the nearly empty bottle of rye hanging from his hand. Once the Ranger had passed and turned his attention to the dark street ahead, Wright walked through the batwing doors and stared out toward the restaurant. He stepped through the doors, but then stopped and continued to stare along the dark, empty street.

At the bar, Frank Abbadele nudged Parker Dennison and said, "Look at this. He's thinking about it awfully hard."

Dennison looked up from his glass of rye, his eyes red-rimmed, his shirt collar unfastened, his necktie hanging loosely. "Think he'll do it?"

"I believe he will," said Frank. "I did a pretty good job on him." He gave Dennison a look. "I thought you couldn't be hearing any of this?"

"Ethically, morally and legally, I shouldn't," said Dennison rubbing his hands together with a sly grin. "But one can only resist temptation so far. Is a wager in order?" he asked.

"But of course," said Frank.

"Then I wager ten dollars that he doesn't attempt it," said Dennison. "I believe he has thought about it long enough that he's talked himself out of it."

"Your bet's covered," said Frank, staring at Fuller Wright. "Although I almost feel bad about taking your money."

"Don't worry about *my* money," Dennison said. "Wait until you see what my legal services are going to cost you." He raised his shot glass in an unsteady hand, as if in a toast. Whiskey spilled over the edge of the glass and dripped on the bar top.

★ ★ ★

It was sunup when the Ranger finished his breakfast and began his walk back to the hotel. On his way, Sheriff Hugh Boggs stepped out of his office and met him as the Ranger stepped down off the boardwalk. "Morning, Ranger," Boggs said, closing his office door behind him. Seeing Sam come from the direction of the restaurant, Boggs added, "You're up awful early, or do you ever sleep?"

"A man who sleeps past sunup doesn't have much planned," the Ranger replied, touching his fingers to his hat brim without stopping.

"I'll have to try and remember that," Boggs said wryly, moving down to the street and along beside him. "You know, I've been doing some serious thinking, Ranger," he said. "I figure now that things are cooling down here, the judge coming and all, there's no reason for you and me not to be friends, is there?"

Slowing his pace slightly, turning his gaze to Boggs, Sam said, "If you figure things are cooling down here, Boggs, you haven't done much serious thinking at all. This town is ready to blow sky-high. You've been too friendly to the bad elements. Somebody should have taught you better."

Boggs frowned, overlooking the Ranger's accusation. "All right, I'll admit things are still a little tense here and will be until the judge gets here and settles things. But, Ranger, you have to admit that the Abbadeles are doing things according to our legal process — to the letter of the law, the same law that you and I swore to uphold. Is that so wrong?"

The Ranger slowed and took a breath. "No, Boggs," he said, "it's not wrong, except for the spirit of why they do it. Sometimes a lawman gets sick of the way a no-account will break every law in the book, then, as soon as he feels the flames of justice licking at his back, all of a sudden he wants to make sure everything's done real legal-like." He offered a patient smile. "But as far as you and me go, you're right. We've no reason to be enemies. And we won't. Not as long as I can do my job and you can do yours. We don't have to agree, but we can still try not to step on one another's toes." He extended his hand as if forming a truce. "Is that a deal?"

Sheriff Boggs looked relieved, shaking hands vigorously. "Yes, it is, Ranger, and I'm glad we're getting the air clear between us. And as far as you dunking me in that water trough the day you got here, I don't hold that against you. I was drinking too heavily, and I got belligerent. So it was partly my fault. Since then, I've managed to curtail the whiskey."

"That's good to hear, Boggs," said the Ranger. "In my opinion, whiskey and law work have never mixed well."

Boggs started to say something more on the matter, but before he could, Deputy Fuller Wright shouted as he stepped sideways into the middle of the street, forty feet ahead, "Ranger, I'm looking for you!"

The Ranger's eyes hardened first on Sheriff Boggs. So fierce was his gaze that Boggs took a quick step backward. His face turned stark white. "Ranger, so help me God, I've got no hand in this," he said. He swung around to face Fuller Wright. "Deputy, what the blue living hell is wrong with you? Back away from here! That's an order!"

"I'm through taking orders from you, Boggs, you big tub of guts! You back away yourself, if you don't want the same thing! I'm sending the Ranger straight to hell!"

"Ranger, he's drunk or crazy, either one," said Boggs, talking fast, trying to settle things. "Let me talk him down!"

"Careful, Boggs," said the Ranger, seeing that the sheriff was telling the truth, that he had no hand in this. "He's wound awfully tight."

"Deputy," Boggs called out to Wright, "this man hasn't wronged you in any way. I haven't even heard a cross word between you. Settle yourself down, please! This ain't a fight you want to be in. He will kill you deader than hell!"

"Out of the way, Boggs!" said Wright with finality. "I don't need a reason, not this morning." He stared at Sam. "Ranger, I've heard too damn much about how much sand you've got in your craw. I'm sick of hearing it. I'm twice as fast as you are!"

"Better listen to your boss, Deputy," said the Ranger, stepping forward, wide of Boggs, giving himself plenty of room in the street. "I don't want to kill a lawman."

On either boardwalk, early store patrons took cover quickly. Pip Richards had started to sit down early in his spot out front of the harness shop. But seeing what was about to take place, he kicked the skinny hound to get it started toward an alley, then followed it hurriedly, looking back at the street as he went. "You sound too damn sure of yourself to suit me, Ranger!" shouted Fuller Wright, spreading his feet shoulder-width apart.

"It's my job to be sure of myself, Deputy," said the Ranger, seeing no good outcome. The deputy was strung high and tight. Sam saw that someone was going to die in the street. It wasn't going to be him, not if he could help it. "Whoever talked you into this wasn't doing you a favor," he said, searching for anything he could say to stop it. "Like as not you're drunk on whiskey. Maybe you need to sleep on this, clear your mind. Then, if you still feel like —"

"Shut up, Ranger! I didn't come here to talk! I came here to kill you!" Fuller Wright's shoulder bowed slightly. It was coming any second, the Ranger warned himself. He'd seen this too many times. As he listened to Fuller Wright, he made a quick check on the street. Crowded into the batwing doors of the Hung Dog Saloon stood Frank Abbadele, his brothers Bob and Dick, and the attorney, Parker Dennison. But across the street from them the Ranger saw Maria, her hand on her rifle, poised and watching, waiting for the slightest sign of involvement from them.

"All right then, Deputy," said the Ranger, his words sounding strange to him, "if it's killing you came for, let's get it done." It seemed wrong, standing there, facing off with a lawman. He tried not to look at the badge on Wright's chest.

There it came, the stiffening of the shoulders, the right shoulder dropping slightly as the deputy's hand went down to his pistol butt. He was fast; the Ranger saw that already, saw it clearly as his own hand made that same plunge and closed around the butt of his big, tied-down Colt. He saw the slick, practiced speed of the gunman, the crisp upturn of the barrel tip swinging free of the holster's edge, starting to level toward him. But everything the Ranger saw Wright doing, he knew that he himself had already done . . . only he'd done it a split second faster.

Inside the Ranger's mind all sound and feeling and motion stopped abruptly, as if life both within and around him had been suddenly frozen in time and place. There was tight, crushing silence. Then the world around him exploded back to life as the Colt bucked in his hand and the smell of burnt powder rose to his nostrils. At the hitch rail to his right, a frightened horse neighed wildly. A townsman rushed out to calm the animal as Sam cut his eyes from Fuller Wright's lifeless body in the dirt to where Maria stood prepared to back his play. He knew she was there, yet he had to see her anyway. He had to reassure himself that in the interim of killing, something had not come along and caused her to vanish.

"Lord God!" Boggs said in a hushed tone. He ventured back to the middle of the street, still cautiously not getting between the Ranger and the lifeless body in the dirt. "I swear I don't know what came over him." Boggs shook his head. "Wright was testy and had a broodiness to him that was hard to put up with, but damn . . ."

"I know what got into him," said the Ranger. He stood staring at the Abbadeles, who'd stepped out of the batwing doors and stood bunched together on the boardwalk.

"Now, Ranger," said Boggs with a worried look, "you can't prove that the Abbadeles had anything at all to do with this!"

"I know it so strong, I don't have to prove it," said the Ranger. He opened the big Colt as he spoke, poked the spent cartridge from the cylinder and replaced it without taking his eyes off Frank Abbadele.

"Ranger, don't go doing something rash!" Boggs said, hurrying along beside him as the Ranger walked straight to the Hung Dog Saloon.

"I'm not, Boggs," Sam said, his eyes still fixed on Frank Abbadele, who returned his harsh stare. "Something rash would have been to shoot Frank Abbadele before your deputy hit the ground. He's the one who brought this on."

On the Hung Dog's boardwalk, Parker Dennison stepped to the side, his hands purposely in full view, a black cigar between his fingers. Bob and Dick Abbadele flanked their brother closely as the Ranger stopped in the middle of the street, facing them.

From the side, Parker Dennison's words sounded well rehearsed as he said in a smooth, clear voice, "Ranger Burrack, as legal counsel for Mr. Frank Abbadele, it is my duty to point out to you that my client is unarmed." As Dennison spoke, Frank Abbadele grinned and opened his coat slowly with both hands, showing the Ranger that he was not wearing a gun belt.

The Ranger ignored the lawyer and said directly to Frank Abbadele, "If I wanted to kill you, Abbadele, I would have done it from over there and saved myself the walk. I just wanted to look you in the eye while I tell you what kind of low, twisted coward you are. You had no call whatsoever to send that man out and get him killed. You did that just for pastime."

"I don't know what you're talking about, Ranger," Frank said, his dark grin not wavering in spite of the Ranger's cutting words. "But if you think you can goad me into a gunfight, you're wrong."

The Ranger looked past Frank Abbadele at the rest of the gang crowded into the batwing doors behind him. "I didn't think I could goad you into a gunfight, Frank. I figure you're not going to do any fighting for yourself, not as long as you've got your pick of fools to do your fighting for you."

"Be warned, Ranger," said Parker Dennison. "Everything you say and do here today is being witnessed by these gentlemen." He swept a thick, soft hand along the street and the front of the saloon. "I fully intend to mention your conduct to the judge as soon as court convenes." He pointed a finger at Sam. "If you persist in this threatening manner, be warned, sir, that I will instruct the sheriff here to arrest you for —"

"Hold on, Mr. Dennison!" Boggs cut in, a worried look on his face. "You can't expect me to arrest this man! You saw what he done out there!"

"Are you saying you cannot fulfill the obligations of your office, Sheriff?" asked

Parker Dennison, intimidating Boggs.

"I'm not saying that; no, sir!" said Boggs, his face looking pasty beneath a sheen of sweat as he ran a trembling hand across his forehead. "Jesus, is there ever any letup? The Ranger hasn't broken any law!"

"I beg to differ with you, sir," said Dennison. "If he continues to act in a threatening manner toward Mr. Abbadele, I must insist you arrest him for the safety of my client and that of this entire community."

"For God sakes, Frank!" said Sheriff Boggs, turning an appeal to Frank Abbadele.

But before Frank Abbadele could answer, the Ranger said, "Calm down, Boggs. Be a lawman. Quit letting these people turn you into their lackey."

"Ranger, I'm just trying to keep peace here," Boggs pleaded.

"Good for you," said the Ranger. "You don't have to worry about arresting me. I'm leaving. I'll be by your office later to fill out a report on what happened between me and Wright, just to keep the record straight." He gave Parker Dennison a sharp stare, then turned and walked to the hotel.

Chapter 15

April stood in the hotel window, looking out at the stagecoach as it lumbered toward town through the wavering midmorning heat. She wore a new dress and hat that Maria had brought her from the mercantile store earlier. While Maria did April's clothes shopping, April had stayed at the hotel, tending the baby. Toot Abbadele came by with whiskey on his breath and tried to explain to her how important it was for him to stick close to his brothers right now. But April would hear none of it. She'd asked him to leave. She'd told him not to bother coming back. She and the baby, accompanied by her grandfather, would be leaving on the stagecoach for Circle Wells. Toot had stormed out of the room, slamming the door behind him. So be it. Toot had gone straight back to the Hung Dog Saloon to join his brothers.

She turned from the window with the baby in her arms. "The stage is arriving," she said softly to her grandfather, who stood near the door, a new small canvas travel bag sitting at his feet. "I see it coming along the trail."

"Perhaps we better wait until it has fully arrived before we walk down there," said Reverend Bullard. "Tension is running high. Let's not give Toot an opportunity to create a public scene when you and the baby get ready to leave." Looking for support, he glanced at Maria, who stood beside the bed, folding a small blanket she'd purchased for the baby.

"Your grandfather is right," said Maria. "There is no hurry." She stepped over as she spoke and laid the folded blanket atop the canvas travel bag. "It would be wise to wait here until the stage is prepared to leave. It will take a while for them to change horses and for the driver and guard to rest and eat." She gave April a searching look. "Unless, of course, you are going down early deliberately, so Toot can see that you are truly leaving . . . that you meant what you said."

"Toot knows that I meant what I said," April replied with resolve. "But I'll wait a while longer to keep the baby out of the heat."

"That is a good idea," said Maria. "While you wait, I will walk down and see how Sam is doing." She picked up her rifle from against the wall and excused herself with a touch of her hat brim.

Downstairs, out front of the hotel, the Ranger stood where he had been standing the past ten minutes — on the boardwalk, keeping an eye on the saloon across the street. In the window of the saloon he saw Toot Abbadele watching him through the cleaned circle on the glass. The Ranger stared coldly at him until Toot finally stepped back out of sight. Then the Ranger turned at the sound of the hotel door opening. He saw Maria step out onto the boardwalk with her rifle under her arm. "April saw the stage from Circle Wells coming," Maria said. "Her grandfather thinks there could be trouble when she tries to leave."

"There could, I suppose," said Sam, "but I doubt it. I believe if Toot Abbadele was going to give her a hard time, he already would have. Something tells me he's not as bad as the others. He just hasn't found the guts to stand up to his brothers yet. If he ever does, he might just turn out to be a decent man after all. Too bad that it looks like it'll be too late for him and the young woman to make a go of it, though."

"*Si*," said Maria. "April is determined

that she and the baby are leaving without him. She says he has chosen his brothers over her and the baby."

Sam shook his head without answering, then looked out toward the stagecoach growing larger through the sand and sunlight. Something didn't look right to him, so he cocked his head slightly and eyed the stagecoach more closely as it swayed and bounced along the trail. Seeing the Ranger's curiosity, Maria asked, "What is it, Sam?"

"I can't say yet," he replied, already taking a step toward the stage depot, "but something doesn't look right."

Now, walking beside him, Maria also studied the coach as it drew nearer. Halfway to the depot, she said, "It has no freight atop it — no luggage or anything else." Then, without taking her eyes off the stage, she recognized Big Shod and said, "Look, Sam! The man driving it —"

"Is Jefferson Eldridge Shadowen," the Ranger said, finishing her words for her. They both quickened their pace to the depot and stood out front watching anxiously. As the coach entered town and slowed down, the Ranger and Maria saw where the many bullet holes had left fresh splinters sticking out all over the coach's body. One of the coach horses was missing. In its place stood Shod's big gray. "This looks bad," said the Ranger, stepping forward and opening the door as he looked up at the big bounty hunter. "Are you hit?" he asked.

"No, nothing worth mentioning," said Shod, setting the wooden brake arm and wrapping the reins. "But the judge is back there. He's badly wounded," he added, adjusting his spectacles as he jumped down from the seat, his rifle in hand. Already, onlookers had begun to gather, looking in awe at the splintered coach. Calling out to a livery boy who came running, Shod said, "Get the gray out of there and stable him separate — he's mine."

Pulling the bullet-shattered door open, the Ranger looked at the faces of the two worn-out, battle-weary women. "Here, ladies, let us help you," he said, reaching in for Swan Hendricks, seeing that Clare-Annette had the judge nestled to her bloody breast. Passing Swan along to Maria, the Ranger gently reached beneath the judge and scooped his limp body off Clare-Annette's lap.

"Watch his head," Clare-Annette said, her voice sounding parched and raspy. "God, he's shot bad, Ranger," she whispered. She cradled the judge's head to keep it from flopping limply over the Ranger's forearm.

"Yes, ma'am, I see he is," the Ranger whispered in reply. The big bounty hunter squeezed halfway inside the coach and helped the Ranger with the judge. *"Comadrejas?"* Sam asked as they stepped down from the stagecoach.

"Yes," said the bounty hunter. "More than I've ever seen at one time. They've gotten together in force. You can bet we haven't seen the last of them."

"They killed one of the stage horses?" the Ranger asked.

"No," said Shod, as they continued on with their task. "We had a horse come up lame less than five miles back. I turned him loose, put my horse to the team. We're lucky we made it here at all." He gave the Ranger a look. "If it hadn't been for Kirby Brooks and his daddy, we'd all be dead."

The Ranger paused for just a second. "The man you were dogging saved your life?"

"Yes," said Shod. "Think about that one for a while."

"I've already started," said the Ranger.

From the gathering onlookers, someone called out, "The judge has been shot in the head! My God, somebody get a gurney! Get him to Dr. Lovedale's!"

"*Please* watch about his head," Clare-Annette repeated, swaying terribly as she stepped down.

Maria stepped in and looped Clare-Annette's arm over her shoulder. "Here, let me help you," Maria said, steadying her.

"I can walk," said Swan Hendricks bravely, even as she staggered in place. But Big Shod caught her with his free hand and lifted her easily into his arms, still holding his rifle. "Oh my, on second thought . . ." Swan said, trying to offer an exhausted smile. She let her cheek fall against the bounty hunter's thick chest.

From the hotel window, April had watched the coach pull up in front of the depot. Seeing the condition of the passengers as the Ranger, Maria and the big bounty hunter pulled them out, April left her grandfather watching over the baby and hurried down to the street as quickly as her tired, sore body would allow. She arrived in time to see the passengers escorted toward the doctor's office, a few townsfolk bunched closely around them. For a moment she stood staring in disbelief at the bullet-riddled coach, watching the boy from the livery stable begin to unhitch the sweaty, froth-streaked horses.

April didn't see the men from the saloon walk up and assemble behind her until Toot Abbadele said quietly, "I suppose this means you're not going anywhere after all."

April turned and saw the serious look in his eyes. She saw concern; she saw much more. But then, before she could say anything, behind Toot she heard a ripple of drunken laughter at what he had just said to her. "Tell her she's not going anywhere unless you say so," said Lenbow Decker with a wide, drunken grin. Farther back behind Decker, Walsh and the Knox brothers stood the Abbadeles: Frank, Dick and Big Bob. Next to them stood Parker Dennison, staring off in the direction of the wounded judge with a concerned look on his face.

Toot heard Decker and turned. "Shut up, Decker. I'm talking here."

At first, April thought he'd spoken up against his friends butting into his business, into *their* business. But as he turned back to her, she saw the grin on his face, the expression he'd just shown Decker and the others. April flared at the sight of him smiling to appease his drunken friends. "You think this is funny, Toot?" she said, not trying to hide the confrontational tone of her voice.

"Jesus, April." Toot's smile faded; his voice dropped to a whisper to keep the others from hearing him. "Nobody's saying it's funny. I didn't mean it to be. I was just commenting. Surely you're not leaving now! Look at that stagecoach. What about the baby?"

"If you're worried about the baby, be a father to her," said April, not trying to keep her voice down. Toot's face reddened with embarrassment. The drunken outlaws tried to stifle their laughter; still, some of it came through.

April glared at the men, then turned back to Toot. "As soon as the stage is ready, so am I. My baby and I can't leave this town soon enough." She turned and walked stiffly back to the hotel, not allowing Toot to see that her eyes had filled with tears that were about to spill down her cheeks.

"Damn it," Toot said to himself under his breath. He started after her, but she was moving quickly. Passing his brothers on his way to the hotel, Toot felt Frank's strong hand close around his forearm, suddenly stopping him.

"Take a look at yourself, little brother,"

said Frank. "You're chasing after a woman like some lovestruck fool. She ain't your kind. Hell, boy, she ain't even your color."

"You go to hell, Frank," Toot shouted, shaking his arm free of his brother's grip then walking on a few steps toward the hotel before stopping, realizing how hopeless the situation had become between him and April.

"That's it, Toot," Frank called out to him. "You stop right there and think about it for a minute. You'll see that I'm right." He pointed a finger at his brother. "It's time you decide one way or the other. Either you stick with us or you go throw your life away with some colored girl and her half-breed baby!"

"*My* half-breed baby, Frank!" Toot shouted at him, turning, facing his brother. He pounded his hand on his chest. "That baby is my daughter, too, Frank! Can't you get that into your head? I am the father of that precious little baby!" Tears glistened in Toot's eyes.

Big Bob whispered, "Jesus, Frank, leave him alone. He's falling apart on us."

But Frank ignored Bob and said to Toot, "Are you sure of that, little brother? Maybe that dark-skinned gal has you seeing things that ain't there. What makes you think you're the only man she ever —"

"Stop it right there!" Toot's hand snapped instinctively to his pistol butt. But then he caught himself, realizing he was about to draw on his own brother.

Seeing Toot's reaction, Frank dropped his hand and kept it poised. "Oh, now you're ready to shoot it out with your family over her?"

"No," said Toot. "You're my brother. I won't shoot you!" Barely under control, he advanced on Frank, his hand sliding away from his pistol butt to the buckle of his gun belt. He unfastened it and let it fall in his tracks. "But I will beat the blue living hell out of you!"

"Hold it," said Big Bob, stepping forward, prepared to come between his brothers. "There'll be none of that."

"Get out of the way, brother," said Frank, unfastening his gun belt and letting it fall. "Toot has needed a good ass-kicking for as long as I can remember."

In the doctor's office, Maria stepped over and looked out the window at the scene in the street. Frank and Toot Abbadele clashed against one another like two powerful, enraged animals. Fists flying, they battered one another to the ground, then rolled back and forth in the dirt. The onlooking outlaws cheered them on, shuffling quickly out of their way. Parker Dennison stood with his head slightly cocked. He stared at the combatants with a bemused expression on his face, his cigar hooked loosely between his fingers. Big Bob Abbadele had made an attempt to separate his brothers, but upon slinging them in opposite directions, the two lunged back together like rabid pit dogs. Big Bob threw up his hands in disgust and stood back out of their way.

"No self-respecting sheriff would allow this to go on," Maria said, watching Frank Abbadele rise to his feet with Toot over his shoulder. As Toot kicked and pounded him, Frank ran to the boardwalk and tried to hurl his brother through the large window of the mercantile store. The store owner ran out, waving his hands in protest. But Terrence Knox jumped in and shoved the man backward over a stack of nail kegs as Toot rolled to his feet and made a dive at Frank.

"Uh-oh," said Maria. "Now it is spreading. One of them has started man-handling the store clerk." Even as she spoke, she made a move toward the door. "This has gone far enough," she said.

"Wait up, Maria," said the Ranger. "I'm going with you."

The black bounty hunter looked up from watching the doctor swab thick pasty blood from the judge's head. "Want some company out there?" he asked, gesturing his rifle barrel toward the street.

"No, we've got it," said the Ranger. "You look like you could use some rest."

"That's right," said Swan Hendricks, tired but still able to pass along a flip remark. "You stay right here. We might need some big strong man to carry us around the room." Clare-Annette sat slumped against her, half-conscious, the front of her ragged dress covered with the judge's dried blood.

In a no-nonsense tone, the doctor cut in. "The fact is, she's right. I could use some help getting everybody bedded down here." His eyes went to the sound of cheering and catcalls in the street. "From the sound of things, I'll have more business any minute now."

"Let's hope not," said the Ranger. He and Maria headed out the door.

As they walked along the street, the Ranger saw the mercantile owner pick his way out of the midst of spilled nail kegs and loose pick handles and hurry back inside his store. Noting the wild, angry look in the store owner's eyes, Sam quickened his pace and veered toward the mercantile store. "Trouble coming from the store," he said to Maria.

While the two brothers rolled in the dirt and the outlaws stood circled around them, no one paid any attention to the Ranger as he stepped up onto the boardwalk, kicked a spilled nail keg out of his way and stood back flat against the front wall beside the open door. Neither did anyone pay attention to the store owner when he came charging out the door with a shotgun in his hands. But skillfully, the Ranger snatched the shotgun from the man's hands with such suddenness that the man lost his balance and fell into a pile of nails. As quickly as the Ranger grabbed the gun, he raised the double-barrel in the air and fired a loud blast of buckshot straight up. The blast ripped off the outer edge of the wooden overhang and showered the outlaws with splinters and bits of roofing tin.

"God almighty!" shouted Terrence Knox, the whole group ducking instinctively at the sound of the blast. Most of them reached for their pistols, then froze at the sight of the Ranger leveling the shotgun toward them, the barrel he'd just fired curling smoke.

The Ranger stood rigid, poised in anticipation. "Wait!" Parker Dennison shouted at the men, seeing the look on the Ranger's face, also seeing Maria flanking the crowd, her rifle aimed and ready. "Don't draw on him! That's exactly what he wants! Don't oblige him!"

On the ground, Frank and Toot had stopped fighting and lay staring at the Ranger. Frank gave his brother a shove, then said to the others, "Dennison's right, men. The Ranger can't wait to face off with us. Ain't that right, Ranger?" he sneered with contempt.

"Call it however it suits you, Abbadele," said Sam. "But the brawling stops, or else the next shot is going to take some meat off of somebody." He moved the shotgun back and forth slowly across the men.

"You heard the lawdog," said Frank Abbadele. As he spoke, he stood up, dusting his knees and the front of his shirt. "Don't nobody make a move." He took a step backward and, without looking down, extended his hand to Toot, still sitting on the ground spitting dust. Toot took his hand and rose to his feet, a trickle of blood running down the corner of his mouth.

"Are you all right, little brother?" Frank asked without taking his eyes off the Ranger.

"Yeah, I'm all right," Toot said, still spitting dust. He rubbed his hand across the trickle of blood. "This is family business. We don't need no lawman meddling in it." He shot a glance toward the second floor of the hotel where he knew April might be standing. He thought he caught sight of her stepping back to keep from being seen.

"It becomes my business when innocent people are about to get hurt," said the Ranger, realizing that none of the Abbadeles had seen the store owner coming out the door with fire in his eyes.

Having heard the shotgun blast, Sheriff Boggs came hurrying along the boardwalk from his office. The outlaws nudged one another at the sight of Boggs buckling his gun belt around his thick waist as he struggled toward them. "What now?" he said, slowing to a halt a few cautious yards back from the Ranger, not about to get caught between him and the Abbadeles.

"It's law work. Nothing that would concern you, Boggs," said the Ranger. "Just some fighting in the street — disturbing the peace and causing a public nuisance."

"Yeah, Boggs," said Frank Abbadele,

making no effort to hide his contempt for the sheriff, "go on back to your office, see if you can find your bottle of rye. We've got things under control out here." He turned his gaze back at the Ranger. "Now that the judge has a bullet in his head, I expect you'll be able to look out here and see our faces a lot, Ranger. You might just as well get used to us. We'll be here taking it easy till another judge shows up."

Sheriff Boggs looked at the Ranger. "Is that true, Ranger? Is there a bullet in his head?"

"No," said the Ranger. "It knocked a hole in his skull, but luckily the bullet glanced off."

"Jesus, that poor bastard," Boggs whispered, picturing it. He ran a shaky hand along the side of his head.

"The doctor says he might make it," the Ranger said to Boggs, still keeping his eyes and the shotgun on the Abbadeles. "But it's not likely he'll be sitting on the bench judging any cases from now on."

"Then we'll just have to wait for another judge to replace him, won't we?" said Parker Dennison.

The Ranger didn't answer.

"Are we through here?" Dennison asked boldly, spreading his hands as if making peace between the Ranger and the outlaws.

"We're through as far as I'm concerned," said Frank Abbadele, eyeing the Ranger closely. "All me and the boys here care about is peace and quiet, being the good-natured gentlemen that we are." He spread a flat grin. Laughter rippled across the men.

"What about this mess?" said the mercantile owner, who had struggled up from the nails scattered all over the boardwalk. He held a hand to a spot of blood on his forearm where a nail had stuck him. "I suppose I have to clean all this up!"

"Sure looks like it to me," Frank Abbadele said. Laughter rippled again.

The irate store owner reached around, snatched up a broom from against the front wall and began sweeping briskly, shoving the loose nails into a pile. "I don't deserve this. I never bothered nobody in my life! All I do is try to —" His words stopped. He stiffened and froze in place as the sound of a rifle shot resounded in from the desert floor.

Frank Abbadele said, "What the hell?" The store owner's chest turned red, a large spray of blood splattering the store window behind him. In the street, Parker Dennison's cigar dropped from his fingers as he felt a shot whistle past his head.

Maria saw what was happening and acted without hesitation, running forward and diving into the stunned lawyer, knocking him to the ground as more rifle shots whipped past him like angry hornets. She caught a glimpse of the Ranger taking cover as she lay atop Parker Dennison and fired her rifle toward the swirl of dust that seemed to have sprung up instantly across the desert floor. Rifle fire blossomed through the wavering heat. After her third shot, she grabbed the lawyer by his arm and pulled him along, saying, "Quickly, come with me!"

"Maria, get out of the street!" the Ranger shouted from his thin cover along the edge of the boardwalk, where he hugged the ground and fired his pistol toward the oncoming horde. Even as he shouted, the Ranger saw that she had already begun to make her move, half-dragging the lawyer along with her. Through the sound of gunfire, the Abbadeles had begun to spread out, taking cover and firing on the large body of riders racing toward town.

"I demand to know what the hell is going on here!" Parker Dennison shouted, holding his derby hat on his head with one hand as he hurried along in a crouch behind Maria. Only when they had collapsed behind the cover of a water trough did Maria answer. First she took a breath and crossed herself. *"Santa madona,"* she whispered. Then she said to Parker Dennison beneath the rapid, relentless barrage of Gatling gunfire, *"Comadrejas del desierto —* the desert weasels. They are here!"

Chapter 16

Seeing the large number of riders charging the town, the Ranger's first concern was for Maria's safety. Once he saw that she and Parker Dennison had taken cover from the heavy gunfire, he turned his attention back toward the billowing cloud of dust and fired his pistol empty. Then, reloading cartridges from his belt, he chastised himself for having left his big Swiss rifle at the Miller Hotel. His eyes went to the upper windows of the hotel, catching a glimpse of Reverend Bullard before he ducked out of sight as a bullet hammered the clapboard siding. Sam knew he had to get his hands on a rifle, and quick. If he couldn't get to the big Swiss rifle, he'd have to settle for whatever was available. His eyes darted back and forth along the street, seeing the Abbadeles and their men hunkered down, taking whatever cover they could find as they returned fire on the *comadrejas*.

At the hitch rail out front of the Hung Dog Saloon, Sam saw one horse lying dead on the ground. Two other horses kicked and pulled wildly, trying to free their reins as bullets whistled past them. Seeing a rifle butt sticking up from one of the horses' saddles, Sam raced across the street in a crouch, bullets kicking up dirt at his boot heels. Behind the nail kegs out front of the mercantile store, Frank Abbadele saw the Ranger making his move toward the horses. Turning to his brother Bob, Frank shouted above the gunfire, "Stay here, Bob. I'm going to get us some rifles!"

Bob nodded and continued firing on the quickly encroaching horde. Frank ran across the street to where the Ranger hurriedly yanked a rifle from the saddle scabbard of both of the spooked horses. "Those rifles belong to my men!" Frank shouted, seeing the Ranger shove the rifles under his arm. With his free hand, the Ranger unhitched the terrified animals. They bolted away, neighing wildly.

Shoving the rifles into Frank's hands, the Ranger said, "Here, you're welcome to them. Get to using them."

There was no time for Frank Abbadele to respond. The *comadrejas* had concentrated their fire on the two of them, forcing lawman and outlaw alike to drop down and take cover behind the dead horse. Sam snatched the rifle from the dead horse's saddle scabbard, levered a round into the chamber and began firing. Beside him Frank Abbadele gave him a look, then looked at the two rifles the Ranger had shoved into his hands. He seemed to be at a loss for words, taken aback by this strange turn of events. "I — I better get over there with these rifles."

"Where are the rest of your men's horses and gear?" the Ranger asked between firing shots at the riders.

"Some are in the livery," said Frank Abbadele. "Some are out back of the saloon."

"They better get all the rifles they can round up," said the Ranger. "It looks like we've got a fight on our hands." He gave Frank Abbadele a quick stare as he levered a fresh round into the rifle chamber.

"Right," Frank nodded. Without another word, he turned from the Ranger, ran back across the street and slid in beside his brother Bob, pitching a rifle into his waiting hands.

"Did he give you any trouble?" asked Bob, talking about the Ranger.

"No," said Frank, having no time to elaborate. "Why would he?" Without expecting an answer, he turned and shouted at the Knox brothers and the rest of his men. "Get to your horses and get some long arms! These sonsabitches ain't riding over us and getting away with it!"

Inside the doctor's office, Shod had acted fast at the first sound of rifle fire. From the front window, he'd seen the oncoming riders in the boiling dust. "My God," he'd said under his breath.

"What in tarnation is going on out there?" Dr. Lovedale asked, his forearms damp with Judge Henley's blood.

Turning to the doctor, the bounty hunter said to him, Swan Hendricks and Clare-Annette, "It's the *comadrejas!* Get some mattresses, furniture, anything you can find! Get something piled against this door that'll stop bullets!"

Seeing the bounty hunter head for the rear of the building, Swan Hendricks said, "Wait! Where are you going?"

Shod spoke fast. "I've got to get to the mercantile store, get as much ammunition as I can lay my hands on. This could last awhile."

"I'm going with you," Swan said quickly.

"No!" said Shod. Hearing bullets hit the front of the building, he pulled Swan away from where she stood near the window. "Do like I told you," he commanded. "Stay here and help the doctor. I'll be right back."

"Be careful," said Swan, her tone turning gentle.

Shod just looked at her, then turned away. Clare-Annette and the doctor had already begun shoving a large oak desk up against the front door. "Here, Clare, let me give you a hand," said Swan, stepping over to the desk as the bounty hunter hurried along a hall toward the rear of the building.

Outside, Shod ran to the mercantile, his rifle in hand, amid bullets whistling in from the *comadrejas* and guns exploding all around him from men returning their fire. In the middle of the street, a buggy had been abandoned when the shooting began. The Knox brothers had scrambled out to it, cut the horse free and turned the light-weight rig onto its side. They sat huddled behind it, firing with their pistols. Catching a glimpse of Shod as he ran past them, Terrence Knox swung his pistol toward him, taking aim on his broad back. "There goes that bounty hunting bastard!"

But Hirsh Knox grabbed his brother's arm and pulled it down. He tried to speak. "Don't-da-da — sho-sho — he-hi —"

"Shut up, Hirsh!" said Terrence. "I

291

wasn't really going to shoot him! We need every gunhand in town right now!"

Shod ducked inside the mercantile store just as bullets slammed into the door frame. Without stopping, he ran to a large ammunition cabinet, jerked the doors open and grabbed a large box of rifle cartridges. Shoving the box under his arm, he reached for a box of pistol cartridges and had just started to pick it up when a sound from behind caused him to turn quickly, drawing and cocking his Colt. He saw someone duck down behind a dry goods counter and heard them crawling quickly along the floor. Following the sound with his pistol barrel, he called out, "Stop right there. Stand up and show yourself, or I'll shoot!"

"I have a rifle in my hand," a nervous voice said. "What am I supposed to do with it —"

Shod cut the voice off. "Either lay it down or raise it high over your head, one-handed. Now, hurry up!" Outside, the firing grew more intense. The sound of hooves growing closer caused the ground to rumble slightly.

"Oh my goodness, don't shoot!" said the voice. "I'm standing, I'm standing."

Shod watched as two hands rose above

the counter, one trembling as it held up a shiny new rifle. The other hand held a box of cartridges. Shod looked on curiously as the Reverend Bullard stood all the way up, an embarrassed look on his face. Seeing the big bounty hunter, the reverend let out a short sigh and shook his head. "My, my, what a terrible person you must think I am," he said.

Shod let the hammer down and lowered his pistol into its holster, seeing Reverend Bullard's clerical collar. "Not at all, preacher," he said, hastily going back to the gun cabinet. "I've got plenty of terrible people to think about right now. They're coming here to kill us all. Are you going to be able to use that rifle when the time comes, or is killing against your calling?"

"Killing is against the calling of any sane human being, sir," said the reverend. "But which is worse, killing or allowing innocent people to be killed and doing nothing to save them?"

"I like your religion, preacher," said Shod, adjusting his spectacles.

"Allow me to introduce myself, sir. I am the Reverend Bullard." The old clergyman stepped around from behind the counter. Lowering his hands, he placed the rifle up under his arm. "You must be the bounty hunter my granddaughter told me about. The one who rode out looking for two wanted men."

"I'd bet I am, preacher," said Shod. "But there's no time for introductions." He nodded toward the sound of gunfire and roaring hooves sweeping in from the desert floor. "If you're staying here, you better find yourself a spot and start shooting. I've got to get some shooting gear back to some people who're waiting for me."

"Oh, of course!" said the reverend, already moving toward the rear door. "I'm leaving, too. I'm going to the hotel to defend my granddaughter and her baby. I pray that God be with you, sir."

"Much obliged," said Shod. "I'll take all the help I can get." He watched the reverend leave, then hurriedly threw open some larger drawers beneath the cabinet as fighting erupted on the street.

Lying prone behind the water trough, Maria returned fire, watching the swell of man, horse and dust grow larger, the sound of their gunfire growing louder. She saw the wagon emerge out of the dust, streaks of fire flashing like lightning from the Gatling gun barrels. "Can't I do something?" Parker Dennison asked, huddled beside her, shouting above the terrible din rolling toward them.

"Stay alive," Maria shouted in reply without turning her face away from her rifle stock. She could see Sam lying behind the dead horse twenty yards away. Bullets had torn chunks of raw meat from the horse's carcass and sliced across its upper side, exposing pink flesh beneath its dark skin. "Sam!" she shouted. "Get out of there! Hurry! You can't stay there!"

The Ranger barely caught Maria's voice through the roar of battle. But as soon as he looked around and caught a glimpse of her behind the trough, he scooted back a few feet from the dead horse, then rolled to his feet in a flat-out run. Maria gave him covering fire until he came diving in beside her. Their eyes met for a second, long enough for each to understand that the other was all right. Then the Ranger said to her and Dennison, "You can't stay here, either. Get over to a store building! I'll cover you!"

"No!" said Maria. "You go. I'll cover you!"

The Ranger saw that this was not the time to argue. In seconds, the *comadrejas* would be in the main street. "Come on, we'll all go together!" he said.

They raced as one to the door of the town barbershop. The Ranger was heartened to see rifle and pistol barrels firing from upper windows and doorways along the boardwalk. But amid the firing, he also saw bodies draped over the edges of two of those windows; and in more than one doorway he saw townsmen spin in place, their guns flying from their hands as bullets ripped through them. On the boardwalk out front of the barbershop, the Ranger turned and fired while Maria and Parker Dennison lunged through the door. Upon seeing his boss enter the barbershop, Sturgen came running in a crouch, one hand holding his derby hat down on his head. Bullets nipped at the dirt behind his heels. "Get inside, quick!" the Ranger said, giving him an extra shove as Sturgen raced past him.

Once inside the barbershop, the Ranger closed the doors and bolted them. "Dennison, can you shoot?"

"Yes, I can shoot," said the lawyer, all haughtiness gone from his voice. "Just give me something with bullets in it."

The Ranger raised his Colt from his holster and pitched it to him, the roar of horses' hooves vibrating beneath the floor. Before turning to the window with his rifle, the Ranger heard Sturgen say in a meek voice, "May I also have a pistol?"

"Sturgen, have you ever fired a gun?" Dennison asked, taking position at the other corner of the window.

"Oh, certainly, sir! As a child, that is," said Sturgen.

"Here, take this," said the Ranger, lifting another, smaller pistol from the holster tucked up under his arm. He pitched it to Sturgen, then turned back to the widow. "Here they are!" he said, raising the rifle in his hands and slamming the butt of it into the window, breaking it, then firing into the oncoming riders almost before the shattered glass hit the floor.

Sturgen looked at the pistol in his hands as if it had just dropped out of the sky. He looked around at the scene before him as if it might all be a wild, strange dream. But when a barrage of bullets from the Gatling gun swept across the barbershop, Sturgen seemed to snap out of a trance. Dropping down and taking cover behind the window, he fired shot after shot until the pistol clicked on an empty chamber. Without being asked, the Ranger pitched his gun belt to the floor beside him. Sturgen looked up in thanks, then snatched bullets from the belt and reloaded.

From the hotel window above the street, Reverend Bullard fired repeatedly at the oncoming riders, gasping as he saw one of his shots lift a man from his saddle and send him sprawling in the street. As soon as the old minister had returned from the mercantile store, he'd put April and the baby into a corner of the room, snatched the mattress from the bed and thrown it over them for protection. But now that the fighting had commenced, he caught a glimpse of April moving in beside him, the Ranger's big rifle in her hands. The reverend gave her a startled look. "Where's the baby?" he asked.

"The baby is fine, Grandfather," said April, extending the big Swiss rifle, resting it on the window ledge.

Reverend Bullard gave a quick glance at the mattress, realizing she had left the baby well-wrapped and protected. Then he looked at April and grabbed the big rifle before she had a chance to fire it. "That big-bore rifle will knock you across the room, child!" he said. "Here, give it to me. You take this one!" They switched rifles and began firing. Below them, the *comadrejas* filled the street. The reverend and his granddaughter followed the frontmost riders until they saw them reach and overrun the position where Frank and Bob Abbadele had first taken cover and returned their fire.

"Lord have mercy on us," Reverend Bullard whispered, seeing what looked like a swarm of ants pour over the street and boardwalk and continue on toward the livery barn.

Inside the livery barn, where Tommy Walsh and Lenbow Decker had gone to get their rifles, they had joined two armed townsmen and taken up good firing positions from the hayloft doors above and through a wide crack in the front doors. The four men pounded out round upon round of deadly rifle fire. Out front, the main body of *comadrejas* was forced to swing in a wide circle rather than confront the heavy rifle fire head-on. Even the onrush of the Gatling gun was slowed down when a bullet killed the wagon driver and one of the gun operators had to leave his spot to get the team of horses under control.

From the hotel window, the reverend saw several riders drop from their ragged saddles and run from door to door along the storefronts. The old minister shouted, "Watch the door!"

April swung the big rifle around toward

the door and fired just as it began to swing open. The bullet struck the door frame an inch from the side of Toot Abbadele's head as he hurried inside.

Toot let out a sharp yelp and grabbed his ear. "Jesus! April!" he shrieked, a rifle hanging in his right hand.

"Oh, Toot! Oh my God, no! I've shot you!" April cried out, seeing him cup his hand to his ear. She dropped the rifle and ran to him.

"No, I'm all right," said Toot, plucking a splinter from his ear. Blood ran from a graze across his shoulder. His cheeks were smudged with rifle smoke. He slammed the door as April threw her arms around him. "Quick, let's barricade this door. They're all over the place!"

"Oh, Toot," April sobbed, still clinging to him. "You came here to be with us!"

"I'll never leave you, April," Toot sobbed in reply. "I realized . . . I'd rather *die* with you than try to *live* without you." Toot hugged her to him as he and the reverend moved to a heavy oaken dresser and shoved it against the door.

"Hurry," said the reverend, shoving the dresser, "or you'll be dead either way." The sound of boots and bare feet resounded on the floor below them, through the sound of shattered glass and broken furniture. The three moved quickly, piling furniture against the bottom half of the door, then moving back away from it as the boots and bare feet thundered up the stairs.

In the hallway, a dozen *comadrejas* ran from room to room, testing the doors, kicking them open and firing shots in every direction. Upon seeing their door tested, then lunged against to force it open, April, Toot and Reverend Bullard fired as one. Their bullets ripped through the door above the furniture. From the hall came a scream of pain. Then return fire ripped through the door, causing the furniture to jump with the impact. "You sonsabitches!" Toot Abbadele raved in anger, hearing the baby scream in terror beneath the mattress in the corner. But even amid the heavy fire, the *comadrejas* continued to pound against the door, scooting the heavy furniture an inch at a time until one managed to shove himself halfway inside the room, firing with a pistol.

Toot Abbadele made quick work of the man, putting one shot through his forehead. But no sooner had the man slumped dead in the partially open door than four *comadrejas* shoved his body into the room, opening the door farther before they charged in, shrieking and firing wildly. A shot hit the reverend high in his right shoulder, causing him to drop his rifle and fall to the floor before catching himself on one knee. Paying no regard to the shoulder wound, he immediately reached for the rifle, but the gripping pain stopped him. April snatched the rifle. Two *comadrejas* advanced on the reverend, both of them grinning until the big Swiss rifle exploded in April's hands. One flew backward in a spray of blood; the other turned his pistol away from Reverend Bullard toward April. She screamed, but it was not in concern for her own life. Across the room, she saw a *comadreja* aiming his pistol toward the mattress in the corner where he heard the shrill cry of the terrified baby.

Toot Abbadele shot the man aiming the pistol at April; then, seeing the one aiming at the mattress, he spun and fired. His shot hit the *comadreja* above the ear, splattering blood and brain matter high up the wall.

"The baby!" April screamed, running to the mattress and throwing it to the side. Seeing that the baby was not injured but was badly frightened, she grabbed it up from the floor and held it against her.

Toot fired again; this time his rifle shot a *comadreja* in the gut as the man came charging in, firing wildly, letting out a loud war cry. The shot picked him up and sent him slamming backward into another gunman. The two flew out of the room and tumbled along the hall. Toot ran to the door and slammed it shut, seeing other *comadrejas* hurrying down the stairs. "They're leaving!" he shouted. Then his eyes went to the Reverend Bullard, who sat slumped on one knee, his left hand pressed against his wounded right shoulder. "Reverend! Are you all right?" he cried out.

"I'll . . . be all right," the old minister said haltingly. From outside the window, firing raged from the direction of the livery barn. "Get me over to the window. We've got to help them down there."

Toot helped Bullard to the window and propped his rifle out across the ledge. Looking down at the far end of the street, he saw that the fiercest fighting had concentrated on the livery barn. He gave a quick glance to the spot where his brothers Frank and Bob had been earlier, but there was no sign of them. *Good, they might both still be alive,* he thought, taking a breath of relief. "Can you shoot, Reverend?" he asked.

"Yes, I can shoot," said Bullard, his right arm hanging limp, useless. "I can't promise I'll hit anything, but at least they'll know they're under fire."

"Good enough," said Toot, cocking the rifle in Bullard's hand.

April stepped in beside Toot, holding the side of the baby's head pressed to her, her hand and her breast shielding the tiny ears from the sound of the gunfire as much as possible. The baby's shrill cries of terror had lessened a little. In April's other hand she held a bloody pistol she'd picked up from the floor where one of the dead *comadrejas* had dropped it. "I can still shoot," she said with determination. "They haven't killed me yet."

Chapter 17

The main body of *comadrejas* on the street concentrated their fire toward the livery barn, causing a brief lull in the fighting at the barbershop where the Ranger, Maria, Dennison and Sturgen had taken cover and put up strong resistance. Dead *comadrejas* lay strewn out front of the shop and along the boardwalk. A man's body lay draped across the large window ledge, his knees on the boardwalk, his face and arms dangling in broken glass on the shop floor. Noting the attack had turned to the livery barn, the Ranger hurried over to a bullet-riddled barber chair, threw it aside and helped Maria to her feet. She stood up, shaking splinters and broken glass from her shirt. Seeing a trickle of blood run down her forehead, Sam wiped it away with his thumb and, seeing it was only a scratch, dismissed it.

"Are you all right?" he asked, looking Maria up and down, at the same time keeping his rifle turned toward the broken window, ready for anything.

"*Sí*, I am all right," said Maria. "What about you?"

"I'll do," said the Ranger. Behind them, Parker Dennison stood up, reloading the Colt with bullets he'd taken off a dead *comadreja*. At his feet, the dead man lay in a wide puddle of blood. "What about you, lawyer?" Sam asked, looking over at Dennison.

Staring down at the body, Dennison spit on its back, then kicked its blank, lifeless face before answering. "Yes, I'm fit. I think these scoundrels have begun to realize they made a terrible mistake attacking us." Although the lawyer's voice sounded steady and under control, the Ranger noticed that his hands shook so badly he had difficulty loading the pistol. Outside, the firing continued to rage.

"It's not over yet," said Sam. He turned to Sturgen, who stood slumped, holding the pistol Sam had given him with both hands, as if it weighed a ton. "What about you," Sam asked him. "Are you all right?"

Sturgen nodded, then said, "But I will need some bullets if we're to continue defending this position."

"They're hitting the livery barn hard. We need to get out of here," said Sam, looking out through the broken window.

"Good idea," said Dennison. "But where will we get some horses?"

"Beg your pardon, sir," Sturgen said to Dennison, "but I don't think the Ranger means we're *leaving* town. I believe he meant we're going to seek a better position."

Dennison's face reddened. "Of course. I knew that, Sturgen!" he snapped. "I simply meant, where would we get horses if we . . ." His words trailed. "Damn it, man! Never mind what I meant! I know we need to help the men defending the livery barn!" He turned to face the Ranger. "What do you have in mind?"

"I've seen shooting coming from the second floor of the hotel and the mercantile store," said the Ranger. "Either position puts the *comadrejas* in a cross fire." As he spoke, Sam levered a round into the rifle chamber and stepped toward the back door. Maria walked beside him.

"Which one should we go to?" asked Dennison, close behind the two, followed by Sturgen, who kept an eye toward the firing out in the street.

"I heard my Swiss rifle firing from the hotel," said Sam, "but I didn't see it doing much good. I need to get my hands on it and do some real damage to these buzzards."

"Then we're with you, Ranger," said Dennison, quickening his step as they moved out into the alleyway, looking cautiously in both directions. Two dead *comadrejas* lay facedown in the alley. Ten feet away from one of them lay a dead townsman, the back of his head blown away, a big walker Colt lying near his dead fingertips. "Why haven't they kept this entire stretch of buildings surrounded?" Dennison asked, almost in a whisper.

"The desert weasels are not the smartest bunch in the world. They're just common cowards, thugs and murderers," the Ranger replied, the three of them moving along with caution. "They looted the stores and the bank. Now they want the horses in the livery barn. That's all they're thinking about right now. They probably figure we're dead by now."

"Desert weasels?" said Dennison.

"*Comadreja* means weasel in Spanish," said Maria. "*Comadrejas del desierto*. They are desert weasels."

"Hear that, Sturgen?" Dennison said over his shoulder. "We're getting ourselves a Spanish lesson in the bargain." Then he said to Maria, "This is madness. They've sacked the whole town. What if we negotiated with them, maybe gave them all the horses in the livery barn? Would that stop this and get them to leave?"

"You cannot negotiate with the *comadrejas*," said Maria. "They are animals. They do not want to negotiate. They kill because they are killers, nothing more. Killing and stealing is all they know how to do."

"Well, isn't that just dandy," said Parker Dennison, looking all around for any sign of the enemy. "Hear that, Sturgen? They kill because it's all they know how to do."

"Yes, sir. I heard, sir," said Sturgen dutifully, keeping an eye on the alleyway behind them as the fighting roared out in the street.

"Hurry up," the Ranger said to them in a hushed tone, moving along in a crouch, his rifle cocked and ready. "We don't want to get caught out in the open like this."

His words caused Dennison and Sturgen to quicken their pace. All four of them moved along in a slight trot, crouched low and staying close to the backs of the buildings until they reached the open rear door of the hotel. The Ranger crept inside first, stepping over the body of a dead *comadreja*, then the body of the hotel clerk. They slipped quietly along the hall to the front stairs, then hurried upward until they neared the second floor. There the Ranger halted everyone behind him with a raised hand, hearing the sound of labored breathing along the second floor hallway. "Wait here," he whispered. With the rifle pointed ahead of him, he eased upward the next two steps and crept along the shadowed hallway toward the door riddled with bullet holes. On the other side of the door, he heard rifle and pistol fire, the big Swiss rifle sounding louder than the other two guns.

Against the wall sat a wounded *comadreja,* both his hands pressed tight against his stomach, blood oozing between his fingers. The Ranger eased forward and kicked a pistol out of the dying man's reach, then motioned for the others to join him. As Maria led Dennison and Sturgen along the hallway, the Ranger stooped down and looked the *comadreja* over for any other weapons. The man wheezed deeply and said in a growl, "What are jou . . . staring at, jou pig? If I . . . could shoot jou, I . . . already would have. What I can . . . get to my gun, I will shoot jou. If jou are smart, jou will kill me."

"Fair enough," said the Ranger, reaching down, aiming his rifle barrel at the center of the man's forehead.

"Wait," said Parker Dennison, stepping in beside the Ranger. "Let me see if I can get some idea of how we might reason with these people. Maybe we *can* negotiate some sort of peaceful settlement to this after all." He gave Maria a confident glance. Stooping down beside the man, he leaned in close and said, "What if we could get the doctor over here and save you?"

The *comadreja* offered a weak, dirty grin. "Save me? Jou would save me for to hang, or to go to the prison . . . and rot there?" He let his attention go for a second to the sound of gunfire coming from the direction of the livery barn, as if relishing the idea of all the death and destruction going on there. "Why I would want for jou . . . to save me?"

"What if you wouldn't have to hang or go to prison, though?" said Dennison. "What if I said I could be your lawyer, represent you in court? You and all your friends, if we can work this out."

"No . . ." The man's words trailed as he shook his bowed head slowly. "It is better . . . that we kill all of jou."

"But why?" Dennison shrugged.

"Because we hate jou so much," the man growled.

"See? Now let's get going," said the

Ranger, nudging Dennison back from the bloody *comadreja*. "We're wasting precious time here."

"One second, please," said Parker Dennison. Leaning even closer, he said to the dying *comadreja,* "You don't mean that. I can't believe you mean that. Surely you have some humanity, some decency —"

"Ayiee!" Dennison's words turned into a cry of pain. The Ranger acted quickly, pulling the trigger on his rifle and nailing the *comadreja*'s head backward against the wall. The *comadreja* had slipped a dagger from one bloody sleeve, raised it and plunged it into Dennison's shoulder halfway to the hilt. From his other sleeve, he'd also pulled a knife; this one was on its way toward Dennison's belly when the Ranger shot him. The man slid down the rest of the way to the floor, a smear of blood on the wall behind his head.

"Jesus! He stabbed me!" Dennison said, stunned by the sight of the knife protruding from the front of his shoulder. "I don't understand this. What kind of people are these?"

"These are *comadrejas,* Dennison. Do you *understand* that?" said the Ranger, helping the startled lawyer to his feet. Dennison stood on wobbly legs. "They are cowards, backstabbers, murderers, every single one of them. Don't try to figure them out. Just shoot them. Now come on. Let's get you looked at." He helped Dennison toward the sound of gunfire on the other side of the bullet-riddled door. "April! Reverend Bullard!" he called out, hoping they would hear him through the gunfire. "It's us — the Ranger and Maria. We've got the lawyer and his helper with us. The lawyer's hurt. Don't shoot, we're coming in!"

Helping Dennison along the hall, the Ranger saw the door open a crack, then open wider. He was surprised to see Toot Abbadele come quickly out into the hall to help him with Parker Dennison. "Damn, this is a mess," said Toot. "I've got the reverend in there. He's wounded, too."

Inside the room, the Ranger let Dennison sit down on the floor. Maria went to April and her grandfather at the window, checking the old minister's wound. Toot held Dennison in place on the floor so the Ranger could pull the knife blade out of the lawyer's shoulder. They worked quickly, the Ranger taking the bandanna from around his neck and pressing it against Dennison's bleeding shoulder. "That's all we can do for now, so hold tight," Sam told the gasping lawyer. Dennison rocked back and forth in an effort to still the pain. "Where's your brothers, Toot?" Sam asked, already walking away from Dennison to the window.

Toot stayed right beside him. "I'm not sure, Ranger, but I hope to God they got away before these bastards overran them." He raised the rifle to his shoulder as he spoke. "From the sound of all the firing coming from the barn, I'm thinking maybe they made it there someway." He began firing the rifle.

Looking down at the street, seeing dead townsmen lying along the boardwalks and in doorways, the Ranger winced. Flames rolled up the side of the telegraph office. At the livery barn, the fighting continued furiously. Reaching down, the Ranger took the big Swiss rifle from Reverend Bullard's hand. "The best thing I can do is put that Gatling gun out of commission before it chops that barn to the ground."

Maria moved the wounded minister back out of the way and sat him beside Dennison on the floor. The Ranger adjusted the sights on the big Swiss rifle, then raised it to his shoulder, aiming it into the thick of the fighting. But then he lowered it and took a breath. "This won't do. I've got to get above that gun wagon to do what needs doing."

"Whatever you are getting ready to do," Maria said with resolve, "I am going with you."

"Not this time, Maria. I'm going up along the roof line. I just need one good shot." He turned and headed for the door. "You stay here, help Toot keep up the firing. The men in that barn need all the help they can get." He stopped at the door long enough to ask, "Have you seen any sign of the bounty hunter down there?"

"No," said Toot, still firing from beside the window frame, "I haven't seen him."

"He was in the mercantile store," said Reverend Bullard. "He said he had to get back to the doctor's office. But things began to happen so fast, I don't know if he got the chance." As the minister spoke, Maria stepped over to the door beside Sam, to lock it behind him once he'd left.

"I hope he made it," said the Ranger. "We need him." He opened the door a short distance, checked the hall, then slipped out and closed the door behind him. Maria bolted the door and returned to the window, making the sign of the cross while she whispered a short prayer under her breath.

Swan Hendricks ventured a look through the curtained front window of the doctor's office. Clare-Annette, hovering at her shoulder, asked, "What can you see out there? Do you see the big fellow?"

Swan didn't answer at first. She studied the terrible scene of bodies strewn along the streets as if lying in the afterpath of some killing storm. She studied the large group of armed horsemen and men afoot crowded in a half circle around the livery barn. Back and forth along the street she saw several *comadrejas* who had left the fighting at the barn and were running amuck, looting, shooting at anyone or anything that moved. "No, I don't see him," she said at length, easing the curtains back together. "Let's face it, he's not coming back. He might be dead." Just beyond the window, a long war cry and the sound of running feet moved along the boardwalk. The two women held their breath for a second.

"Why haven't they broken in here?" Clare-Annette asked, whispering in a trembling voice lest she be heard through the thin walls that separated them from the raging madness beyond the bolted door.

Seeing how badly shaken Clare-Annette

had become, Swan drew the frightened woman into her arms, comforting her. "Shhh now, take it easy. We're doing all right so far. Who knows? They might miss us altogether." Looking around nervously as if searching for anything the looters might want, she added, "There's not much here to interest them. Maybe we'll manage to sit this out." She looked past Clare-Annette's shoulder into the doctor's tired, worried eyes, knowing full well that at any second the door could crash open and their lives be taken quickly, almost effort-lessly.

In the other room, the wounded judge babbled insanely, like some lunatic out of control. Swan said, "He's not going to get loud and give us away is he, Doc?"

"No, I don't think so," said the doctor, speaking softly. "I gave him something to keep him from drifting off to sleep. If he goes to sleep right away, I'm afraid he'll never wake up." The doctor's fingertips were tinted red from a thin sheen of blood.

"That poor man," Swan whispered, still holding Clare-Annette in her arms. "If he lives, what will ever happen to the hole in his head? I mean, will it ever heal?"

"To some extent, yes, it will," the doctor whispered, managing to talk while keeping one ear turned to the shooting and yelling outside his small world of mending and healing. "The bone matter will replace a lot of itself. Of course, there will always be an indentation there, a soft spot, if you will, like that of an infant, you see?"

"That's enough, Doc," said Swan. "I get a bad image of all that."

"Yes, of course, I understand," said Dr. Lovedale. He stood silently staring at the front door, as if preparing himself for what would come at any second.

But no more than a second later, Swan let out a short gasp as the silence was broken by a loud banging on the door. "Oh my God!" she cried out, hugging Clare all the more tightly against her.

"Doctor!" said Shod, banging harder on the wooden door. "It's me, the bounty hunter! Open up, quick!"

"It's him!" Swan squealed with surprise and delight. Turning Clare-Annette loose, she hurried to the door, loosened the bolt and pulled the door open. "It's about time you —" She stumbled backward, the big bounty hunter shoving her out of the way just in time. A bullet whistled past her face and thumped into the wall across the room.

"They've seen me," said Shod, ducking

inside and kicking the door shut behind him. A bullet sliced through the door and spun past the doctor's chin like an angry wasp. "Everybody down!" Shod demanded. As he spoke, he set a small wooden crate on the floor and gave it a slight shove with his boot as he drew his pistol and cocked it. Turning to the door, grabbing the handle, he shouted, "Stay down — here goes!"

On the street, three *comadrejas* raced toward the door to bust it down. But they slid to a stunned halt ten feet away when the door flew open and in it stood the big bounty hunter, his pistol blazing as rapidly as he could cock and fire it. The frontmost *comadreja* let out a war cry, raising his rifle, but his cry was cut short when Shod's first shot put a dark hole where his left eye had been and sent his brain matter flying in a fine red mist out the back of his head. The second shot sent one of his companions spinning like a top until he bored downward on the hard ground. As Shod slammed the door after the third shot, the last of the three attackers went crawling away, screaming, a hand trying to press back a thick pouring of blood from his belly.

"They know we're here," said Shod.

"They'll be coming!" He punched three bullets from his belt and hastily replaced the ones he'd just fired. "Did you find us any guns?" Swan asked, breathless.

Shod nodded. "Yep, they're already loaded." Reaching inside his vest, he pulled up a big Colt pistol and pitched it to Swan. Then he asked Dr. Lovedale, "Is the judge dead or alive?"

"He's alive," said the doctor.

"Can you carry him?" asked Shod, pulling up another pistol and pitching it to the doctor. Then, from his trouser pocket, he produced a third, which he tossed into Clare-Annette's eager hands.

"Carry him? Well, I . . ." The doctor stalled, considering it for a second.

Seeing the urgency in Shod's face and voice, Swan cut in, "We can carry him. What do you want?"

"Get him and get out the back door . . . fast!" said Shod, stepping over, spreading the curtains and looking outside. At the livery barn, the battle raged on, giving no notice to what was happening a block away at the doctor's office. But across the street, three *comadrejas* stood huddled around the man with the blood flowing from his belly. From his spot on the ground, the man raised a bloody hand long enough to point his finger toward the doctor's office.

"What about you?" Swan asked. "We're not going to leave without —"

"Get the judge and get out!" Shod ordered. "I'll be along! Get through the rear of the hotel. Somebody's making a stand from there."

Across the street, he saw a half dozen *comadrejas* gathering, looking his way. "Here they come!" he shouted at Swan. "Now get the hell out of here!"

"All right, all right! You don't have to shout!" Swan grabbed Clare-Annette by her arm, pulling her along. "Come on, Clare, Doc! Let's get that furniture off the back door! Doc, you pick up the judge. I'll help you with him!"

"This could kill him," said the doctor.

"This could," said Swan, hurrying him and Clare-Annette along. "They *will* for sure!"

Shod stared grimly out the window, hearing the women and Dr. Lovedale toss furniture aside in the other room. *You don't have to shout . . . ?* He managed to smile to himself, recalling the woman's words. *Strange thing for her to say at a time like this,* he thought. He felt the tense seconds tick away inside his head. Yet he noted that his hand was calm and steady as he pulled a thin black cigar from his pocket, bit off the tip and lit it as more *comadrejas* gathered and began moving across the street, spreading out as they came. He took a deep draw on the cigar and let the smoke out slowly, savoring it, as if noticing for the first time the richness of a fine nickel cigar. Reaching down, he drew a long skinning knife from his boot well and gripped it firmly in one hand, his big Colt in his other. "All right, weasels. You want a fight? Come and get it."

Chapter 18

The Ranger climbed upward from a back window to the roof of the hotel. He hurried along the back edge of the roof line, his big Swiss rifle in one hand, his Colt in the other. In the alleyway below, he saw dead townsmen and *comadrejas* strewn about like bloody rag dolls in their various poses of death. He saw the doctor and the two young women run across the alley from the rear of the doctor's office, the three of them sharing the burden, carrying equally the limp, pale judge in their arms. He wondered if the bounty hunter was dead, since he saw no sign of him. But there was no time to spare finding out right now. He continued on, feeling the heat of the roof through his boot soles.

From the direction of the livery barn, the Gatling gun chattered relentlessly, the constant pounding of it causing a vibration beneath his burning feet. He traveled the roofs as far as he could, leaping across from one to the other until the procession of buildings stopped. He looked at the wide alley running between the mercantile and a restaurant, knowing he couldn't make such a leap. "This is as close as you get," he said to himself. Crouching, he hurried upward to the facade overlooking the street and sank down against it for a moment, checking the sights on the big Swiss rifle. He heard heavy gunfire erupt from the direction of the doctor's office. He was thankful that the doctor and the women had gotten out safely, yet it dawned on him that the bounty hunter might have stayed behind to buy them some time. Whatever the case, there was nothing he could do about it now.

Taking two additional rifle cartridges from his pocket and placing them between the first two fingers of his left hand, the Ranger eased up to the edge of the facade and laid the rifle barrel over the bend of his left arm, locking his cheek to the stock to steady it. He adjusted his body slightly as he honed his sight onto the gun wagon. Watching the tip of his front sight travel up the gun operator's back, he reminded himself that while this wasn't a hard shot — not at a distance of less than seventy yards — there were a lot of lives riding on it.

He took a deep breath and held it, settling in for the shot, easing his finger back on the trigger. As soon as he killed one gun operator, he knew another would take the man's place. The trick would be to kill this operator, then take out the gun itself. He knew that once the *comadrejas* heard this first shot, all hell would break loose in his direction. So be it, he thought, feeling the impact of the shot, the big gun slamming back against his shoulder. Seeing the gun operator fall forward and tumble to the ground, Sam worked fast. He jerked the rifle chamber open, slipped in one of the cartridges from between his fingers, closed the rifle chamber and settled it for the next shot. This one had to be perfect.

He took another deep breath and held it, feeling the rifle grow dead still, his front sight locked on its target, a perfect aim, even as the *comadrejas* turned their attention upward toward him, firing and cursing wildly. The Ranger did not so much as flinch as a blast of splinters from the edge of the wooden facade nipped at the side of his neck. Bullets sliced the air on either side of his head, reminding him of the thin tightwire of chance he'd placed himself upon. Well . . . He was old enough to die, he thought, feeling the rifle kick again. Hadn't he realized coming up here that this would probably be the last thing he'd ever do? *Maybe,* he thought, seeing most of the *comadrejas* turn their guns from the barn toward him.

Before jerking himself back out of the gunfire, he had to see what good he'd done. They would be upon him soon enough, in force, too many for him to handle. Before he died, he had to see for himself. Gazing hard at the Gatling gun, he saw that the tall metal crank which had stood there before was now missing. He thought he'd caught a glimpse of it blow away when he'd pulled the trigger. As bullets pounded the facade, he pulled back and dropped down on the roof, offering himself a thin, tight smile. If there was ever a single shot worth his life, that one was it, he thought. Now the rest of the town had a chance. That was worth dying for, wasn't it? He asked himself that question as he laid the big rifle down and drew his pistol.

He could make a run for it, but running never was his style. And of course it was worth it, he told himself. He'd made his life's work out of trying to somehow make things better, give someone else a better chance . . . righting some wrong that only he could right. It better have been worth it, he reminded himself, because any second now the enemy would be swarming over the edge of that roof like ants. Any second now, whatever good or bad he'd done in life, he'd better be prepared to account for. Any second now, whatever he might have, or might not have —

God almighty! His thoughts were interrupted not by a swarm of *comadrejas,* but rather by a hard upward blast that actually lifted his hat from his head and caused him to flatten himself to the roof to keep from being hurled off it. His eyes went to his left, in the direction of the blast, just in time to see smoke, fire and building material shoot upward over a hundred feet and spread out as it rained down, covering the entire town. He huddled against the facade, both arms wrapped around his head, hearing chunks of flaming debris fall hard all around him. As soon as the deadly rain dissipated, he sprang up, bracing himself with both hands on the facade, and looked down at the far end of the street. Where the street made a slight turn, he saw that the doctor's office was no longer there, nor were most of the two buildings that once stood on either side of it. Along a sixty-foot stretch of boardwalk, all that remained of the three buildings was a black hole filled with swirling smoke and fire.

Down on the street, the Ranger saw the *comadrejas* running in circles, confused, without direction. He breathed deep. This thing wasn't over for him after all. From the livery barn came renewed firing. This time, without the Gatling gun and all those other rifles keeping them pinned down, the men inside the barn picked their targets with accuracy. *Comadrejas* fell like blades of grass to a sickle. The Ranger fired down on the confused men with his Colt, giving the livery barn all the support fire he had to offer. One of the *comadrejas* on horseback managed to rally the men around himself and the abandoned gun wagon. But just as it appeared that he and the others had regrouped and were about to launch a renewed attack on the livery barn, the Ranger saw the big bounty hunter step into the street from between two buildings a half block away and touch the end of his cigar to a six-inch wick on the end of a bundle of dynamite sticks.

"Good move, Mr. Jefferson Eldridge Shadowen," the Ranger said to himself. He ducked down against the facade again and braced himself as Shod drew back and hurled the lit bundle of dynamite in a long, high arc toward the bunched-up group of *comadrejas*. The dynamite landed on the street in the midst of the gathered *comadrejas,* sending them running wildly in every direction, trying to get away from the coming blast. Some of them made it; many of them didn't. The building beneath the Ranger seemed to rise up off the ground and sway backward a little with the impact of the explosion. The Ranger felt his bones ache beneath the terrible concussion of earth and manmade explosive.

For a moment, he covered his head with both arms, feeling and hearing clods of dirt and chunks of horse and man dropping around him with a strange sound on the metal and tar roof. No more than five feet from him, a naked human leg hit the roof and rolled with a soft flopping sound until it disappeared over the edge and fell to the alley below. The Ranger stood up as soon as the air cleared and immediately looked down on the street, his pistol already cocked, ready to resume firing. In the middle of the street lay a large round hole left by the blast. All around the hole lay parts of bodies and bits of boots, shoes and clothing. Farther away from the hole lay whole bodies in twisted positions, man and horse alike entwined in a dance of death. But the Ranger had no time to survey the scene closely. He aimed and fired at the fleeing gun wagon as it sped along the street, headed out of town.

Comadrejas ventured out of whatever cover they'd managed to find. Most of the ones on horseback fled, firing back over their shoulders as they went. The ones afoot ran for their lives, rifle fire from the livery barn nipping at their heels. One of the leaders, still mounted, rode out of an alley waving his hands back and forth and shouting, "Don't jou see, people? We surrender! We only want peace! War is wrong! Let us all live together in peace!" But before he'd finished speaking, he saw the second bundle of dynamite sailing through the air. Spurring his horse hard, he raced away, rifle shots from the livery barn still filling the air around him.

The Ranger ducked down again. This time he covered both ears with his palms. The explosion rocked the building as badly as before. But this time Sam was better prepared. As soon as the air cleared itself of falling debris, he sprang up and took aim on the fleeing horseman as he sped farther away. But before firing, Sam saw some of the *comadrejas* on foot jump up from the ground and make a desperate charge toward Shod's position a half block away. Quickly, he swung his pistol in that direction and fired, sending one man sliding face forward on the hard ground.

From the livery barn, the rifle fire shifted at the same time, dropping many of the charging *comadrejas* before they could get to the bounty hunter.

The remaining desert weasels broke up and scattered in different directions, some heading out of town, others taking cover inside the looted stores along the boardwalk. Looking off at the rise of dust in the wake of the fleeing horde, the Ranger took a deep breath. The attack had been repelled. Now the remaining *comadrejas* had to be flushed out and dealt with. Sam picked up his big Swiss rifle and hurried back along the roof line, this time having to pick his way through the scattered remains left by the powerful blasts of dynamite.

Looking down as he hurried along the back edge of the roof line, Sam saw Pip Richards stepping out of a small tool shed, looking warily in both directions. "Pip," the Ranger called out, the sound of his voice startling the old whittler until he looked up and saw who it was. "Catch this rifle for me — I'm coming down."

"Lord, Ranger!" Pip looked back and forth again as if he might have missed something the first time. "Well, come on and drop it. I'll catch it." Cradling his arms out for the rifle, he continued speaking. "What in God's name was that explosion? It must have blown half the town away!"

"It saved our lives," the Ranger said, holding the Swiss rifle out and dropping it horizontally into Pip's waiting arms. "Glad to see you're all right."

"Who me? Ha," said Pip, examining the big rifle as the Ranger found a wooden access ladder on the corner of the building and climbed down it briskly. "I do the sensible thing for an old geezer like me to do — I hide and stay out of the way."

"That seems to work for you," the Ranger said, giving Pip a slight grin, reaching for the big rifle.

But Pip held on to it. "Mind if I carry it for you, Ranger? I'm going whichever direction you are. It might make a weasel think twice before shooting at me. They hardly tangle with an armed man, you know."

"Carry it, if it suits you," said the Ranger, already turning, walking toward the alley that led to the street. "It's loaded, so if a weasel sticks its head out, blow it off."

"I'll sure do it," said Pip, hefting the rifle, raising it slightly to his shoulder for practice as they walked out to the street.

At the large blast crater in the middle of the street, a few townsfolk had already begun to gather, most of them carrying a firearm of some sort. Others had already passed by and looked at the craters on their way toward the sound of gunfire from where some of the remaining *comadrejas* had taken cover. Stopping at the spot where the two craters overlapped, the Ranger looked to his right and saw Shod walking toward him from an alley, carrying the small wooden crate under his arm. To his left, the Ranger saw the livery barn doors open slowly. From inside came the Abbadeles and their men, along with a few townsmen who'd joined in the fracas. From that same direction came Sheriff Hugh Boggs, his shirt torn and smudged, his hat missing. "Here we go again," Sam whispered to himself.

"Gonna need this rifle, Ranger?" Pip asked, seeing the Abbadeles coming.

"No, Pip, hang on to it," said the Ranger. He took a searching look at the second floor hotel window and saw Maria lean forward enough to wave and let him know she and the others were all right. Dozens of bullet holes surrounded the hotel window.

"I swear, Ranger," said Pip Richards, looking all around with a forlorn expression. "It'll take us all day just to count up the dead."

"Don't start counting yet; it might change," said the Ranger, adjusting his big Colt in its holster as the Abbadeles walked up and stopped across the craters from him, twenty feet away. Looking down at the two-foot-deep center of the craters, Bob Abbadele whistled low. "Whooieee, that bounty hunter can put holes in the ground, can't he?"

Coming from the other direction, Shod slowed to a halt and said across the craters, "I can fill them, too." He stood poised, his hand near his pistol butt, ready to back whatever play the Ranger made.

The men began spreading slowly behind Bob, Dick and Frank Abbadele. But Frank raised his hand slightly, stopping them. Then he said to Shod, "My brother meant no offense, bounty hunter."

A tense silence passed. Then Frank continued. "The fact is, these holes couldn't have come at a better time. We was near out of ammo in the barn." A tired smile came to his face as he looked back and forth between the Ranger and the bounty hunter. "I was beginning to think you lawmen didn't like us anymore."

A short laugh rose and fell among the tired men. Shod managed to offer a trace of a smile himself. "Glad I could help," he said, raising his hand away from his gun butt and adjusting his spectacles on the bridge of his nose.

The Ranger saw a sort of a truce being offered by Frank Abbadele, and for the town's sake, he decided to let things cool between all parties. But he thought he should test the situation a bit just to make sure everyone was in agreement. Nodding at the Knox brothers, he said to Frank Abbadele, "Think you can spare a couple of your men long enough to help root out what's left of the weasels?"

Staring at the Ranger, getting an idea of what he was up to, Frank said to Terrence and Hirsh Knox, "Boys, what do you say? Feel like killing some more *comadrejas?*"

Hirsh Knox spoke up. "We sss-sur-sure wou-wou-would li-like to —"

"Jesus, shut up and come on, Hirsh," said Terrence, pulling his brother by the arm. "It'll be nightfall before you get it said." The two hurried off toward the sound of isolated gunfire at the far end of town.

"In case you're wondering, Ranger," said Frank, eyeing him closely, "the only thing that's changed between us is the time of day. I figure you wouldn't want it any other way. Neither would I. But for now, we got some serious business to settle with those desert weasel sonsabitches."

"That suits me," said Sam. "We need to get on them out there, not give them a chance to regroup and hit us here again. We should have seen that raid coming, but we were all too busy fighting one another. Now good people are dead because of it. I figure I owe this town something. I'm ready to go after the weasels."

The Abbadele men listened to the Ranger, but none of them showed any interest until Frank said, "You're right, Ranger. They caught us by surprise, but they'll play hell ever doing it again. Far as I'm concerned, we can check this town out, make sure it's rid of those vermin, then get on their trail and ride them straight to hell."

"The Gatling gun is their main weapon," said the Ranger. "It's broken now, so we need to get to them before they find a way to get it fixed."

"Yeah," said Frank. "What happened to that gun, anyway? One minute it was working fine, the next it wouldn't fire a lick."

The Ranger wasn't going to answer. But Pip reached down and picked up the broken metal handle and held it up, examining where a bullet from the Swiss rifle had snapped it off the gun. "Here's what happened to it. Somebody shot it off clean as a whistle!"

Standing across the crater, Frank Abbadele and his men walked around and took a closer look at the long handle. Standing beside the Ranger, he looked at him and said in earnest, "I'm obliged to whoever done it, whether I like it or not. Another few minutes, that gun would've cut us to ribbons."

"Had it not been for you and these men in the livery barn, the weasels would have torn this town to the ground and kept riding." The Ranger picked his rifle up from Pip's arm and held it at his side. "So I reckon we're all obliged to one another, whether we like it or not."

"I meant no offense, Ranger," said Frank Abbadele.

"None was taken," Sam replied.

Standing beside the Ranger, Pip Richards nudged him. "Uh-oh, look what's coming here!" He pointed toward the far edge of town.

All heads turned toward a slow-running horse, its slumped rider and the horse he led behind him. Guns cocked among the Abbadele men, but Frank spoke up. "Don't shoot, boys. It's Kirby!"

"Kirby?" said Terrence Knox, eyeing the

rider. "I hope that ain't his pa strapped across the saddle."

Upon hearing Kirby's name, Shod took a keen interest and stepped forward.

Everyone in the street watched the worn-out horses approach. Struggling hard, but past the point of being able to create any speed for themselves, the poor animals veered back and forth unsteadily, Kirby's boot heels batting the sides of his mount. Nearing the crater, Kirby slowed the animals to a halt, turning them sideways to Frank Abbadele and the men. Spilling from his saddle into Frank's arms, Kirby spoke in a dry, raspy voice, nearly delirious. "We outran them! Didn't we, Pa? Did you see that? They . . . never caught us . . . never outfought us." He faded out for a second.

The Knox brothers stepped in and helped Frank drag Kirby to the shade of a board-walk. Frank raised his hand from Kirby's side and saw the thick, dark blood on his palm. "Somebody find the doctor, quick!"

"Ain't . . . no hurry," Kirby said.

"Yes, there is, Kirby. You hang on, boy," Frank demanded. "You're going to be all right!"

"So damn thirsty . . . ," Kirby said, fading.

Beside Frank, Dick Abbadele shouted at

Sheriff Boggs. "Boggs, go get Kirby some water! Hurry it up!"

Sheriff Boggs just looked at him. Then he turned and said to the rest of the men, "You heard him. Go get some water, pronto!" Turning back to Dick Abbadele, Boggs said, "I've done my last stooping and fetching. From now on, I'm the sheriff here, doing my job the way I should have been all along." He shot the Ranger a glance. "If I'd been tending to business all along, maybe none of this would have happened."

"Is that a fact?" said Dick Abbadele. All three of the Abbadele brothers gave Boggs a cold stare.

"Yes, it is." Boggs looked worried, but he stood his ground. "That's how it's going to be from now on. This attack has changed everything, far as I'm concerned. There's good people dead that shouldn't be. From now on, I'm going to be too busy to fetch water. If something like this ever happens again, it won't be because I left the door open."

Frank Abbadele turned back to Kirby, his brothers doing the same, as if dismissing what Boggs had to say. "What happened, Kirby?" Frank asked.

Before trying to answer, Kirby looked out toward the two winded horses standing with their heads low, white froth glistening on them. "Get my pa . . . out of the sun! I don't want him . . . swelling up."

Frank Abbadele said over his shoulder, "Somebody get Lester down off that horse. Get him into some shade!"

As men scrambled to obey Frank's order, Sheriff Boggs stepped in and leaned down near Kirby. When Frank gave him a menacing look, Boggs said, "I'm the sheriff. I need to hear what he's got to say."

When a canteen appeared and was passed along until it came into Frank Abbadele's hands, Kirby drank from it, then tipped it until he poured a cool stream of water all over his burning face. "God, that . . . feels good," he said haltingly. Then, instead of trying to tell them anything, he gave a tired gesture toward Big Shod, then relaxed in Frank Abbadele's arms and closed his eyes. "Ask him. He was there."

"Hey, Kirby, wake up!" Frank shook him.

A thin smile came to Kirby's exhausted face. He said without opening his eyes, "We whupped them, didn't we, bounty man? Saved them gals?"

Shod stepped in and stooped down beside Frank Abbadele. "You sure did, Kirby. You and your pa. Those gals are fine.

They're around here somewhere. You hang on; they're coming. They'll be wanting to thank you themselves."

Still speaking with his eyes closed, Kirby said, "We all . . . just love them ole gals. We wouldn't let something happen to them . . . for nothing in the world."

"We know that, Kirby. We love you, too," said Swan Hendricks, having hurried along ahead of the doctor, Clare-Annette right behind her. She placed a hand on Kirby's forehead, and he opened his eyes a little, trying to focus on her. Clare-Annette laid her hand on his chest.

"Oh, Kirby," Clare-Annette said, struggling to keep her tears from spilling. "That was so brave and good, what you and your pa did for us. Nobody ever done anything so sweet and kind for us like that." She ran a hand beneath her eye. "That was the nicest thing ever!" She leaned down and kissed his pale lips.

Kirby tried to grin as he licked his lips slowly. "Bet had I . . . lived, I'd never had to pay for nothing in this town . . . ever again."

"That's right, Kirby," said Swan, leaning down, pressing her cheek to his, tears glistening in her eyes, too. "Never again."

"What about it . . . bounty man?" Kirby

asked, managing to open his eyes a bit more, staring up at Shod past Swan's cheek. "You ready . . . to take me back . . . to Texas, get that *re*-ward?" He raised his bloody, trembling hand to Shod.

Shod grasped his hand firmly in both of his. But for a second he couldn't answer. The big bounty hunter stared out for a moment across the desert floor. Finally, he said, "No, Kirby. I think Texas will just have to do without you." He looked back down, but in doing so noticed that Kirby's hand had stopped trembling and gone limp. "Much obliged, kid," Shod whispered, laying the dead outlaw's hand on his chest and patting it. He stood up and looked away again, this time adjusting his spectacles on the bridge of his nose as the old doctor came shouldering his way through the men gathered around Kirby Brooks.

"It's too late, Doc," said Frank Abbadele. "He's dead."

Shod saw Maria, Reverend Bullard, Parker Dennison and Sturgen coming along the street from the hotel. To the Ranger, he said quietly, "Sheriff Boggs is right. This weasel attack changes everything."

Chapter 19

April finished feeding the baby, wrapped it loosely in a thin blanket and laid it on the bed between two pillows. The baby slept peacefully. When Toot Abbadele stepped into the room, she raised her finger to her lips, keeping him quiet. Parker Dennison and Sturgen had joined the Abbadeles and accompanied them to the livery barn to prepare horses for the trail. Reverend Bullard sat in the corner of the room reading his frayed Bible. But upon seeing Toot enter, he stood stiffly, closed the book and reached for his black hat. "I believe I'll just walk over to the barn and see how things are going," he said. "Give you young people a chance to talk."

Whatever tension there was between the reverend and Toot had been suppressed by both of them in order to deal with the situation at hand. "Grandpa," said April, "don't try riding out of here with this posse. I mean it. We need some good men here to protect the town, too, don't forget."

"Child, I know my weaknesses as well as my strengths. I wouldn't ride with the posse, knowing I might slow them down and might put someone's life in danger." Holding his hat and Bible in one hand, he walked to the door. "I do want to see that young man with the affliction in his voice before he rides out of here, though."

"You mean Hirsh Knox?" said Toot in surprise. "Why do you want to see him, Reverend Bullard?" Toot caught himself, seeing the stern look on Bullard's face. Reminding himself that in spite of their unspoken truce he and the reverend were still not on the closest of terms, he added quickly, "I mean, if you don't mind my asking, sir."

Reverend Bullard replied, "That poor young man has suffered enough. It's time he comes to terms with himself and reconciles the tongue-twisting demon that plagues him." Reaching for the door, Reverend Bullard nodded good-bye.

"Whoa, Reverend," said Toot, not entirely sure what the old minister had in mind but realizing that whatever it was, it could go terribly wrong for him in a hurry, "I don't know what you think you might do or say to Hirsh Knox, but I best warn you, he will shoot a man for very little reason!"

"I realize that," said Bullard. "All the more reason why I need to reach out and enlighten him as to why he is in this demon's grasp." He walked out the door, closing it softly behind him as Toot tried to hurry forward and stop him.

"Wait, Reverend!" said Toot, trying to keep his voice low so as not to wake the baby.

April grabbed Toot's forearm. "Toot, you must let him go. The more you try stopping Grandpa from doing the Lord's work, the more stubborn he'll become."

"But Hirsh Knox won't listen to any religious nonsense — he'll kill him!" Toot said.

"Take my word, Toot," said April, giving a tug on his arm. "Nothing you or I say or do will stop Grandpa. All we can do is hope for the best."

Stepping over to the window and looking down, Toot and April watched the reverend walk toward the livery barn, side-stepping the last of the dead *comadrejas* as two men dragged the body away. "Jesus," Toot whispered. "I feel like I ought to do something to stop him."

"I know," said April. Then, as if dismissing her grandfather, she turned her face up to Toot and said, "Did you get your horse ready for the trail?"

"Yep," said Toot. "I was lucky; my horse was okay. Some of the horses were dead in their stalls from the Gatling gun getting through the wallboards."

There was a silent pause. Then Toot said, "Are you sure it's all right with you, me riding out with my brothers?"

"Yes . . . under these circumstances, of course," said April. "I know the town needs you. You have to go."

"Well," said Toot, "I could stay here if you want me to. There's going to have to be some good gunmen here to protect the town while the posse is out there."

"No," said April, drawing herself closer to him. "I've thought about it. Maybe this is the best way for you to break away from your brothers . . . riding with them one more time — this time to do something good. To save innocent people's lives."

Toot shook his head slowly in bemusement, wrapping his arms around her. "This has been the strangest thing. We were ready to lose one another over me riding with my brothers. Now here I go, riding with them with your blessing." He took a breath in contemplation, then said, "Want to hear something even more strange? In the livery barn, the Ranger,

346

Sheriff Boggs and my brother Bob, all three working together, helping the posse get their horses and gear ready for the trail."

April smiled and laughed softly under her breath. But then she stopped and looked into Toot's eyes. "Do be careful out there, Toot," she said.

"I will, April. I promise," he replied. "Now that I've got you and the baby depending on me, you can bet I won't be taking any unnecessary chances."

They were startled by the sound of two pistol shots ringing out close together down on the street. They both ducked slightly, even as they turned and looked down. "Jesus! what was that?" said Toot, holding April against him protectively.

On the street, Maria slumped to her knees, the red stripe of a bullet graze showing across the back of her shoulder. Her pistol smoked in her hand. Less than twenty feet away lay the *comadreja* she'd just shot, facedown, smoke rising from the exit wound on the back of his bloody head. Looking down from the hotel window, Toot said, "I better get down there." He looked around and noted Reverend Bullard's big pistol lying on a dresser. "Lock the door and keep that pistol at arm's length. It looks like we're going to have to give this town another going over before we leave."

The Ranger ran all the way from the livery barn, seeing Maria down on one knee with a bloody stripe across her shoulder. He held his pistol cocked and poised until he came to a halt and stooped down beside her. "Are you all right?" he asked, keeping his voice calm and even as his eyes scanned the street in both directions. Then he looked closely at the bullet graze. "That was too close for comfort," he said.

"*Sí*, it was," said Maria, both of them standing up, the Ranger assisting her. "But it is only a graze, I can tell." She arched her head around for a glimpse down her shoulder. "Luckily, I saw him make his move. He was playing dead, but I saw his hand go for the pistol lying near him in the dirt."

Two townsmen who'd been moving bodies off the street came up and stopped with frightened looks on their faces. "He was just waiting for us to come get him," said one man, shaking his head. "I swear, I never understand these weasels. They would rather die killing innocent people than they would live in peace."

"*Sí*," said Maria. "He might have slipped away unnoticed, but he preferred to lie in wait for his own death. What does the world do with such people as this?"

"Sooner or later it spits them out," said the Ranger. "Let's get you to the doctor, wherever he's at right now. Looks like you're not going to be riding posse. You'll have to stay here with Boggs and watch about the town." Thinking about it, he said, "Maybe that's for the best. I still don't have a lot of confidence in that drunken sheriff."

"He is sober now, Sam," said Maria, "and it appears he is trying to do his job. Let's give him the benefit of the doubt."

"That's hard to do when there are lives depending on that benefit," said the Ranger. They walked toward the board-walk out front of the harness shop, where Pip Richards stood watching the doctor attend to a wounded townsman.

"Anything I can do?" Toot Abbadele asked, running up beside the Ranger and Maria. "I didn't see the whole thing, but I saw you were hit and came running."

"*Gracias*," said Maria. "I am all right, just grazed." She looked at Toot and asked, "How are April and the baby?"

"They're both fine," said Toot. "April is more scared than she's letting on, but that might be for the best with these damned weasels still prowling around. It'll keep her from letting her guard down." He stopped short, seeing there was nothing he could do. "Well, I best get back up there till we leave, Ranger," he said. "I hate leaving her and the baby alone."

"Much obliged, Toot," said the Ranger. "You'll know when we're all leaving."

As Toot trotted back toward the hotel, the Ranger said to Maria, "It still feels odd, everybody acting like old friends. Wasn't that long ago we were all on the verge of throwing down on one another. This could take some getting used to."

"*Sí,*" said Maria. "And by the time we get used to it, everybody will be back at one another's throats." She shook her head, walking on.

At the boardwalk out front of the harness shop, Dr. Lovedale stood up from the wounded townsman, wiping his hands on a small white towel he'd carried over his shoulder. "Keep that arm in the sling now, Oscar, like I told you," he said, looking down, seeing the man struggle with the sling tied up around his neck. Then, looking at Maria as she and the Ranger walked up, the doctor said, "There seems to be no letup today." Nodding toward the *comadreja* in the street, he asked, "Is he dead?"

"Yes," said the Ranger.

"Good," said Dr. Lovedale. "I hate attending to them after what they've done here." He spit in the dirt along the front of the boardwalk. Then he asked, looking at Maria, "What about you, young lady? Are you hurt?"

"I caught a graze," said Maria, stepping up onto the boardwalk. She looked at Pip Richards, then said to the doctor as she began unbuttoning her blouse, "Perhaps we should step inside somewhere private?"

"Oh, of course," said Dr. Lovedale, reaching over and fumbling with the door of the harness shop. "There's no one in here. Let's step inside and take a look."

The Ranger waited on the boardwalk, looking back and forth along the street for any sign of remaining *comadrejas* lurking in the shadowed alleyways. Pip Richards stood beside him wearing a cracked and worn holster with a battered-looking Grandville revolver sticking up from it. "Do you think I should get myself a horse and ride with you, Sam?" he asked, using the Ranger's first name as if they were partners in upholding the law.

The Ranger looked him up and down. Not wanting to hurt his feelings, he said, "I'd be proud to ride with you, but don't you think the town might need you worse right here, in case the weasels come back while we're gone?"

Pip seemed to consider it, hooking his thumbs in his belt and using the side of his boot to push the skinny hound away from him. "Get out of here, dog," he said. "You're getting hair all over my pants leg." Then he sucked his teeth and nodded. "Yep, it might be best if I stay here. This town could become a hotbed of fighting."

"That's right," the Ranger said. "If something happened here while we were gone, you'd never forgive yourself for not —"

He stopped at the sound of two pistol shots from the livery barn. "Wait here, Pip!" the Ranger said. "Tell Maria I said to stay put!"

As the Ranger hurried toward the livery barn, he heard the door to the harness shop swing open and heard Pip deliver his message to Maria. "Sam, wait, I'm coming," Maria called out to him. But the Ranger only raised a hand and waved her back.

As he approached the barn, the large

doors swung open and Reverend Bullard came tumbling out backward. Hirsh Knox stepped out with his pistol drawn and fired a shot into the ground three feet from where the reverend landed. Upon seeing the Ranger's pistol come out of its holster, Hirsh lowered his pistol into his holster and raised his hands chest high in a show of peace. He stood silent. Reaching one raised hand to his mouth, he wiped it back and forth vigorously across his lips. Behind him, the Abbadeles and their men crowded in the open barn door along with some townsmen. Seeing the Ranger approach with a bandanna wrapped around his wounded arm, Terrence Knox spoke up on his brother's behalf. "Ranger! It weren't Hirsh's fault! Ask anybody! That old preacher went nuts on us! Grabbed Hirsh by the mouth and commenced shaking his head like it was on a spring!"

"I came to save and cleanse that man of an unclean spirit!" Reverend Bullard shouted, rising to his feet. Dusting his seat, he pointed a thick finger at Hirsh Knox and said, "Brother in Christ, I forgive you for thwarting my efforts. You're being misused by that vile, loathsome demon inside your mouth!"

Hirsh Knox took a step toward the old

minister, still wiping his lips, an angry look on his face. Terrence grabbed his arm, stopping him, and said to Reverend Bullard, "Old man, he's getting ready to do more than *thwart* you, if you don't keep your mouth shut!" Terrence looked at the Ranger with a baffled expression. "What's wrong with that old fool? He can't go around grabbing folks by their mouth! You can't blame Hirsh for shooting at him!"

Frank Abbadele spoke up, saying to the Ranger, "The fact is, Ranger, if Hirsh meant to kill him, he'd be dead right now."

"I know that," said the Ranger, stepping closer to the reverend, dusting his frayed black coat with his gloved hand. "You're going to have to settle down, Reverend Bullard," he said quietly.

"I — I must have my Bible," the reverend said, picking his hat up off the dirt at his feet, dusting it off and placing it on his head.

Looking around on the ground and back up at the men, the Ranger said, "Where's his Bible? Anybody see it in there?"

Lenbow Decker came from amid the group and held the Bible out, wiping a hand over it, freeing it of dirt and bits of straw from the barn floor. "Here it is, Ranger," said Decker. "He must've dropped it when Hirsh shoved him backward."

The Ranger looked at Hirsh Knox, who stood tight-lipped, staring coldly at Reverend Bullard with a puzzled expression on his face, his lips red from the reverend grabbing him with tremendous force. "Hirsh, is this thing over for you?" Sam asked.

Hirsh nodded in silence without taking his cold, puzzled stare off the reverend.

Having to pull Reverend Bullard away to get him started, the Ranger walked close beside him back toward the hotel. When Bullard kept half-turning and looking back at Hirsh Knox, Sam said, "Reverend, leave those men alone. I admire your faith, but pull it out some other time."

"I'm sorry, sir," said the reverend indignantly. "But the spirit dictates my actions in such cases as this. All I can do is obey."

"I understand," said the Ranger. "But we've got a tense situation here. I need you to help me keep things under control, for everybody's sake."

"I'll do all I can, Ranger. You have my word," said Reverend Bullard.

"Good. Just stay at the hotel until we leave," said Sam. "Stay out of that man's sight for a little while. Let him cool down some."

"Indeed I will, sir," said the reverend. "Although I daresay we'll have no more trouble with him or that insidious demon that has so long plagued him."

"Oh?" the Ranger asked, eyeing him. "Why's that?"

"Because that terrible demon is gone!" Reverend Bullard said, his voice trembling with excitement. "God be praised!" He hastened his step and straightened the front of his frayed black coat. "Hallelujah! Hallelujah!" he chanted under his breath.

Back at the barn, Terrence and Hirsh walked inside as the men disbursed and went back to readying their horses. "The nerve of that meddling old man!" Terrence said, brushing his shirtsleeve as if to clear it of some unseen matter. Turning to his brother, Hirsh, and noting the redness around his mouth, Terrence chuckled and said, "Damn if that old preacher didn't come near to ripping your lips off! You doing all right, brother?"

Hirsh didn't try to answer. Instead, he shook his head, turned and walked out through the rear barn door into an empty corral where he stood staring out across the desert floor, his eyes welling with tears. Inside the barn, Terrence said to Frank Abbadele, "Truce or no truce — that crazy negro preacher does anything like that again, me or Hirsh, one is bound to kill him." Terrence tightened the cinch on his saddle angrily. "Poor ole Hirsh has been teased and ridiculed his whole life because he stutters. I admit I even give him a hard time myself." He dropped the stirrup and stood, facing Frank and the others. "But I'll be damned if some negro is going to belittle him that way, especially in front of everybody. Don't be surprised if Hirsh don't mull it over and over till he snaps and kills that man."

Frank looked around as if to make sure the Ranger wasn't present. "This truce is only good as long as I say it is, Terrence. But for now, we're living by it." He stepped over to the front door and gazed along the street in time to see the Ranger and Bullard step up onto the boardwalk out front of the hotel. Then his eyes moved out across the desert floor. "I wish to hell we'd hear something from Tillis. I don't like the idea of him being somewhere out there with all these *comadrejas* raising hell." He considered it for a moment, then added to himself under his breath, "Especially with him holding that Riley bank money." He searched the distant horizon as if his brother Tillis might appear. Then he turned and walked back to his horse's stall.

Inside the hotel and up in the room, once the Ranger had explained to April and Toot what had happened, April stared in shock. "Grandpa! No! You didn't!" she said, as if unable to believe her ears. Toot Abbadele stared down at the floor, not knowing what to say.

"I had no choice in the matter, child," Bullard said in his own defense. "My calling is to do the Lord's work, and so I must." He slumped down into a chair, took out a handkerchief and mopped his sweaty brow.

"Keep him here," the Ranger said to April and Toot, keeping his voice lowered just between themselves. He looked at Toot and asked, "Did you know where he was headed?"

Toot replied, "I knew he was going to the livery barn, but I had no idea he'd do something like that."

"It's not Toot's fault, Ranger: It's mine," said April. "I told him to let Grandpa go." She looked at Reverend Bullard sitting slumped in the chair and added, "But my goodness, I wasn't expecting him to do that!"

"Hirsh could've killed him," said Toot, a serious expression clouding his brow. "He might yet." He turned to April. "Be sure and keep the reverend here till we're all out of town."

Listening, the Ranger nodded in agreement, then gestured toward the door, motioning for Toot to follow him. "Come on, let's get going. It might be up to you and me to hold this bunch together long enough to get rid of the *comadrejas*."

The Ranger turned, left the room and waited outside the door while Toot and April said their good-byes. When Toot joined him, they walked down the stairs, out the front door and toward the livery barn. On their way, Toot said, "Ranger, I might not get a chance to say this later, so I want to get it said now. I'm much obliged to you for cutting me loose on that bank robbery charge."

The Ranger looked at him as they walked on. "I didn't cut you loose, Toot. April said you were with her. I believed her."

"Yeah, I know," said Toot. "But you didn't have to. You could have been hard-nosed about it. I've always heard that's how you play it."

Ignoring the remark, the Ranger said, "I weighed it out, and I believed her, Toot. That's how it shaped up. Nothing more to it."

"All right, but much obliged anyway." Toot smiled to himself as they walked on, passing Big Shod and Swan Hendricks, who stood beside Shod's horse at a hitch rail.

"There's a sight that takes some getting used to," Swan said as the Ranger and Toot Abbadele made their way to the front door of the livery barn. "This is what you could call a calm before a storm. Once the weasels are wiped out, the Ranger better watch his step. If I know the Abbadeles — and believe me, I do know the Abbadeles — there's a double cross in the works right now."

"Every one of the Abbadeles?" Shod asked, checking the cinch on his saddle.

"Huh?" said Swan. Then, realizing the implication of his question, she put a hand on her hip and cocked her head slightly. "What is it you're asking?"

Shod shrugged. "Just being curious."

Swan looked bemused. "Just curious? Well, in that case: Yes, I know each and every one of them. I also know just about every other man within fifty miles of here."

"I bet you do," Shod said a bit sullenly, dropping his stirrup easily, running a gloved hand back along the big gray's side.

"Hey, big fellow!" Swan shook him by

his thick shoulder. "Is that jealousy I hear in your voice?"

Shod caught himself, let out a breath, then said, "Yes, maybe it was. I'm sorry. I'm not your judge. I had no right commenting."

"Damned right you didn't," she said. Then, stepping in close, she slipped her arms out around his waist and looked up into his eyes. "But it was flattering." She smiled. "Even a whore likes to hear that somebody —"

"Don't call yourself that," Shod said, cutting her off, laying his big gloved hands on her shoulders.

"It's what I am," said Swan. "I make no pretense about it."

"Just don't call yourself that when you're with me, all right?" said Shod. "It might be what you do, but it doesn't fit what the people here think of you — you or your friend Clare, either one. This town looks up to both of you, no matter what you do for a living. So don't say it in front of me."

"Yes, sir!" Swan smiled. "But what does the town caring for us have to do with it?"

"It means you both matter," said Shod. "It's good to matter, don't you agree?"

She saw a yearning in his dark eyes and realized there was much more he wanted to say. But she knew that this was all she would get for now. She raised her hand and touched his cheek. "Yes, it's good to matter. And you matter to me."

"You don't have to say that," Shod said.

"I know," said Swan. "But I mean it. You do matter to me. I want you to be careful out there."

Shod nodded. "Yes, ma'am," he said, mimicking the way she'd been answering him of late. He turned her loose and un-hitched his horse. Then he stopped and looked at her again. "When I get back, think you might take some time off your work? Maybe we could spend some time together. See what comes of it."

She made a pretense of considering it, then said, "I'm sure I could. Why don't you look me up when you get back?" She smiled.

"I might just do that." He returned her smile, then stepped up atop the gray, turned it in the street and heeled toward the livery barn, where the Ranger and others led their horses out and mounted them on the dirt street.

Chapter 20

As the riders filed two abreast along the street leaving town, Terrence Knox raced his horse back and forth alongside the column, calling out as his eyes searched in all directions. "Hirsh, where are you? Come on, Hirsh! We're leaving now!" But when there was no response, Terrence spurred his horse to the front of the column, beside the Ranger and Frank Abbadele. "Something ain't right, Frank! Hirsh has up and disappeared on me!" There was a puzzled, concerned look in Terrence Knox's eyes. "We've got to stop and go find him!"

Frank Abbadele looked at the Ranger riding beside him. Sam said in a lowered voice, "We need to get to the weasels before they figure a way to fix that Gatling gun."

Frank Abbadele looked at Terrence Knox without slowing his horse's walking pace. "Keep moving, Terrence. The Ranger's right. I don't want that Gatling gun spitting in my face again."

"But Frank," Terrence protested. "I've got to look for Hirsh! If it was one of your brothers, wouldn't you?"

"Look for him then, damn it," said Frank. "As soon as you find him, both of yas catch up with us."

The riders continued along the street, people on either boardwalk silently watching them pass. There was no fanfare from the onlookers, only the grim, determined expressions of people who knew that a dark task lay ahead. Swan Hendricks started to walk out beside Shod's horse as he rode past, but upon seeing him shake his head slightly, telling her not to, she hesitated then stepped back and stared as he heeled his big gray to the front of the column and joined the Ranger and Frank Abbadele. "I'll ride on ahead and scout the trail in case they have any surprises waiting for us."

Both the Ranger and Frank nodded. "If you find yourself in trouble, remember the signal," Sam said.

"Got it," said Shod. "Two pistol shots means I've got weasel problems." Then, without another word on the matter, he heeled his horse forward and up into a run, raising a wake of dust out onto the desert floor.

"I hope he didn't take all that dynamite with him," said Frank Abbadele.

"No," said the Ranger. "Most of it's right here in my saddlebags."

"Oh . . ." Frank Abbadele looked surprised, then put a little more space between his horse and the Ranger's.

From the hotel window above the street, Reverend Bullard looked down, seeing April standing along the street as Toot Abbadele veered his horse over to her, leaned down and kissed her gently. When Toot heeled his horse back into the passing column of riders, Reverend Bullard sighed in resolve, then turned and looked at the sleeping baby on the bed. With a faint smile, he shook his head and walked to his chair in the center of the room. No sooner had he seated himself than he heard the sound of boots walking toward the door. Only then did he notice he had failed to bolt the door when April had gone downstairs to see Toot and the others off. Upon seeing his mistake, the reverend tried to spring up from his chair to correct it. But he was too late. "Jesus help me!" Reverend Bullard murmured aloud the second the boots stopped outside the door. On the dresser a few feet away lay the big pistol, but before he could even think of reaching for it, the door burst open so violently that it hit the wall and bounced back. It would have slammed itself shut were it not for the hand of Hirsh Knox catching it midswing and holding it.

Hirsh stood staring wild-eyed at the elderly clergyman, his cheeks streaked with tears. His beard stubble glistened wet; a string of saliva hung from his lower lip as if he were an animal gone mad. His right hand was balled tightly into a fist near the handle of his holstered Colt. His words were halted but clear as he said, sobbing, "Old man . . . what in God's name . . . have you . . . done to me?"

"Oh my!" said Reverend Bullard in a trembling voice, clasping his hands together into a steeple at his heart. "It isn't what I've done, my son! It's what the Lord Jesus has done *through* me! He has chased your demon on down the road! You are *healed*, praise God!" The old minister sank to his knees on the wooden floor, gesturing for Hirsh Knox to join him.

Hirsh started to sink slowly down but then stopped himself, straightened up abruptly and shook his head. "No! *Hell, no!* I'm not . . . doing this. I don't believe in . . . all this religious malarkey! I never did!" Yet even as he said the words in bitter denouncement, Hirsh could not stop the tears from streaming down his cheeks.

"It don't matter none at all whether or not you believe in God, son. God believes in *you!*" said Bullard.

But Hirsh would have none of it. "Damn it to hell! What's happened to me?" he shouted, clasping his hand to his chin as if he might undo whatever repair had been made to him. "You did . . . this to me. Now you've got to stop it!"

"Stop it?" The old reverend couldn't believe his ears. "Stop it, you say?" He rose slowly halfway, resting his hands on his bent knees. "Son, don't you see? The Lord Jesus Christ has cured you! Has chased out your terrible affliction! There's no stopping it! He has cured you! Son, praise him for it!" Bullard's thick finger pointed upward as if stirring something up in heaven.

Hirsh's hand clasped around his pistol and yanked it from its holster. "Yiiieee!" he screamed, cocking the hammer as he lunged forward at the old preacher.

At the bottom of the stairs, Terrence Knox heard his brother's scream from the second floor and hurriedly raced upward, taking three steps at a time. He'd seen Hirsh's horse hitched out back of the hotel and followed his hunch that in rage and humiliation Hirsh had gone looking for Reverend Bullard. Rounding the corner of the landing, using the newel post to make his turn, Terrence raced along the hall and into the room, drawing his pistol on his way. "Turn him loose, you sonsabitch!" he shouted, charging through the doorway, pointing the gun at Bullard but seeing no way to fire without hitting Hirsh.

"Easy, young man," said Reverend Bullard gently to Terrence, looking at him past Hirsh's bowed shoulders as he held the weeping outlaw to his bosom. "Your brother isn't being harmed. He's just been witness to the power of the Lord."

But Terrence wasn't convinced. He stepped sidelong around the two men, who stood like exhausted dance partners with the music ended. "Hirsh?" he said, puzzled and shocked by his brother's actions. "Hey, ole boy . . . is everything all right here? I know you can't tell me, so just nod your head." All the while he spoke, Terrence kept his pistol pointed at the old reverend.

Still sobbing quietly, his shoulders shuddering, Hirsh raised his head from Bullard's shoulder enough to look at his brother and nod. "Yes . . . I'm all right," he said softly, his voice recovering from emotion.

"Huh?" Terrence Knox stopped cold, stunned by the sound of his brother's voice. "What'd he say? Was that him talking?" Terrence asked the reverend, not trusting what he'd just heard from his brother's mouth. "I'm getting the willies. You better tell me something fast!"

"Yes, indeed, it truly was your brother speaking," the reverend said peacefully. "The brand-new words of a brand-new man, spoken now by the grace of God!" Patting Hirsh's back, Bullard released his hold a bit, allowing Hirsh to straighten up and wipe his sleeve across his wet eyes.

"Yeah, right," said Terrence Knox, giving Bullard a skeptical look, keeping his pistol pointed at him. Then, turning to Hirsh, he asked. "What's going on here? Did this old negro grab you again?"

"Listen closely, Terrence," Hirsh said slowly, deliberately emphasizing each word. "This man has cured me. I can talk now, as well as anybody." But his mouth, not being used to such articulation, se-creted heavily. Laughing through his tears, Hirsh blotted his sleeve to his lips, saying to Bullard, "Now it looks like I've got a spit problem, Reverend."

"That will pass, my son, as soon as you get more talking practice. You and your new mouth has to get acquainted, you might say."

"I'll be goddamn . . ." Terrence whispered in disbelief, staring wide-eyed at his brother, hearing his voice as if hearing the voice of a stranger. His gun slumped toward the floor, where Hirsh's own gun had fallen moments earlier.

"Don't talk that way, Terrence," Hirsh said, still wiping his teary red eyes. "Not after what just happened here."

"I ain't sure what did just happen here, Hirsh," said Terrence, looking suspiciously at Reverend Bullard. "This is all some kind of strange hocus-pocus, far as I'm concerned. What do you call it?" he asked his brother.

"I'm calling it the same as the reverend here calls it," said Hirsh, sniffling a bit. "God gave me my voice."

"And you really believe that sort of foolishness?" asked Terrence. "Just because whatever was afflicting you is gone, you're going to say it was God's work?" He shook his head. "I always thought you had better sense than that . . . even though you couldn't say the word *shit* without twisting it nine different ways and still getting it wrong."

"I asked you not to talk like that,

Terrence," Hirsh warned him patiently. Then he took a deep breath and, looking at Reverend Bullard, said, "Call it what you want to call it, Terrence. All I know is, I could not speak. Then this man grabbed my lips in the name of Jesus. And now I can speak. Is there any part of that story that's not true or didn't happen just exactly the way I said?" As he spoke, Hirsh touched his already wet shirtsleeve to his lips, his mouth still salivating heavily.

Terrence stared at him, thinking it over. Finally, he relented. "Hirsh, you're right. That is the whole of it. The main thing is, you can talk now." He nodded toward the window. "I reckon we better get going now, catch up to the others."

"I can't go," Hirsh said firmly.

"What do you mean, you can't go?" said Terrence. "Frank and the others are counting on us, Hirsh. We got to go!"

"No. I'm not leaving this man's side," said Hirsh. "He knows about God, and I want to hear everything he can tell me."

"You can go on ahead, my son," said Reverend Bullard. "I'll be here when you return. We can talk then all you want to."

"There, you see?" said Terrence to his brother. "The preacher ain't going no-where. He'll be waiting to talk —"

"No!" Hirsh cut his brother off. "These are dangerous times. I'm staying here to be with this man and protect him. A lot of weasels left here on foot. My guess is they might regroup and come back."

Terrence, getting a little put out with his brother, said, "Hirsh, I don't want to have to knock you in the head and carry you over my shoulder. We all know there's *comadrejas* left around here to deal with. But the biggest part of them is out there. You've got to show up with me. Otherwise, it'll look bad on both of us. We ride with a tough bunch of men. They don't want to hear me making excuses for you!"

Hirsh thought it over quickly. "You're right, Terrence," he said. "They are a tough bunch of men. Maybe I better go with you. I can tell everybody what happened here. Tell them how God reached down and touched me through Reverend Bullard." He nodded as if settling something in his mind. "Yes, that's it. That's where God would need me, there talking to the others about Him."

"Uh, wait a minute, Hirsh," said Terrence, rubbing his chin, giving the matter a second thought. "Let's not get in too big a hurry."

"Why?" Hirsh asked. "What more is

there to think about? They're expecting us. Let's get moving." He started toward the door, but Terrence grabbed his arm, stopping him.

"Damn it, Hirsh! Don't go nuts on me," Terrence shouted. "You're not going to get out there and start talking to the Abbadeles and the rest of the bunch we ride with about God, are you?"

"You bet I am, if they'll listen," said Hirsh. "This is no light thing for me, brother. You saw the shape I was in my whole life. I've gone so long without being able to say things, that my jaws are aching right now from being able to talk the right way." As he spoke, he cupped his cheek in his hand.

"But you don't have to tell them about how God and this old negro did all that, do you?"

"That's right, brother, I do have to," said Hirsh. "Far as I'm concerned, God let this man fix what was wrong with my voice. If I don't use it to say something on God's behalf and his, then God might just as well take it away from me again." Hirsh nodded toward the door. "Now let's get going. Hurry up."

"Maybe you're right," Terrence said. "It might be best if you stayed here and kept an eye on the reverend and the town. You never know what these weasels are going to do next."

Hirsh shrugged. "Are you sure? I really would like to share all this with the rest of that bunch."

"I'm sure," said Terrence. "You stay here, rest your voice, get settled down some. There'll be time later to explain all this to everybody." He gave Reverend Bullard a pleading look as he backed away to the door. "Preacher, you keep my brother here with you, all right? Don't let him come riding out there looking for us. There could be weasels everywhere."

"I will do my utmost to keep him here," said Bullard. He and Hirsh stood watching as Terrence backed out the door nervously and closed it behind him. Then Bullard turned to Hirsh and said, "He is right about the town needing your help, my son."

"I know," said Hirsh. "The fact is, I can't be around the Abbadeles right now. I need to feel clean and religious for a while. That's the only way I can explain it."

"I understand," said the reverend.

Santaglio sat atop his horse along a high cliff overlooking the flatlands where two riders rode along at a strong, steady gait.

His eye moved past them back along the trail until it reached a fork. From there, his eyes moved toward Sabre Ridge in anticipation, expecting to see a body of riders at any moment. Beside him, Merza said, "Perhaps the men from the town will not come," as if he were reading Santaglio's thoughts. A hot breeze moved across them, lifting stands of the horses' manes and the edge of Merza's wide, flat hat brim.

Santaglio looked at Merza with mild contempt. Of course they would come. He had no doubt about it. They would come, and he would ambush and destroy them in this tangle of hills and crevices. Instead of replying, Santaglio nodded down at the two riders and said, "Take some men down there. Bring those two up here to me quickly. Leave some men at the bottom of these hills as lookouts. If we hear gunfire, we will know the men from Sabre Ridge are upon us."

Merza nodded. "I will leave some men down there. Do jou want those two brought up here alive?"

"Of course alive!" said Santaglio, growing impatient. "I want to see if they can fix this Gatling gun for us."

Merza turned his horse and rode away quickly, motioning for a group of mounted men sitting near the gun wagon to join him. Santaglio watched the group ride down the winding switchback trail to the flatland and out toward the two approaching riders. Then he pulled his horse back, turned it and heeled it over to the gun wagon, where many wounded *comadrejas* lay scattered about on the hard, dusty ground. "Do not worry about what happened in the town today," he said to the men. "Soon we will have the Gatling gun fixed and jou will all taste the sweetness of victory."

The men stared blankly at him.

On the desert floor, Merza pushed his horse hard, taking a backward glance up to the edge of the cliff. Seeing that Santaglio no longer sat up there watching his every move, Merza slowed his horse a bit, feeling a little less pressured. A thousand yards ahead, the two riders had seen them come down off the hill trail. Tillis Abbadele stared ahead as he said to Doyle Royal, "What have we here? Looks like someone's been watching us from the cliffs." As he spoke, he drew his rifle from his scabbard, levered a round into the chamber, then laid it across his lap. Beside him, Doyle Royal did the same. Their horses never broke stride, riding onward to meet the band of *comadrejas*.

Moments later, Merza and his riders reined up twenty yards away and began walking their horses the rest of the way to Tillis Abbadele and Doyle Royal. *"Buenos tardes,"* Tillis called out to the dust-streaked riders.

Doyle Royal chuckled under his breath, his thumb across his rifle hammer. "Now you've done it. They hate having to speak *real* Spanish instead of that broken-up talk they use."

"And I'm supposed to give a blue damn what they want me to speak to them?" Tillis replied sidelong to him, keeping his eyes on Merza, leading the riders. "They don't even know what language to speak to one another."

As the *comadrejas* drew nearer, Merza offered a thin smile through dust-caked lips. Raising a finger for emphasis, he said, "I believe jou two are talking about us, eh?"

"Well, no shit now, *segundo*," said Tillis. "How long did it take all of you together to figure that out?"

Merza's smile withered and left him. "All right, then. None of the, what jou call, the polite conversation. Come with me. Santaglio is awaiting jou."

"Is he now?" said Tillis, eyeing Merza

closely. "Did you get the Gatling gun I told you was coming?"

"We got it, but there is trouble with it," said Merza.

"Trouble? What kind of trouble could you have?" Tillis asked. "Couldn't you figure out how to load it?"

Beside him, Doyle Royal snickered and kept himself from laughing aloud. Merza gave him a dark glance, then said to Tillis, "We used it in a raid, and someone shot the handle off it. Santaglio thinks that you might be able to fix it for us."

"A raid? Already?" Tillis said, surprised. "You boys sure don't fool around, do you?" He gave a short laugh, then asked, "Where did you raid?" But as soon as he asked the question, he began getting a bad feeling down in his gut, anticipating what the answer was going to be.

"Sabre Ridge," said Merza, spreading a tight, victorious smile. "We stole everything the town had. We robbed the stores, the bank. We took everything but the horses. We would have gotten them, but someone shot the handle off the Gatling gun."

"So, they must've put up a fight there?" asked Tillis, trying to get a picture of whether or not his brothers might have been in the town.

"Oh, they fought hard, but it made no difference," said Merza. "We killed them without mercy!"

Tillis pretended not to be bothered by the *comadreja*'s words. "Is that a fact? Did you get much money from that puny little bank?" He pretended to shrug off any further interest in the fighting.

"No," said Merza. "It is too small to have much money. But Santaglio tells us that money is not everything." He grinned. "The main thing is we killed many peoples there!" His eyes shined with excitement just recounting it. "The street, it was full of the dead!"

Tillis stared at him blankly, not letting Merza see that he would have much preferred to raise the rifle from across his lap and put a bullet between his eyes. "Hear that, Doyle?" Tillis said without taking his eyes off Merza. "The main thing is they killed a lot of people."

"Yeah, I heard it," Doyle said, also keeping his voice and expression in check. "You can't beat that, I reckon."

"*Sí*, this is what I say," said Merza, without a hint of what Tillis and Doyle Royal were really thinking. "Soon this will all be our land again." He gave a sweeping gesture with his arm.

"Again?" said Tillis. "Not trying to hurt your feelings, *amigo*, but when was this ever your land?"

Merza's smile faded away. He snapped back closer to reality. "It does not matter when it was. Soon it will be!"

"All right, whatever you say, *segundo*," said Tillis, not wanting to spark any problem. "You're all welcome to it, far as I'm concerned." Thinking about the Riley bank money in his saddlebags and not wanting to do anything to draw any attention to it, he nodded in the direction of the high cliffs and said, "Why don't we get on up there and see if me and Doyle here can't do something to fix that gun for yas."

"*Sí*, let's ride." Merza spun his horse and heeled it back toward the upward trail into the hills, the other men gathering around Tillis Abbadele and Doyle Royal and riding in a wide circle surrounding them like escorts.

As they rode along, Doyle Royal sidled close to Tillis and said, "Do you suppose Frank and the boys were in town when all that happened?"

"You heard this weasel say the town fought hard," Tillis said in a lowered tone. "Without Frank and the boys, that town couldn't have put up much of a fight."

"Damn it to hell," said Doyle. "For all we know, our whole bunch could be lying back there dead right now."

"That's right," said Tillis. "But let's keep our wits about us here. We'll see what we can do to straighten this thing out." They rode on, and Tillis added, "I wish to hell I'd never tipped these weasels off about that Gatling gun shipment. I hope I ain't done something that got my brothers killed." Riding along, Tillis Abbadele looked back over his shoulder in the direction of Sabre Ridge.

"What're you thinking about, Tillis?" Doyle Royal asked.

"About how bad I hate doing something to help the law," he said. Then, looking around at the *comadrejas,* he said, "But if Frank and the bunch were there, and they're still alive, they'll be coming. I got to let them know we're here . . . see if we can help them out some way."

Chapter 21

The rest of the men looked on as the Ranger and Frank Abbadele stood up from examining the hoofprints on the trail and looked off toward the long stretch of jagged hills. Night was closing quickly. Looking through the grainy evening light, they saw the big bounty hunter trotting his gray toward them a hundred yards away. They hadn't seen him since he'd scouted out ahead of them on their way out of town. "With a good moon, we could push on all night, Ranger," said Frank, the two of them waiting for Shod to join them. "My men are used to riding by moonlight on empty bellies." He looked the Ranger up and down. "How do you feel about it?"

"It suits me," Sam said. "The harder we keep pushing them, the more apt they are to make mistakes. It wouldn't be wise to ride onto those switchbacks tonight and maybe get ourselves caught in a crossfire ambush. But we need to get as close as we can. Let them know we mean business."

Frank nodded, realizing that this very well could have been what the Ranger would have been saying about him and his men under a different set of circumstances. "Right," Frank said. He looked back to where some of the men had stepped down from their saddles for a rest. He called out to them, "Stand down for a minute, but don't get too comfortable. We're going on."

"All night?" asked Lenbow Decker.

"Yep, all night, if need be," Frank said. "Or at least until we get to the hills."

The big bounty hunter brought his horse down and turned it sideways to the Ranger and Frank Abbadele. "I spotted some bare feet and some boot prints falling in with the riders closer back to town. I know you saw them, too."

"Yes, we saw them," said the Ranger. "Stragglers that got cut off and left town in the other direction, we figured."

"That's what I figured, too," said Shod. "I just wish we had seen more of them. The more who made it back to the main body, the less there are lurking back around town."

"I know," said the Ranger, a troubled look coming to his brow before he managed to put it aside and deal with their situation. "How far ahead are they now?"

"The wagon has slowed them down considerably," said Shod, taking off his hat and slapping dust from it against his leg. "We could catch up to them by midday tomorrow if we keep moving."

"We already planned to," said the Ranger. "What else?"

Shod nodded back along the trail he'd ridden. "About three more miles, there's a fork in the trail. Looks like two riders rode in on it not long ago, coming from the south. They would have had to be blind not to see all the wagon tracks and hoofprints."

"More weasels?" asked Frank.

"Either more weasels or somebody friendly to them," said Shod. "I can't imagine anybody wanting to run into them otherwise."

The Ranger looked into Frank Abbadele's eyes intently. "Do you have any idea who those two might be?"

Frank returned the intense gaze, but spoke sincerely. "No, Ranger, I don't. Everybody that rides with the Abbadeles is here, except for my brother Tillis, and his pal, Doyle Royal. But they both know better than to run into *comadrejas* by accident. They sure wouldn't be taking a chance on doing it on purpose."

The Ranger nodded. "Let's get some water, rest these horses a few minutes and get moving."

"I rested mine a while ago, waiting for you," said Shod. "I'll push on from here. Next time you see me, I'll have everything scouted along the base of the hills. I'll make sure there's no surprises waiting there for you."

"Good," said the Ranger. "We'll make a dark camp once we get there, then get up the switchbacks at first light."

"A dark camp is a good idea," said Shod. "If you see a campfire near the bottom of the hill line, then it'll be mine. Stay away — it'll only be a decoy."

"We will," said the Ranger. "If anybody comes riding into your camp, it won't be us."

Without another word, Shod touched his gloved fingertips to his hat brim, turned the big gray and heeled it into a quick trot. He pushed the big gray harder in the cooler air of late afternoon. By the time he'd reached the sloping base beneath the hill line, the sun had dropped completely below the western edge of the earth. He gathered dried deadfall of piñon, mesquite brush and juniper and built a small fire in the belly of a dry wash. In the outer glow of the small circle of the firelight, Shod grained the big gray, watered it with canteen water he'd poured into his hat, then led the horse silently away from the camp, rifle in hand, until he found himself a piñon tall and full enough to block out the light of the moon and stars.

Shod lay as silent as stone in the blackness, listening for any foreign sound on the quiet desert floor. The big knife from his boot well lay on the ground by his side. At midnight, while resting soundly without sleeping, Shod heard the first rustle of clothes against brittle dried mesquite brush. Without moving a muscle or flickering an eye, he continued to listen until the slightest whisper of a human voice came wafting to him on the still night air.

Shod moved like a crouching shadow across the desert floor, leaving the horse behind, hitched to the trunk of the piñon. With his rifle and his knife, he traveled outward, circling the sound of brush and whispers until he moonlighted three figures against the bright purple sky. Lying flat on his belly, having laid his rifle beneath a creosote bush, he snaked forward silently inches at a time until he stopped almost within arm's length of the crouching *comadrejas*. He heard their voices clearer now, and what he heard made him feel justified in what he knew he had to do. The voice came from a dark figure who had just crawled back from the edge of the dry wash where he'd looked down and seen the saddle on the ground. Shod had wrapped his saddlebags and personal belongings in a blanket and propped his hat at one end of it against the saddle.

"Here is only one man, and he sleeps. Jou two spread out in the half circle," said a voice. "We will all pounce at once and kill him. Shoot him full of holes. It will let Santaglio and the others know these pigs are upon us."

"But if there is only one man there," a voice replied in a nervous whisper, "how do we know they are upon us, that others will be coming?"

"He is the scout, jou fool," the first voice said harshly. "Now go, both of jou, and do like I told jou!"

As the three spread out, Shod followed the one in the middle as the dark figure snuck straight ahead toward the glow of firelight down over the edge of the dry wash. Nearing the edge, Shod quickened his pace, coming up off his belly into a low running crouch. The *comadreja* heard the softly running footsteps and had started to turn around at the sound of them. But Shod struck fast and with deadly force. His left hand clasped tight on the man's throat, cutting short any chance to scream for help. At the same second, his right hand plunged the big knife blade deep into the *comadreja*'s chest, where his ribs met, the impact lifting the man onto his toes, where he stood as if suspended, his hand grasping and clawing at Shod's forearm for only a moment before all energy and life dissipated from him.

Shod jerked the knife hard to release it from the man's chest, then eased the body to the ground, hearing the last breath of air escape from the pierced lungs. As soon as he'd wiped the blade back and forth on the dead man's chest, he hurried forward, veering left toward the other figure in the dark. "Vesah, is that jou?" the voice whispered, turning toward the slight rustle of brush behind him. When he heard no answer, he asked again, this time his voice a bit stronger, his hand lifting a pistol from his belt. "Vesah, jou better answer me, damned jou! I am serious —"

The big blade found its mark, sinking to the hilt as Shod's free hand clasped around the pistol and its hammer in such a manner as to keep it from firing. The *comadreja* managed a long grunt, but the blade would not allow him to shout aloud for help. Shod sank to the ground with him, keeping a grip on the pistol as the dying man made an effort to jerk it away from him. As the man struggled in his death throes, he lunged forward, sank his teeth into Shod's thick shoulder and hung on, slicing deep, drawing blood.

Shod clenched his jaws tight against the pain, then pried the man loose when he felt the life leave his body. "Damned weasel," Shod whispered to himself, pressing his hand to the severe bite wound.

But there was no time to stop and check himself out. On the other side of the half circle surrounding the dry wash, Shod saw the outline of the third figure in the moonlight. The man stood bowed slightly at the waist, holding a rifle across his stomach, looking back and forth for any sign of the other two. "Vesah?" he whispered in Shod's direction. "Ramal?" He took a cautious step toward the edge of the dry wash and peered down at the campsite. While he looked back and forth, Shod hurried, racing as fast and at the same time as silently as he could across the sand. At ten yards away, Shod saw the *comadreja* spin around in his direction. Knowing he could not get to the man in time to keep him from pulling the trigger and having the shot resound a warning to the rest of the *comadrejas,* Shod dropped to the ground and lay in a deathlike stillness, almost feeling the man's eyes move back and across him.

"Jou damn cowards!" the man whispered to his friends, not realizing they were beyond ever hearing his insults again. "Get over here — help me kill dis pig!" He waited and, when no answer came, he whispered in exasperation, "All right, I will shoot him full of holes all by myself! But then his stuff is mine, all mine!"

Seeing him raise the rifle to his shoulder as he started to step down the edge of the dry wash, Shod called out in a whisper, "Wait, I'm coming."

"Is about time," said the *comadreja,* turning toward him again, squinting to help himself see in the darkness. "I thought I would have to —" He stopped short, seeing the dark, grimacing face draw nearer into the outer glow of firelight. Shod's cheeks and spectacles were splattered with fresh blood, his eyes appearing large and sinister through the thick lenses. "Stop!" the *comadreja* demanded, his voice trembling in sudden terror at what had swept in upon him like some fiend from the lower regions. He tried to raise the rifle, but Shod backhanded it away, sending it sailing from the man's shaking hands.

"This is not your night, you murdering weasel," Shod whispered, throwing a powerful arm out around the man, drawing him close into death's embrace.

The Ranger and the Abbadeles had seen the small glowing campfire throughout the night as they rode closer to the base of the hill line. They had deliberately kept their distance when they made their own dark camp in the early hours of morning. Less than two hours later, when they had rested both the horses and themselves, they mounted and rode quietly along the trail leading past the campfire. As night lifted in a grainy, gray mist from among the brush and rock on the desert floor, the Ranger was the first to catch sight of the big bounty hunter sitting on an upturned boulder above the dry wash, leaning back against the side of a larger boulder, his rifle lying loosely across his lap.

"Hold up," Sam said barely above a whisper to Frank Abbadele and the others. Leaving them behind, he rode up to the boulder and looked up at Shod. Now he saw the knife lying beside the big bounty hunter. He saw the dark dried blood on his gloved right hand. "Are you hurt?" the Ranger asked quietly. He took a canteen strap from his saddle horn and pitched it up to him.

"I'm all right," said Shod, also speaking softly as he stood up, catching the canteen. He peeled his right glove off, uncapped the canteen, took a sip, then squatted down and poured a thin trickle of water over his hands. "They were here keeping a watch for us," he said, nodding toward the dry wash where he'd rolled the bodies over the edge. "Now that they don't know we're down here, if we move quick, we might get the drop on them before daylight."

As the two spoke, Frank Abbadele ventured forward, away from the others, and sidled up to the Ranger. Seeing the bloody glove lying at Shod's feet as he washed his hands, Frank said in a grim, lowered tone, "Where's the bodies? I'd like to see them."

"See the bodies?" the Ranger asked, as if he might have mistaken Frank's words.

"That's right." Frank's eyes slid back and forth between Shod and the Ranger. Seeing the look on their faces, he said, "I want to make sure they're *comadrejas*."

"You can take my word for it, Abbadele," Shod said. "They were desert weasels." He stood up, drying his hands on a dusty bandanna he'd taken from around his neck. "Who else would they be?" he asked.

"I'd like to see them anyway," said Frank, facing them each in turn, "just to satisfy it in my own mind."

"He asked you a question, Frank," said the Ranger. "Who else could it have been?"

"All right," said Frank, letting go of a tense breath, "I'm going to level with you. Those two sets of prints coming in from the other fork in the road — one set looked like they might belong to my brother's horse." Unable to face the Ranger or Shod now, Frank Abbadele looked down and off to one side. "Tillis put some store-bought shoes on his horse a while back. I recognize the marking. I should have said something when we first spotted them. I suppose I just couldn't bring myself to do it."

"The bodies are lying over the edge there — go help yourself," said Shod, giving a nod toward the dry wash. "But I can tell you that they're all three *comadrejas*."

Shod and the Ranger gave one another a

curious glance as they watched Frank Abbadele ride his horse over to the edge of the dry wash and look down at the three bodies lying sprawled in the sand. Satisfied with his findings, Frank rode back and stopped beside the Ranger. "What would your brother be doing riding with the weasels?" Sam asked.

"I don't know," said Frank. "But riding with them doesn't mean he's in cahoots with them. For all I know, they could have him prisoner." He studied the stoic expressions facing him, then said, "All right, I doubt if he's their prisoner, but I can't see Tillis having anything to do with them, either."

The Ranger crossed his wrists on his saddle horn and considered it. Then he said, "Since he's not one of those bodies over there, it stands to reason that he's still with the *comadrejas*." He gave Frank Abbadele a pointed gaze. "Where does this put us once we trap those weasels and it comes time to do some killing?"

Concern clouded Frank's brow. "I don't know, Ranger. But I ain't crossing Tillis off just because his horse's hoofprints showed up along the trail. Who knows? The *comadrejas* could have stolen his horse. Maybe even killed him for all we know."

But both the Ranger and the bounty hunter kept quiet, neither of them believing that to be the case. "Just give me some room to deal with my brother, find out if he is riding with these weasels," said Frank. "That's all I ask."

"And if we find out he *is* riding with them," Shod said. "What then?"

Frank winced. "Damn it, I don't know what then! I'll have to deal with that situation if it comes down." He turned his horse and gigged it back over to the rest of the men. Sam and Shod saw the rest of the Abbadeles draw their horses close around Frank as he spoke to them.

"What now?" Shod asked the Ranger, staring across the few yards separating them from the Abbadeles.

"Now we just watch one another's back a little closer until we see where Tillis Abbadele stands in all this," said the Ranger. "We knew what we were getting ourselves into taking up with the Abbadeles, the same as they knew what they were doing taking up with us, a couple of lawmen."

"I don't like it," said Shod firmly.

"Duly noted," said the Ranger, also staring at the Abbadeles. "Neither do I. But we're in too deep to stop this thing now. There's too many lives counting on us." He gestured upward into the gray, grainy light. "Let's get up into the hills, see if we can't catch them off guard before daylight."

He waited until Shod stepped down the backside of the boulder and came riding around to him on the big gray. Together they rode over and joined the others, taking a position at the front of the riders beside Frank Abbadele. When they had begun riding forward onto the upward trail, Frank Abbadele said to the Ranger, still talking in a lowered voice, "I suppose you'd like to know what we were talking about just now?"

"Only if you feel like you want to tell me," the Ranger replied, gazing ahead along the trail.

"I told them not to hold back because of Tillis. I said Tillis is a big boy and knows how to look out for himself." Having spoken, he gazed ahead grimly for a moment, until he felt the Ranger's eyes on him. "It's the truth," said Frank, looking over at him as they rode quietly upward. "If Tillis has thrown in with that bunch, I reckon he knew what he was getting into. In that case, I don't owe him a thing."

They rode on.

A half hour had passed by the time they reached a point where the trail forked around the hillside in either direction. Straight ahead stood a high abutment of solid rock like an impenetrable fortress wall. "Here's where we split up," the Ranger said, whispering now, knowing they were closing in on their prey. "If we've caught them by surprise, we'll soon know it. If not, they're waiting for us. They'll commence firing down on us over that ridge." He pointed upward through the lingering gray swirl of morning mist. "That's where they are if they think we're coming. It's the perfect spot for an ambush."

Beside Frank Abbadele, Lenbow Decker swallowed a dryness in his throat and said in a hoarse whisper, "So they could be waiting for us right now, staring down at us, ready to pounce?"

"That's right," Frank Abbadele whispered in reply. "Does that scare you, Decker? I've never known you to worry about getting shot at."

"I'm not," Decker whispered. "It's just that we're so damn outnumbered anyway. I hate not knowing if they're waiting on us or not."

"Going up is the only way we'll ever find

out," said Frank, still whispering. "I doubt if they'll want to give us any warning first."

"Sorry, Boss," said Decker. "I reckon I was just thinking out loud."

The Ranger looked all around and along the ridgeline. "If we had any way of knowing for sure that they might be lying in wait, we'd throw caution to the wind, swing behind them, then push them right off the cliff. They'd have no way to escape."

Frank looked around, too, as if doing a quick head count. "That's damn ambitious, Ranger, considering the odds. I figure there's still a good fifty or more armed men, even with all the ones we killed back in town."

"I know," said the Ranger. "We'll go on as planned, try to catch them by surprise in a cross fire. But if anything changes and makes it look like we ought to get behind them, be ready for it, all of you."

"Don't worry about us, Ranger," said Frank. "We'll be ready for whatever comes."

Toot nudged his horse over beside Sam and said to his brother, "If it's all the same, Frank, I'm riding with the Ranger."

Frank looked him up and down, then said in a relenting voice, "Ride with whoever you want to ride with, far as I'm con-, cerned." He turned his horse away.

The Ranger looked at the two parties of riders splitting up, ready to ride up in different directions. "Be careful we don't fire at one another," he added. Then he nudged his horse to the right, Shod and half of the men following him quietly, upward along the narrow trail.

Chapter 22

Atop the cliff on a thirty-yard stretch of rocky, flat ground, Tillis Abbadele and Doyle Royal leaned against the gun wagon and looked back and forth at the *comadrejas* lying along the edge, poised for an ambush. Without going to the edge and checking, Tillis could tell by the shine of bloodlust anticipation in the *comadrejas'* eyes that riders were at that very moment moving quietly upward along the trails below. Tillis took off his hat, ran his fingers back through his hair restlessly, then put his hat back on. "I swear, Doyle," he said in a lowered voice, rubbing his chin with his head bowed, "I've tried swallowing what's going on here every way I can. I just can't make it taste right going down."

"I know what you mean," Doyle Royal whispered in reply. "No matter if it's our bunch coming up that hill or a bunch of strangers. Whoever it is, they're more like us than these gritty-necked weasel sonsabitches."

"Yeah?" said Tillis. They gave one another a questioning look. "That's the very same thing I've been standing here thinking."

Doyle Royal spit and ran the back of his hand across his mouth. "My whole life I've been a no-account, belligerent bastard, and I know it. Hell, I've been proud of it at times." He looked around again. "I ever showed up at heaven, I wouldn't blame God for hunkering down, pretending He ain't at home."

Tillis nodded. "I know the feeling. What's your point?"

"Well, my point is, you and me never should have told these rotten turds about that Gatling gun." Doyle Royal swept his hand back and forth, gesturing toward the *comadrejas*. "Since we did, it seems like we ought to do something to stop this."

Tillis Abbadele considered it as he continued to look around at the armed men along the edge of the cliff. "And you figure that would get you a seat in heaven?"

There was a slight pause. Then Doyle Royal grinned. "Naw, I reckon not. But it would sure give me something to laugh about sitting in hell."

Tillis chuckled under his breath. "I sure would like to be good and drunk right about now, wouldn't you?" He gazed longingly at his horse and saddlebags a few feet away, thinking for a moment about the bank money.

Doyle Royal let out a sigh. "Yeah, I would. But damn it, it just wasn't meant to be." He straightened up from against the gun wagon, rubbed his hands together and touched his hand to his empty holster before remembering that Santaglio had taken their pistols as soon as they had arrived. Then he winced and asked, "What have you got in mind, Tillis?"

Tillis nodded back over his shoulder. "Ole Santaglio has been wanting us to fix that Gatling gun. Let's hop up there and take a look at her." He grinned widely.

"Well, hell, yes!" said Doyle Royal, slyly returning the grin. "I've got no plans made for the day."

Along the edge of the cliff, Merza lay peeping down, watching the riders below move single file up along the trail. When the man beside him nudged him in the ribs, Merza looked around at him. "What do jou want?" he hissed.

"Those two," the voice whispered. "I thought jou better see what dey are up to."

Merza studied Tillis Abbadele and Doyle Royal, watching them move about in the bed of the gun wagon. Tillis held the broken gun crank in his hand, inspecting it closely. "So?" said Merza. "Santaglio know dey are here to fix the gun! Don't bother me!" He turned away in a huff and peeped down over the edge again.

"Right now?" the voice asked, tugging on Merza's sleeve.

"What, *right now?*" Merza asked in response, getting more and more irritated, turning back to face the man.

"Should dey be fixing it right now?" the man asked.

Merza shrugged impatiently. "Right now, tomorrow, yesterday — what do I care? Can jou see I have got something important here?" He cut a quick glance to Santaglio lying in wait with twenty or more men along the cliff line opposite him. "There is the leader. If jou need to ask him, go ahead, but don't tell him I said for jou to!" Again Merza turned in a huff and looked down over the edge.

"All right den," the man said. He slipped backward from the edge and stood up, then turned and walked toward Santaglio, giving Tillis and Doyle Royal a suspicious stare on his way.

Inside the gun wagon, Doyle saw the look on the *comadreja*'s face and said to

Tillis, who stood bowed over the mounted Gatling gun, "Better hurry it up, Tillis. We've got a nosey weasel checking us out."

"I'm hurrying, pard. But this ain't working worth a shit." He wrapped his belt tightly around the broken crank handle, trying to get it to stiffen up enough to turn without bending or coming off.

"Here, try this," said Doyle, snatching a knife up from his boot well and handing it to Tillis handle first. "Use it like a splint."

"Good thinking," said Tillis. He hurriedly released the belt, held the long knife flat against the broken crank handle and rewrapped his belt around it, this time seeing the handle stand more firmly.

"Is that the right deal?" Doyle asked, casting a quick glance at the *comadreja*, seeing him stop and get Santaglio's attention then point toward the gun wagon.

"Yep, that'll do for a while," said Tillis. "Long enough to warn the riders at least."

"Uh-oh," said Doyle. "Santaglio's looking our way now. He's standing up . . . looking, wondering."

"Stall him. Wave at him or something!" Tillis said. He hurriedly snatched up an open crate of cartridges and began loading the gun, keeping his back to the cliff line where Santaglio stood craning his long

404

neck for a better look at what the two were doing.

"Wave at him?" Doyle asked, grinning at Santaglio, touching his finger to his hat brim. "He'll think I'm an idiot!" Even as he spoke to Tillis, he nodded and began raising his hand, waving it back and forth slowly.

"He thinks it anyway," said Tillis, working furiously. "Damn this newfangled shooting gear the army's come up with!"

"All right, here I am, waving, grinning," Doyle said to Tillis, still nodding. Then, under his breath, he said through his broad grin, "Right over here, Santaglio. That's right, here we are, fixing this Gatling gun just like you wanted us to. Here we go, getting it ready to shove it right up your rotten, stinking —"

"Got it!" said Tillis, slapping the lever into place.

"Just in time!" said Doyle, still grinning, waving. "Here he comes!"

As Tillis swung the big gun around toward Santaglio's side of the cliff, Doyle ducked over to the side, revealing the Gatling gun with its handle standing tall. Seeing the handle repaired, Santaglio's first response was a trace of a bemused smile. But then he saw Tillis crouch down and take a steady firing position. "Rush him!" Santaglio screamed, shoving two men forward toward the Gatling gun while he himself began running away, his rifle flying from his hand as if to lessen his weight.

"*Yeeeehiiii!*" Doyle Royal yelled, grabbing the big gun from the side, steadying it as Tillis began turning the firing crank. "Ride it, cowboy!"

The impact of the explosions caused the whole wagon to vibrate violently. Doyle's hat rode down his forehead until the band nearly covered his eyes. Yet he refused to turn loose of the Gatling gun. He held it in a death grip, keeping it steadied even as the *comadrejas'* bullets grazed and punched him brutally. "Stay with me, pard!" Tillis shouted, taking on wounds himself, the two of them swinging the big gun back and forth, spraying the ambushers with a deadly hail of bullets.

On the trail circling upward on the left, the noise came suddenly. Frank Abbadele jerked his horse to a halt so quickly that the spooked animal reared high, causing the others to bunch up against them. "Jesus!" Frank shouted, trying to settle the horse and hold his hat on his head. As soon as the horse calmed, a bloody *comadreja* came screaming out off the edge of the cliff and landed with a thud in the middle of the trail. The horse went crazy again; this time Frank kept it in check. The men stared upward, stunned by the relentless chatter of the Gatling gun, the screams and curses of dying men. Another body hit the trail, then another.

"Lord! It's raining weasels!" Lenbow Decker shouted wide-eyed, working at keeping his own horse under control.

"There's no doubt about it now!" Frank shouted at his brothers Dick and Bob and the rest of his men. "Tillis is the only *loco* coyote in the world could cause something like this!" He raised his rifle and swung it back and forth as some of the *comadrejas* along the cliff realized their surprise had been discovered and began firing down on them. "What are we waiting for? Get behind them — shoot the bastards off this hillside!"

On the other side of the hill, the Ranger and his party stopped and looked up at the sound of the Gatling gun, the screaming and cursing above them. He shot a glance at Toot and Shod and saw them thinking the same thing he was thinking. "It's got to be Tillis," said Toot. "He's warning us!"

"Whoever it is, this is the break we

needed!" said the Ranger, already heeling his horse, gesturing forward with his hand for the other riders to follow him.

Pushing their horses hard along the two hundred yards of upward trail before them, the Ranger and his half of the riders began firing at *comadrejas* as a few tried climbing down the steep, rocky ledge from the cliff line to escape the deadly Gatling gunfire. But as they reached the point where the trail turned back, leading out onto the stretch of flatland, the Gatling gun fell silent. As the Ranger's group and the Abbadeles' group rejoined, gunfire from the *comadrejas* began to seek them out. Without discussing the turn of events, the Ranger said with urgency, "Don't stop! Take all the ground we can while the gun's not firing."

"You heard him, men!" Frank shouted over his shoulder, both he and the Ranger turning their horses onto the flat hilltop. "Somebody opened the door for us — don't let these weasels get it closed again!"

They charged along the flat hilltop cavalry style, the Ranger, Frank Abbadele and the big bounty hunter in the lead, riding three abreast, the others spreading out behind them. Two men flew from their saddles as shots from the *comadrejas* hammered them: one was a townsman, a cattle buyer named Martin Baugh, the other was the cattle rustler and outlaw Lenbow Decker.

Seeing his good friend Decker fall, Tommy Walsh cried out to him a few feet away. But there was nothing else he could do for Decker. He rode on, firing his pistol rapidly amid the sound of bullets streaking through the air near his face.

Beside the gun wagon, on the ground where Tillis Abbadele had landed beside Doyle Royal when the *comadrejas'* gunfire had overcome them, Tillis managed to reach out with a bloody hand and drag Doyle and himself back beneath the gun wagon. As the firing raged above them and heavy boots scrambled around in the wagon bed trying frantically to find the gun handle, Doyle opened his eyes slightly and whispered through bloody lips, "Look . . . what I . . . brought." His other trembling hand pulled his shirttail up, revealing the Gatling gun handle he'd yanked loose before shots drove him out of the wagon. "I did good, didn't I?" he rasped.

Seeing his friend's eyes starting to glaze over, Tillis patted his chest with a weak, bloody hand, saying in his own injured voice, "You damned sure did, ole pard. I'm proud of you."

Seventy yards away, at the thickest point of gunfire, when the Ranger saw he could force his way no deeper into the *comadrejas'* firing positions, he reached back with his boot knife, cut his saddlebag straps, grabbed the bags and flung himself from his saddle. He gave the horse a hard slap to send it out of the fighting. As the horse hurried away to safety, the Ranger ran to where Frank Abbadele and his brother Bob lay behind the cover of a flat rock that only reached a few inches above the dirt. Shots ricocheted off the rock as Sam came sliding in. Frank scooted over a few inches, crowding Bob in order to allow cover for the Ranger.

"We've got to keep moving!" the Ranger said, raising his voice beneath the heavy gunfire. He began firing as he spoke. "We can't stay here!"

"I know!" Frank said. "I landed here when Bob's horse got shot and threw him! I'm ready when you are!" Eyeing the saddlebags the Ranger held to his chest, Frank said, "Need a good cigar?"

"Yes, much obliged!" said the Ranger, raising a gloved hand as Frank Abbadele pulled a black cigar from inside his coat pocket and handed it to him.

The Ranger looked past Frank at Bob

Abbadele, who lay firing, giving no regard to the blood and the long sliver of bone showing through his trouser leg. Looking back along the way they'd come in, he saw the bodies of man and horse strewn about. But from behind the bodies of some of the horses where other men had managed to take cover, rifle and pistol shots exploded. The Ranger turned his gaze to the right, where a short stretch of rocks lay filled with gunmen firing at the gun wagon, forcing the *comadrejas* to abandon it. Among these men lay the bodies of *comadrejas* who had fought hard but in vain to hold that rocky ground. Past the stretch of rocks stood a thicket of cedar and scrub juniper where Toot Abbadele and some of the men and horses had found cover.

Lighting the cigar from a match Frank Abbadele held out for him, the Ranger asked through puffs of smoke, "Did you see where that bounty hunter landed?"

"Yep, he's right up there!" Frank pointed to the right, where Shod lay flat at the frontmost point of the stretch of rocks, snaking his way forward beneath the firing from both sides.

"He likes staying right on top of things, doesn't he?" the Ranger said, shaking his head as his hand opened the saddlebags and took out a short coil of fuse.

"Damned if he doesn't!" Frank replied, firing as he spoke. "Must be because he can't see from far off!" He managed a wry grin.

"I suppose." The Ranger nodded. He cut a few short pieces of the fuse and stuck them into his shirt pocket. Then he took out a single stick of dynamite and slung the saddlebags over his shoulder.

"Think you ought to risk carrying those saddlebags?" Frank asked. "One shot, and it'll blow you sky-high."

"I know," said Sam, ready to stand into a crouch and make a run for it. "If that happens, I just want to be as close to the weasels as I can get." He took a last quick look around before going and said, "When you hear the boom, bring everybody forward."

"You've got it, Ranger!" said Frank. Then he said to Bob, "Here he goes, Bob. Let's keep him covered."

The Ranger raced in a crouch forward and diagonally across the flat hilltop toward Toot Abbadele and the men firing from among the rocks. But halfway there, a concentrated volley of fire sent him diving behind the body of a horse whose carcass had already been ripped and pounded by countless bullets. As soon as Sam slid in behind the animal, his cigar clamped between his teeth, he saw the drawn, haggard face of Terrence Knox huddled against the horse's belly. "I'm hit pretty bad, Ranger," Terrence gasped, his face ashen, his eyes shiny with fear. "And I'm out of bullets." He shook his head sadly. "Gut-shot and out of bullets. Ain't this a hell of a way to play out a string?"

The Ranger saw the dark blood on Terrence's hand as he raised it slightly from against his stomach wound. "I'm sorry, Knox," Sam said sincerely. His hand went quickly inside the saddlebags and brought out a fistful of .45 caliber cartridges. "Here, take all you want."

Terrence held out his gloved hand and let the bullets fall into it. "This is plenty, Ranger," he said in a strained voice. "It's enough to give you some cover. I ain't going to be here much longer."

"Are you sure?" the Ranger asked, realizing he was losing precious time.

"I'd bet on it," said Terrence. "Do me a favor?"

"Whatever I can," said the Ranger.

"Tell my ole brother, Hirsh, I'm damned happy for him. That he was the very last person I talked about."

413

"I will do that," said the Ranger. "Now I've got to get going."

"Go on, Ranger," said Terrence, loading his blood-streaked pistol with a trembling hand. "I've got you covered here."

Sam leaped forward into a crouch just as a lull in firing came from the *comadrejas*. Then, as he raced toward Toot Abbadele, the firing directed back toward him, and he took a dive forward and crawled the remaining few feet with bullets kicking up dirt along his side and into his face. "Lord!" said Toot Abbadele, grabbing the Ranger's back and pulling him the rest of the way into the cover of rock. "I thought sure you was done for, Ranger!" He looked over toward where Frank and Bob lay pinned behind the flat rock. "Are they all right?"

The Ranger puffed on the cigar, making sure it was still lit. "They're neither one hit. Bob's got a leg busted pretty bad, though." He looked around quickly at the faces of the men among the rocks. "Has everybody here still got some fight in them?"

"We're all game," said Dick Abbadele, looking up from beside Toot. "The sooner the better, as far as I'm concerned. Toot's hit and needs attending."

"No, I don't, Dick, so shut up about it," Toot said.

"Where are you hit?" the Ranger asked.

"If I thought it was serious, I'd tell you so," said Toot. "Now, what's our plan? I want to see these bastards pay for what they've done."

The Ranger started to answer, but his words were stopped by an earthshaking explosion that caused him to duck then look forward to where Shod lay flat with his arms still over his head, having just thrown the first stick of dynamite toward a crowded position of *comadrejas*. "There's the plan," said the Ranger. "Next explosion, everybody get moving while they pick rock out of their hair!"

Before the firing restarted from the *comadrejas*, the Ranger had already jumped up and run forward through the drifting smoke and dust from the blast of the explosion. As soon as he reached the rock where Shod lay, he touched the cigar to the short fuse on a stick of dynamite in his hand and hurled it hard, ten yards to the left of the last explosion, then hit the ground.

"There's not as many of them now as when we started," Shod said, jamming a short fuse into a stick of dynamite in his hand. "How many of us are left back there?" he asked, tossing a nod back over his shoulder.

"We've lost as many as a dozen men," the Ranger said. "But we've taken down a big part of these sand weasels. How many you figure are left?" As Sam spoke, he also prepared another stick of dynamite.

"We started out badly outnumbered," said Shod, taking a second to straighten his spectacles on the bridge of his nose. "After those two blasts, I figure we're just about working with some manageable numbers."

"That's good to know," said Sam. "Some of our men are down with wounds. You and I are going to blast our way through these devils. The others are ready to come in behind us." He puffed the cigar, then blew on the end of it, stoking it red. "We're going to have to hit hard and stop for nothing — it's a win-or-die battle."

Shod rose slightly, poised to charge, a cigar between his teeth, a stick of dynamite in his broad fist. "Is there any other kind?" he asked beneath a renewed volley of heavy gunfire.

Chapter 23

Dick Abbadele shook his brother Toot's forearm as the rest of the able men moved forward firing. "Damn it, Toot! You ain't passing out on me, are you?"

"Hell, no!" Toot said, snapping to and seeing the concerned look on his brother's face. "I just had to close my eyes for a second, get myself collected. Come on, get going, Dick! I've got you covered."

"Covered?" Dick looked even more concerned. "I mean for you to go with me! Toot, are you all right?"

"No!" said Toot, feigning an exaggerated expression, raising his slightly bloodied hand from low on his side. "Look — I'm bleeding to death, *ayiii!*" As Dick's eyes grew wider, Toot shook his head with a dark laugh. "I'm all right! Damn it, go on, Dick! It's just going to hurt like hell if I have to get up and run! I'm hoping you won't make me do it!"

"Hurt?" Dick's expression turned skeptical. "You never could take it, could you, brother? You always was the first one to give out."

"Go to hell, Dick," said Toot, giving his brother a friendly shove to get him started.

Taking advantage of a double blast of dynamite that Shod and the Ranger had hurled into the *comadreja* positions, all the men pressed forward at once. The *comadrejas'* gunfire shrank to a minimum as they hugged the ground, the impact of the blasts immobilizing them for a moment. And that moment was all the advantage the gunmen needed to take the upper hand in the battle. Within minutes, the *comadrejas'* resistance came unraveled. The Ranger and Shod had split up, each taking a side of the cliff line, each followed by a group of fighters who concentrated on preventing any fleeing *comadrejas* from slipping around them and escaping.

When the Ranger had thrown his last stick of dynamite headlong into a small group of charging *comadrejas,* he dropped down flat, then rose up onto one knee and began firing his pistol. When he'd fired his pistol empty, he had no time to reload. Instead, he snatched up a rifle that had spilled from the scabbard of a dead horse lying near him. He levered a round into the chamber and continued firing until he heard Shod shout, "Ranger, look out!" Turning the rifle quickly toward the sound of the bounty hunter's voice, the Ranger fired, lifting a charging *comadreja* off his feet and dropping him dead. But as soon as he'd fired, he saw three more *comadrejas* lunge up as if out of the ground and attack Shod like wolves.

The Ranger charged, unable to risk a shot. Using the rifle like a club, he swung it hard by the barrel and caught one attacker full in the belly with a blow so powerful it broke the gun stock and left the man lying limp on the ground. As he turned to grab one of the other two, Shod sent one flying past him like a rag doll. The third man hung in the air, his feet thrashing wildly but not touching the ground. On the ground lay a knife that had fallen from his hands. His hands gripped Shod's wrists for a moment as the big bounty hunter held him up at arm's length. Sam saw another rifle lying discarded on the ground, ran to it and picked it up. He looked back at Shod in time to see that the *comadreja*'s feet had stopped thrashing and his hands had fallen loosely to his sides. The big bounty hunter flung the body away, then clasped a hand to a long knife wound across his upper arm.

Levering a round into the rifle chamber, the Ranger stood close to Shod, looking all around. "It's bleeding bad — take care of it."

As he stood watching out for more attacking *comadrejas,* the Ranger noted that the fighting had been pushed to the farthest tip of the cliff line, and even there the return fire had turned sporadic, shots fired in desperation and retreat. "Listen to that," said Shod as he stripped a bandanna from around his neck and used it to hold the gaping wound closed. "Sounds like the weasels are calling it a day." They both turned toward the sound of a long scream as one of the combatants leaped from the edge of the cliff to his death on the hard trail below.

Lowering the rifle, the Ranger turned and saw the bounty hunter trying to tie the bandanna around his thick upper arm to hold the wound closed. "Here, let me get that for you." Handing Shod the rifle, the Ranger took over the task of tying the bandanna. As soon as he had finished and had started to reload his pistol, the Ranger caught sight of two *comadrejas* running in a crouch toward the spot where most of the horses had taken shelter in the cedar thicket past the stretch of rocks. "There goes some more!" he said, already dropping the empty cartridges from his pistol. "They're headed for the horses!" Without taking the rifle back from Shod, the Ranger ran toward the horses, his pistol still not loaded, but time not allowing him to stop and finish the job.

Inside the thicket, the Ranger saw the *comadrejas* start to step up onto two horses. Not about to let them get away, he instinctively raised his empty pistol and cocked it. "Hold it right there!" he shouted, hoping his bluff would work until the big bounty hunter caught up to him with the loaded rifle. "Raise your hands and step away from the horses!"

The two acted as if they didn't understand. They gave him a bemused look. "Don't even try to tell me anything — just get your hands in the air."

The two looked at one another, one glancing down at the pistol in his belt as if considering his chances. Behind him, the Ranger heard Shod's running footsteps across the rocks. But even a split second counted, he thought, standing there with an unloaded pistol.

But then, to his surprise, the Ranger saw the pair step away from the horses and raise their hands all the way above their heads. As Shod came to a halt beside him and the Ranger let out a relieved breath, the shorter of the two *comadrejas* said unexpectedly, "I am not Santaglio! He is!" He pointed with his raised right hand. "I am Merza! I am only the *second* in command! It is the truth, jou can ask any of the men!"

"Jou son of a bitch!" Santaglio growled, clearly ready to pounce on the shorter man.

"Don't make a move!" Sam said, knowing the whole thing could be a ploy to distract them while one of them went for the pistol. Then, giving Shod a surprised glance, the Ranger stepped forward, lifted the pistol from Santaglio's belt and pitched it to the side. Shod held the rifle on the pair. "What if I told you I don't care who's the leader?" Sam said, taking a step back. "All I care about is that you both hang for what you've done."

"Hang, ha!" said Santaglio. "Why should we hang because we kill a bunch of jou miserable pigs? I am glad that we killed so many of jou. None of jou deserve to live! I only wish that we had killed more of jou than we did!"

"If I was you," said the Ranger, "I'd keep my mouth shut. There's a good many people here who would just as soon not take you back to stand trial as it is." He turned and saw Frank and Dick Abbadele walking toward the battered gun wagon, Frank limping with an arm looped over Dick's shoulder. "To tell you the truth, I don't much blame them," he added.

Beneath the gun wagon, Tillis Abbadele lay propped against Doyle Royal's body, breathing shallowly, an arm slung over Doyle's back, a bloody pistol in his hand. "It's about time you got here . . ." Tillis' weak voice seemed to collapse. "I'd hate waiting supper . . . for you bunch of turds . . . ," he said.

"Aw, Jesus," said Frank, seeing the shape his brother was in. "This is why I always tried to get everybody to stick close to the spread." His voice sounded not much stronger than Tillis'. Holding his wounded side, Frank had Dick lower him to the ground so he could drag himself in beside Tillis. "We got to get you out from under here."

But Tillis shook his head slowly, coughing up a trace of blood. "No way, brother Frank. I'll fall apart if you move me." He gestured with the pistol barrel, moving it over his body. "Have you ever seen anybody shot this much?"

Frank's voice lowered to a whisper. "No, I don't think I ever have." He struggled to keep his voice from breaking up on him. "You saved a lot of lives, Tillis, doing what you and Doyle did with that Gatling gun. That's the fact of it."

"How do you know it was us?" Tillis asked, his voice growing weaker.

Frank managed a trembling smile. "It had your names all over it."

"Well, I knew somebody would have to save you bunch of shirkers." Tillis laughed, and it turned into a cough. When he'd collected himself, he whispered, "Find my horse. My saddlebags are full of money."

"We're not talking about money right now, Tillis," said Frank.

"Oh?" Tillis cocked an eye. "Well . . . What else is there to talk about?"

"Nothing. I just want to sit here with you a minute," said Frank.

"You ain't turning soft on me, are you, brother?" Tillis asked.

"No. The thing is, I'm shot, too, brother. So's Toot," said Frank.

"I'm sorry to hear it," said Tillis. He nodded toward his hand. "Can you take this pistol from me? I feel like I've been carrying one my whole life."

While Frank and Dick Abbadele sat beneath the gun wagon with their dying brother, the Ranger and Shod walked Merza and Santaglio over at gunpoint and stopped a few feet away until Dick helped Frank stand up and turn sadly from the bodies of Doyle Royal and Tillis Abbadele. "What have you got there, Ranger?" Frank asked, looking the two *comadrejas* up and down.

"These men are the leaders, according to this one," Sam said, gesturing toward Merza. "He says he's the second in charge, and this one is the leader. We'll find out more from them once we get back to town, while they're awaiting trial."

"I will not go to a trial! Hang me here!" Santaglio said defiantly. "Leave my bones to bleach in the sun. My people will remember me as the one who came up from the desert sand and killed so many of jou pigs." He stared at Frank Abbadele as Dick led him forward, his arm looped across his shoulders. Nodding at Frank Abbadele's wound and the blood that stained his side and his trousers all the way down to his boot, Santaglio added in triumph, "It is certain that this pig will see me hang." He scoffed and said to Frank, "Jou will be dead yourself long before I will!" His face took on a look of satisfaction.

"Wrong again, weasel," said Frank Abbadele. Leaning against his brother, his left arm over his shoulders, Frank's right hand swept upward effortlessly, raising and cocking his Colt.

"Frank, no!" the Ranger shouted. But there was no stopping Frank Abbadele. A look of terror came to Santaglio's face just as the bullet blasted through his forehead, knocking him backward. Then Shod and the Ranger lunged forward at the same time as Frank recocked the Colt and turned it toward Merza. "So long, *segundo*." He fired again, sending Merza's body pitching backward, where it draped itself limply over Santaglio's.

The Ranger and Shod stopped cold for just a second, each of them with their guns pointed toward Frank Abbadele. But Frank let out a breath and slid his Colt into his holster.

"You had no right to shoot those men!" said the Ranger, his anger tight inside his chest and his gun hand.

Frank offered a tired smile, pressing his right hand to the wound low in his right side. "What are you going to do about it, Ranger, shoot me?" he said.

Now it was Sam's turn to let go of a

tense breath. He did so as he lowered his Colt into his holster. "There's been enough killing for one day." He gave Shod a look, and the bounty hunter lowered the rifle.

Frank had his brother Dick lower him to the ground and lean him back against the gun wagon's wheel. "I never thought I'd die helping a lawman fight desert weasels," Frank said, his voice still strong in spite of his loss of blood. "You have to admit, Ranger, I had you pretty well whipped to a standstill back in Sabre Ridge, bringing in an attorney and all."

"You didn't have me beat, Frank," said Sam. "The law would have won in the end. If I didn't believe that, I would take this badge off and give it a toss."

Frank shook his head. "No, don't you ever do that, Ranger. It looks good on you." He slumped a bit as Dick pressed a wadded-up bandanna against the wound. "Funny thing," said Frank. "I had it all planned, how I was going to beat you in court, manage to look like a big man in front of my men and the whole town. Then here came a bunch of weasels up out of the sand. Everything just stopped in its tracks and started all over. Killing them became more important to me than beating you, all of a sudden."

"I know," said the Ranger. "I felt something similar to that myself. I reckon no matter how bad I thought you Abbadeles were, I saw these *comadrejas* as being a whole lot worse. Maybe when we go to trial, I can mention to the judge how much help all of you were, riding these weasels down."

"He can't hear you, Ranger," said Dick Abbadele.

The Ranger looked at Frank Abbadele's glazed, dead eyes and the slight smile frozen forever on his lips. "That's just as well," the Ranger said quietly. "I reckon he wouldn't have wanted me mentioning his help, all things considered." Everybody stood in silence for a moment, outlaw, lawman and townsman alike. Then the Ranger looked all around and said, "Anybody who rides for the Abbadeles, I'm more obliged for your help than I know how to say. But this is a good time for you to find a horse and ride away from here if you can."

"Why's that, Ranger?" asked Dick. "We've still got that lawyer working for us."

"That's right," said the Ranger. "But like Frank said, everything started all over when the weasels hit town. If you decide to leave here now, make a clean start for yourselves, you've got my word I won't come looking for you. If it was me, I'd rather do it that way than have to hire some lawyer to do my fighting for me. But it's up to each of you. Do what suits you. I'm just making the offer."

"And I'm taking that offer," said Tommy Walsh, stepping forward, a hand clamped to his wounded arm. "Seeing what these weasels done, what rotten bastards they are, has shamed me somehow. I can work as a cowhand for a living. I don't have to outlaw no more." He turned and walked away. In a moment, one man turned and followed him, then another, and another.

"Does that include me?" Dick Abbadele asked the Ranger. "Or does being an Abbadele mean I don't get the same break?"

"Yep, it goes for you, too," the Ranger said.

Dick looked at Bob, who stood to one side, using a rifle for a crutch, his broken leg hanging crooked and bloody. "Can you manage to get back to town without my help?"

Bob looked around and saw Toot, who had limped in and plopped onto the ground beside Frank's body. He'd reached in and closed Frank's dead eyes. "Toot here will help me if I need any help. Won't you, Toot?"

"I'm wounded," said Toot, "but I'll help you all I can."

The Ranger said to Bob, "If you ride back to Sabre Ridge, you know you'll still have to stand trial, don't you?"

Bob chuckled. "Yeah, so what? Either I'll win, and you leave town madder than a hornet, or I'll lose and go to prison for a few years. I feel lucky, Ranger. I think I'll take my chances." He squinted and grinned. "Ain't that the American way?"

The Ranger offered a thin smile. "Apparently so." Then he looked around and saw Dick Abbadele leading his horse forward. Dick stopped, took the saddlebags from behind his saddle and pitched them on the ground at the Ranger's feet. "Since this is a new start for me, take this money back to the bank in Riley." He shrugged. "Hell, tell them Bob turned it in — that ought to shave something off his time, if he gets any."

The Ranger reached out with a boot toe, nudged the flap back and saw the bands of dollars inside. He nodded. "It could make a big difference." Then he looked at Toot and said, "Are you sure you're able to ride and look after your brother? If not, I can set his leg, we can camp a couple of days, let everybody heal up some."

"I can take care of him," said Toot. "I've got a wife and baby waiting for me. I don't want to be out here no longer than I have to."

"All right then," said the Ranger. "Let's dress our wounds, gather our horses and head back to town. We'll load our dead on this gun wagon."

As the men disbursed, the Ranger and Shod walked toward the thicket of cedar, the Ranger carrying the saddlebags full of money over his shoulder. "Bounty hunter, it's been an honor working with you, but I can't say it's been a pleasure," Sam said.

"Same here, Ranger," said Shod.

"Where are you headed now, if you don't mind me asking?" said Sam.

"Back toward Texas, I suppose," said Shod. "As soon as I keep a promise I made to Swan Hendricks. I sure haven't made much money in this territory. There's some reward due for those men I killed in town. But after all that's happened, I feel bad claiming it."

"So you're going to forget about it?" the Ranger asked, looking surprised.

"Whoa!" said the bounty hunter. "There's

no way I'm going to forget about it. I can feel bad and still claim it, too, can't I?" He smiled broadly and adjusted his spectacles on the bridge of his nose.

The Ranger chuckled under his breath. "I reckon so. If I had any say, you'd get paid something for all the *comadrejas* you've killed here."

"No," said Shod. "I wouldn't accept it. Everybody here did their share of the fighting. Besides, there's some things in life worth doing for free."

"I know just what you mean," said the Ranger, the two of them walking side by side back to the cedar thicket where the horses waited peacefully.